FORGOTTEN

THE FORGOTTEN: BOOK ONE

M.R. FORBES

Published by Quirky Algorithms
Seattle, Washington

This novel is a work of fiction and a product of the author's imagination. Any resemblance to actual persons or events is purely coincidental.

Cover illustration by Tom Edwards
tomedwardsdesign.com

ACKNOWLEDGMENTS

THANK YOU in advance for reading this book. I truly hope you enjoy it.

THANK YOU to my beta readers for helping me add a layer of spit and polish. The book needed it.

THANK YOU to my wife. This book wouldn't have been possible without you.

1

"JOSH, DO YOU SEE THEM?"

Sheriff Hayden Duke splashed through the damp alley. His breathing was ragged, his legs burning from the effort. He had lost sight of the suspects almost a minute ago.

He told himself for the hundredth time that he should spend more time on his stamina, but damn if there weren't a million other things to do.

"No sign of them, Boss," his Deputy replied, voice tinny and distant through the star-shaped transceiver on Hayden's collar.

"You're kidding?" Hayden said.

Deputy Bradshaw should have been at the other end of the alley. Hayden had seen his quarry duck down this way, into the slender spaces between the blocks where most of the city's hooligans liked to screw around, rolling and smoking, and getting way too friendly with the mess of wiring and pipes that were the lifeblood of Metro.

It was almost a rite of passage these days to make trouble for Law. To make trouble for him.

And he was getting too old for this shit.

Not that he was old, even by Metro standards. Thirty-six years, one hundred forty-seven days. Natalia still called him the baby because he was two years younger than her.

Thirty-eight? Now that was old.

He came to a stop at an intersection between the blocks, turning his head to look down each of the strands. Dim lighting tried to follow the lines of the Metro's above-deck utilities, but a large portion of them had gone dark over the years while others were reduced to a harsh flicker. For anyone less familiar with the strands it might have been an eerie, frightening effect.

For him, it was business as usual.

He glanced up, letting a couple of raindrops tap him on the cheek. He smiled. Natalia and her team had only finished repairing the elemental generators last week, and this was the first time the randomizer had delivered precipitation. No one in Metro had felt the crisp moisture in nearly four months, and he wanted to savor it because he had no idea how long it would last. The generators were old, like everything else on the Pilgrim, and each breakdown was becoming more time-consuming and difficult to patch.

How old were they? He wasn't quite sure. His grandfather hadn't been able to remember the launch before he passed, and he claimed his grandfather hadn't been able to recall, either. The Pilgrim Assistance Service Station was no help there, either. Its storage units had corrupted at some point, losing troves of data about the origin of the ship, including the date it had left their homeworld.

Earth.

He only knew it from pictures and videos, the ones the PASS hadn't lost. A beautiful place, teeming with life. Not just people. Animals and plants, too. Green and blue and brown and silver. All the water you could ever want to drink.

All the space you could ever need to roam. All the technology you could imagine to live a life of ease and comfort.

The cities there made the fifty-thousand in Metro look microscopic.

"Where are you?" Hayden whispered, squinting his eyes to dull the flickering lights a little more. If his targets hadn't come out the other end of the alley, they had to be in one of the strands, trying to hide.

He reached to the belt at his hip, drawing his sidearm. He was supposed to be off his shift by now, back in his cube and getting a little sleep. Natalia would be there waiting for him. He smiled. He knew she was going to give him shit for being late. She knew he was going to jaw back at her about the miscreants of their society that kept him working overtime.

His grandfather had told him stories about his time as Sheriff of Metro. Back then, they had drones that navigated the strands, keeping an eye out for illicit activity. People those days were a lot better behaved, and a lot more respectful of the delicate nature of the systems that kept them all alive.

It would have been nice if the Block Seven Fire had served notice that entering the strands was always a bad idea, but it was just too damn tempting. There were only a few places to go to avoid attention, and this was one of them.

"Wilson, do you copy?" Hayden said, tapping his transceiver with his chin.

"Roger, Boss," his Second Deputy said, her tone a little too perky for his liking. "What do you need?"

"I'm going Block Eight dash one forty-two dash four," he said, giving her the coordinates of the specific strand to his left, so she would know where he was if he didn't come back out. Not that a Sheriff had ever not come back out, but it was part of protocol. "Get someone at the end of Eight dash one forty-two dash six."

"Affirmative, Sheriff," Wilson said.

"They might have already come out that way, sir," Josh said.

"I know," Hayden agreed. "We do the best we can."

Metro Law was short on deputies, just like it had been since before Hayden was alive. More and more citizens were being guided toward Engineering, since keeping them all supplied with fresh air and water was more important than catching up to every minor offender. There was a continuum to the effort versus the crime, and while Hayden tended to be more tenacious than the Sheriffs that had gone before him, his resources were ultimately limited.

He started down the alley; gun pointed up toward the membrane that simulated a sky. He had only used the weapon three times in eighteen years, and he never wanted to make it four, if for no other reason than there were only so many rounds for it remaining. The weapon was loaded with stunners, but he had discovered during his first year as a Deputy that non-lethal didn't mean never-lethal. Not everyone reacted the same to the electric charge, and there were circumstances where it could kill.

Killing someone, even by accident, and living with it, was one of the hardest things he had to do, every day for the last fourteen years.

Every day for the rest of his life.

He moved slowly, careful not to splash too hard and betray his approach.

He knew from experience that 142-4 intersected with 143-1, and from there led back to the two main splits on either side of the row of blocks. While his suspects could wind through the strands back here like they were in a maze, they would have to emerge on one of the splits in order to get out completely.

Assuming they hadn't already taken 142-6.

Which they probably had.

He was tempted to call off the search. To drop it and go home. He was tired. Natalia was waiting. So what if a couple of kids had wandered back here? He had been young once, too.

He paused, wiping the rain out of his eyes. There was a pull to keep going. There was always the potential for distracted young couples to damage the conduits that ran through the strands and cause serious problems. He had seen it happen twice in the eight years since he had been promoted to Sheriff. If he thought Natalia would give him a hard time for being late, he could guess what she would have to say about him not doing everything in his power to keep the lines up.

Natalia understood the nature of the strands were a flaw in the ship's design. An oversight by the designers, who had probably never considered how the Generation ship would evolve over the years. In their minds, Metro was going to be a utopia. A place where everyone got along just fine, and everyone worked together for the common good as one big happy family, fifty-thousand members strong. A place where no one would wander into the alleys between buildings. A place that didn't need Law at all.

How wrong they had been.

Metro wasn't bad, overall, but a utopia? The records were lost to the PASS, but he didn't think it had ever been that. The more their technology broke down, the more comforts they lost, the less organized things became. Yes, they were still following population control protocols, rationing, that sort of thing, but there was a whole black market beneath the ordered surface where citizens were trading what they had for other things they didn't or wanted more of, and you never could discount human ingenuity.

He sighed and kept walking, reaching 143-1 and transmitting the position back to Wilson.

"Roger, Sheriff," she replied. "Nothing from the splits yet."

"Roger," he said softly.

He glanced up again. The blocks were dark this time of night. Only a few cube lights were on, letting a little bit of extra light filter into the strands. He needed it. The access lighting through here was in bad shape, most of it burned out.

He took a few more steps, resolving himself to ensure the area was clear. It might take another hour, but he was sure Natalia would thank him for it in the end. He reached the junction between 143-1 and 143-3, glancing down the other strands before crossing over.

He froze when he heard a sudden series of pops and pangs from somewhere far off, way beyond the perimeter of Metro, deep in the inaccessible heart of the Pilgrim.

He cursed, kneeling down instinctively, putting his hand on the wet ground to keep himself steady as the entire city started to shake. The vibration ran from what they called the north end of Metro back to the south, traveling across the entire shell of the city. He watched the small puddles on the ground spread in ripples, using the size of the waves to help judge the intensity.

The superstructure was flexing. That's what Natalia said. Something outside the ship was putting pressure on it, causing some kind of turbulence.

The turbs. That's what they had taken to calling them.

What caused it?

He had no idea. None of them did. They didn't have access to that information. They didn't have access to anything outside of Metro. There were corridors. There were passageways. There were conduits. They were all sealed. All locked. All closed off.

They were passengers, all fifty-thousand of them. Pilgrims, as the name of their vessel implied. On their way from Earth to somewhere else, the descendants of a group of settlers that wanted to hand down a new life on the other side of the galaxy to them.

Where? He didn't know.

When? He didn't know.

Why? He didn't know.

There were a fair number of people in Metro who were certain they should have gotten where they were going by now. They insisted the breakdowns in the elemental generators were proof that the journey had already lasted longer than the ship's progenitors had ever intended.

Hayden didn't know if it was true or not, and he didn't care all that much. They hadn't arrived. The seals hadn't opened. There was nowhere else for them to go. Regardless, he did sometimes find himself questioning the purpose of the journey. Having seen the photos of Earth, he couldn't think of a reason why they had abandoned it.

But what could he do about it?

What could any of them do about it?

Nothing.

Dust and small pieces of debris broke away from the blocks and floated to the ground around him. The ship continued to shudder, the initial shudder beginning to subside before a second, more intense trembling replaced it. This wasn't the first time the ship had encountered outside interference, but it had been increasing in recent weeks. Engineering was working on the problem, trying to determine a cause from the limited readings the systems internal to Metro allowed.

Personally, Hayden didn't think the reason for it mattered. Only their preparation.

He remained in place, glancing up at the blocks over his

head. He could see them swaying, shifting with the movement of the Pilgrim. More of the cube lights were going on as the residents awakened to the shaking. There were tolerances built in. The ship's builders had assumed there would be some measure of friction and had designed Metro accordingly. Even so, time and repetition were taking their toll. On their buildings. On their psyches. On their belief that they would ever make it to wherever it was they had been going in the first place.

He dropped those thoughts when he heard the shouting.

2

Hayden pushed himself to his feet. "Josh, I need backup, one forty-three dash three, heading toward one forty-three dash five, asap."

"Roger, Sheriff," Josh replied. "I'm on my way."

Hayden kept running. The cry had been muffled, quieted, leaving him with only the initial sound to go on.

What the hell was happening in here?

He reached the next intersection, crossing through it to one forty-three five without slowing. A loud crack above the membrane sky signaled especially bad turbulence, and he came off his feet as the floor moved beneath him, sending him toward the side of the block. He clenched his teeth, twisting himself to keep his weight from slamming into the conduits that ran along the side, throwing his shoulder out above the lines to take the blow. He grimaced at the flare of pain, bouncing from the wall and regaining his footing.

He heard another cry.

He reached the end of one forty-three five and turned to one forty-three six, passing the change in direction to his Deputy.

"Sheriff," Josh said. "We've got a Code Blue from Engineering."

Hayden noticed the rain had stopped.

Damn. It figured. Poor Natalia.

"Wilson," he said. "Contact Engineering for me. Tell them we're on our way. Josh, stall for me, okay?"

"Sheriff?" Josh said.

"I know," Hayden said. "You don't need to spout protocol at me. Someone's in the strands, and they're in trouble."

What he had heard wasn't normal. He knew it was a risk to ignore the Code Blue, but he had to take it.

"Josh, do you have my back on this one or not?" he said when his Deputy didn't respond right away.

"I'll do my best, sir," Josh replied. "Natalia's going to be pissed."

"I know. She'll forgive me."

He hoped.

He also hoped it was nothing too serious. A fall and a broken bone, maybe.

A sound like that? It was wishful thinking.

He crossed another junction, radioing his position back to Wilson. He made it halfway down the strand, eyes casting out in both directions, looking for any sign of trouble. There. On the ground ahead of him.

What was that?

He came to a stop and knelt down over the object. A knife?

It was homemade, a small piece of machined metal strapped to what looked like the handle of a spoon, wrapped in cloth to soften it to the hand. He had seen similar makeshift weapons a few times before, and they never went along with anything good. He scooped it up and shoved it between his belt and his pants and then stared down the strands.

Nothing.

He froze, considering the problem. There was an access hatch beside him, an entry point to one of the maintenance boxes that dotted the city. The boxes themselves were supposed to be locked, and only Engineering and Law held the codes.

It wouldn't have been the first lock that failed.

He reached for the access panel with one hand, holding his stunner level in the other. The rumbling was beginning to lessen, the turbulence easing back. Code Blue meant he was supposed to drop everything and head to Engineering. But a knife?

He tapped the button to open the hatch. It flashed a message to him on its small screen:

"Locked. Enter code."

He stared at it for a moment. It was still locked. Whoever had dropped the knife couldn't be hiding inside.

He turned away, listening. The turbulence had passed. The city was settling down again. He hadn't heard anything that would suggest catastrophic damage, but he knew all it would take to kill every last one of them would be for the atmospheric generators and their backups to both fail at the same time.

He sighed. He was wasting his time in here.

He took a step away from the maintenance box. He paused and turned back to it. He had been promoted to Sheriff over Josh and the other deputies in part because of his instinct.

Hayden keyed in the code, quickly entering the eight digit sequence.

The door slid open.

He barely had time to react. A large form came out at him, a fist angling toward his face.

He reacted without thinking, dropping away from the

fist, turning aside. His assailant's momentum carried him past, and Hayden moved in behind. He wanted to shove his opponent into the opposite block, but there was too much risk of damaging a conduit. Instead, he kicked them hard in the back of the leg, bringing them to a knee.

"Metro Law," he said. "Stay down."

Most of the time, they did.

This one didn't.

The man lunged sideways at him, reaching for his waist to pull him to the ground. Hayden jumped back, trying to get beyond his grip but not quite making it. A large hand grabbed his ankle, and he slipped. The bigger man grunted, pouncing on top of him, arm back to pummel his fist into Hayden's side.

Hayden didn't panic. He quickly brought his weapon up, placing it against the man's temple and cocking the trigger.

"Don't," he said, looking up at him.

His opponent's eyes narrowed. Hayden could tell he was considering his options. He pressed the barrel a little harder into the man's head.

"Don't," he repeated.

The big man deflated, raising his hands.

"Get off me," Hayden said. "Keep your hands up."

The suspect did as he ordered, backing off him and standing.

Hayden gathered his legs beneath him and rose to his feet, keeping his eyes locked on his attacker.

"One move and I pull the trigger," Hayden said. "I guarantee it'll hurt."

The man was still.

Hayden turned his attention back to the maintenance box. A woman was pressed against the rear of it, dangerously close to the operational circuits there. Her shirt was unbuttoned, her bra hastily pulled back into place. Her pants were around her ankles, but she had enough time during the altercation to get her panties back up.

"Hi, Sheriff Duke," she said.

He knew her. Sarah Kaine. She had been in his lockup for prostitution more than once.

"Damn it, Sarah," he said. "Put your pants back on."

She nodded and finished dressing.

He turned back to the big man. "I don't know you." He reached to his belt and withdrew a small scanning device. "Give me your wrist."

The man held out his left wrist. Hayden ran the device over it. The display on it showed the man's name and address.

"Francis Lira. Block Twenty-four?" Hayden said. "You came all the way across Metro for a quickie with a hooker?"

The man didn't say anything.

"Look, Francis," Hayden said. "Prostitution is illegal. Assaulting a Sheriff, that's a whole lot more illegal. I recommend you cooperate."

"Sheriff Duke," Sarah said. "Can I go?"

He looked over at her again. "Not yet."

Her lips tightened into a thin line.

Hayden returned the scanner to his belt and drew the homemade knife. "This yours, Francis?"

Francis still wouldn't talk.

"Is he mute?" Hayden asked.

"I don't know," Sarah replied. "We just met. Maybe he's afraid of you?"

"He should be afraid of me; he attacked me." He looked back at Francis. "I've got a Code Blue right now. Do you know what that means?"

He shook his head.

"It means something important on the Pilgrim is busted, and I'm supposed to be helping find it so Engineering can fix it. But instead, I'm wasting my time here with you. Now, here's what I know. One, I heard a shout, a man's shout, but it was more of a baritone, and by your size, I'm going to assume you're a bass. If you can produce sound at all. Two, I found this knife outside the maintenance box, and I'm guessing it's yours because why would the guy run away if he had a knife? That tells me that you two weren't here alone, and the third guy took off. But he didn't take off because I was coming. What I think is that he paid Sarah here for her services, but then you showed up, threatened him, and took his place. Sarah, correct me if I'm wrong about any of this."

She remained silent.

"I have a few problems. One, you entered this maintenance box, which has a code on it you aren't supposed to know. Two, you attacked me when I opened it and were ready to pummel me to death despite the fact that I'm an Officer of the Law. Three, you left the knife out here, when it would have been really handy during problem two. Do you see where I'm going with this?"

Francis was motionless, his eyes staring straight ahead.

Hayden sighed again. "Still won't talk? Fine. Francis, you're under arrest. Turn around."

Francis turned around. Hayden dug out his cuffs and put him in them.

"Sarah, let's go."

"Are you arresting me, Sheriff?"

Hayden shrugged. "I haven't decided yet. You're coming down to the Station with me for questioning. Whether you leave tonight or in a few days? That's up to you."

"Come on, Sheriff Duke," Sarah said. "My mom's sick. The med chits they give us aren't enough. What else am I supposed to do?"

"Your mother is seventy-three years old," Hayden said. "I don't want to sound harsh, but you're supposed to convince her to head over to medical. You know the protocols. They'll put her to rest nice and easy. No pain. You know we don't have enough meds left to care for everybody."

"It's my body. I can do what I want with it."

"Sorry, Sarah. Not in Metro, you can't. Not on the Pilgrim, you can't. What if you got pregnant? It is fair to the others if you get to have a kid outside the lottery and they lose their chance because of it?"

She had tears in her eyes. "She's going to die."

"Yes, she is," Hayden agreed. "That's the way things are here." He shrugged out of his coat and handed it out to her. "You can cover yourself up with this. I'll send Wilson over to your place to tell your mother where you are as soon as the Code Blue is cleared."

She took the coat and put it on, still in tears. "I hate this damn ship. I hate this damn life."

"You can hate it all you want. It's what we have, and nothing's going to change it."

3

Engineering was outside of the main Metro perimeter, a two-kilometer hike from the Law Office out to the wall that marked the north side of the city. It sat just beyond Metro Park North, one of the four small parks that surrounded the blocks that offered residents open spaces away from the tall buildings.

Hayden could still remember a time when the park had grass and even a few real, live trees. Those days had passed, the damage to the water circulation systems costing them a few thousand gallons before it was repaired and reducing their levels enough that the greenery had all died.

It was a shame, but that was life. At least the grass remained, though much of it was brown at the moment thanks to the downtime of the elemental generators. The rain had started up again by the time he had finished locking up Francis and Sarah. The rest of his officers had already been to Engineering and had likely already been assigned out.

He was glad the elementals were still working. Natalia

had put so much time and energy into their repairs; it just wouldn't have been right for them to break again so soon.

He reached the hatch at the base of the southern wall. It was the only access point out of the Metro perimeter from this direction, and it led first to Control and then out to various points around the Metro Hold, where the critical systems were located. The ones they could affect, anyway. Atmosphere, elements, waste recycling, water storage, scrubbers and so on were all accessible through the outer corridors, which like the maintenance boxes were only available to Engineering, Government, and Law.

Except that wasn't completely true. Francis had gotten past the locks. Hayden still didn't know how, but his first order of business once things settled down was to find out. The man couldn't stay silent forever, and even if he did, Sarah wouldn't. At the very least she would tell him what she could about the john that hired her, and how Francis fit in with the failed effort to pay for sex.

A part of him felt for Sarah. She wasn't a bad kid. But her mother had won the lottery late. It happened sometimes. It meant Sarah was going to spend most of her life without her parents, and in fact, her father had gone to Medical the day he turned sixty-five when she was only ten. Some people held on with everything they could even as their access to the ship's limited resources diminished, and some people were brave enough just to let go.

He had already decided he was going to let go of his own volition. Natalia said she was going to hold out for two years, to wait for him to reach that age so they could settle out together.

He entered the access code for the hatch, holding his arms behind his back while it slid open. He moved into the corridor, wrinkling his nose as he breathed in.

"Sheriff Duke."

Hayden smiled when he saw Mae, one of the Senior Engineers. She was small and stocky, long dark hair, small eyes, and a cherubic face.

"Mae," he said. "Sorry I'm late."

"You don't need to apologize to me, Sheriff," Mae replied. "It's your wife you should worry about."

"Believe me, I am. What's the smell?"

"That's our problem," she said. "One of the waste recycling lines was ruptured in the turbulence. Maybe in more than one place." She held up a small device. "You can get one of these from Natalia. It measures the air's chemical composition. We can use it to find the source of the leaks."

"Right," Hayden said. "Sounds like fun."

"Waste is the third most valuable thing on the ship, Sheriff," Mae said. "Arguably, it may be the most valuable. Without recycling, we would have all been dead a long time ago."

"Roger that," Hayden said. "If you'll excuse me."

He continued, entering Control less than a minute later.

He stopped just outside the room, pausing there to take it in. It was filled with screens, at least three dozen of them, though a third were dark and dead forever. The ones that were still functioning displayed the status of different portions of Metro's life support systems. A dozen people sat at various stations around them, monitoring the data and communicating with both the Engineers and Law Officers who were navigating the waste recycling shafts in an effort to locate the leaks.

Meanwhile, his wife was moving from station to station, collecting status reports and issuing commands, overseeing the entire effort in a whirlwind of controlled chaos. He watched her for a few seconds, admiring the way she danced from point to point, the way her hair bounced on her shoulders, the way her uniform creased and flared and rippled with each step. The shape of her face, the sparkle in her eyes. He could feel her passion for the job emanating from her.

Twenty years after the first time he had laid eyes on her, she was still the most amazing thing he had ever seen.

He wiped the distracted smile from his face before he stepped into the room. She was facing away from him, but she seemed to sense his presence, turning around and glaring at him with an expression he knew all too well.

"Hayden," she said, not missing a beat. "It's about time."

"Sorry, Nat," he said. "I had a situation-"

"Later." She grabbed a sniffer from a nearby counter. She approached him, already holding it out. "The Governor stopped by to check on things," she said, interrupted for a moment by his lips. She returned his kiss and then brushed him lightly back. "He knows you weren't here."

Hayden sighed. "What did you tell him?"

"I didn't tell him anything," she replied. "You're a big boy. You'll figure it out."

He laughed. "Right. How bad is it?"

"Bad enough to trigger the Code Blue," she said. "But not the worst we've seen. The sensors are suggesting three broken seals in the waste recycling system. We've already located one. Theroux is down there welding it now. But we're still losing about three ounces per hour."

"That's not a lot."

"Not this time, but every ounce counts, especially since we don't know if or when we'll ever reach our destination."

"Where do you want me to look?"

She took Hayden's hand, leading him over to one of the stations.

"Sheriff Duke," the operator said, glancing back at him.

"Caroline," he replied, greeting the fresh-faced Engineer.

She was one of their newest graduates, only sixteen years

old. He could barely believe he and Natalia had ever been that young.

Natalia leaned over Caroline, pointing to at the screen. "You can reach this segment through Section C. There's a small secured access door there that feeds into the system." She looked at him. "It's a tight fit, but you haven't gained too much weight, yet."

"Are you saying I'm fat?"

"No, I'm saying you're old." She put her hand on his stomach. "And you're getting a little soft in the middle."

"Not in front of the Yeoman," he said, smiling. "I know where that is. I'll go check it out."

"Thank you," she said.

"Just doing my job, miss," he replied. He had left his hat back at the office, but he motioned like he was tipping it to her. Then he took her hand, squeezing it once. "I love you."

"I love you, too," she replied. "Be careful out there."

"Of course."

4

IT DIDN'T TAKE HAYDEN LONG TO FOLLOW THE MAINTENANCE corridors along to Section C. He had been in the area plenty of times before, both with and without Natalia. Code Blues weren't common, but they weren't uncommon either. They happened often enough that he had been down these passages before. He was pretty sure he had even been through the small access door that connected the larger passage with the waste recycling line.

He had to enter his code again when he reached the door, typing in the eight digits and waiting for it to slide to the left. The space was smaller than he remembered, and he had to take off his utility belt to even think of slipping through. He dropped onto his stomach, pulling himself forward on his elbows through the hatch. If there was one part of his job that he hated, it was this. He could handle the small spaces of the strands. He hated feeling like he didn't have room to maneuver.

And he didn't. Not in here. Natalia was right about his expanding gut. He barely managed to fit into the small tunnel, which sank between two larger conduits that carried air and water to Metro. Sometimes it seemed to him as if the builders had designed the ship in a hurry, throwing it together instead of thinking about how all of the pieces fit. The narrow space was a perfect example, because once he bypassed the two meter wide conduits, it opened into a regular, human-sized space again, albeit a small one.

He held the sniffer up near his face, checking to make sure it was turned on. Then he started walking along the maintenance aisle, holding it out ahead of him. He watched the readings on it change as he moved, even though he had no idea what any of them meant.

"Hayden." Natalia's voice came out through his transceiver, interspersed with static. He was surrounded by the metal of the ship's innards, and it was interfering with the signal.

"Hey, Nat," he replied. "I'm in Section C."

"I figured you would be by now."

"How do I know if we have a leak down here?"

"Do you smell anything?"

Hayden laughed. "Good point." He paused and breathed in through his nose. "No." He looked down the corridor. The access lighting was in better shape here than it was in the strand. It looked like the pipes continued for a fair distance.

"That segment goes half a kilometer east," Natalia said. "Then it'll hit a junction and vanish up to Section B and down to Section D, which leads directly into the recycling unit."

"I knew that," Hayden said.

"I'm sure you did," Natalia said. "Can you walk it and radio back if you smell something?"

"For you, anything."

She laughed. The soft crispness of it always made him smile. "Thank you, Sheriff."

"Anytime, Boss," he replied.

He continued walking alongside the pipe, pausing every few meters to sniff again. The Pilgrim's typical recycled atmosphere had an unnaturally fresh smell to it, created by the layers of filters that scrubbed out the CO2 and any wayward particles. It was a smell he didn't notice most of the time, not until it was replaced with something else, like the scent of a nice cultured steak.

He licked his lips at the thought, wondering if they had any steak in their cube. The luxury meal was one of the perks of being a Sheriff married to a Lead Engineer, and a hell of a lot better than the processed nutrition shakes that were the main staple of their diet.

It was also part of the reason he was getting soft.

"No steak," he told himself, continuing down the passage.

He reached the end without registering anything out of the ordinary. He tapped his badge. "Engineering."

A shrill beep told him they were connected.

"Nat, wherever your damage is, it isn't down here," he said.

"Roger, Sheriff," she replied. "I think Deputy Bradshaw located the last of the leaks, but since you were already down there, I figured I'd let you finish. Just in case."

"No problem. Does that mean you'll be heading home soon?"

"As soon as I finish up the report for the Governor and clear the Code Blue. I'll meet you there?"

"Affirmative. I've got Sarah Kaine and a kid from Block Twenty-four in lockup, but I can deal with them in the morning."

"Is Sarah selling herself for meds again?"

"I'm afraid so."

"I wish her mother would just head to medical and get it over with. She's really bringing her daughter down."

"I know, but what can you do?"

"Go easy on her, will you, Hayden? It's hard for a lot of people in Metro. We're two of the lucky ones."

"I know it."

He paused. He hated to think of his home without the filter of his job. It could be a tough place to live, and it was only getting tougher. Not that they had a choice.

"I'm going to head back out. Hopefully, since I got into the passage, I can get out of the passage."

"As long as you weren't daydreaming about steak."

"You know me, Nat."

"That's what I'm afraid of."

He laughed. "I'll see you back at our cube."

"Roger."

Hayden tapped the badge to disconnect, moving more quickly back to the access tunnel.

Tap. Tap. Tap. Taaaap.

He froze, the sound of something pinging on metal giving him pause. What was that? He hadn't noticed it a second ago.

He waited, listening for it. Ten seconds passed in silence. Twenty.

Tap. Tap. Tap. Taaaap.

He leaned over, putting his ear against the sewage pipe. It could have been liquid dripping into it. If it were clogging up that could become a huge problem.

Tap. Tap. Tap. Taaaap.

He heard it further back, and it wasn't reverberating in the pipe, which meant it was external to it. But then, where the hell was it coming from?

He walked toward the sound, trying to trace it as he heard it two more times. It was the same noise each time. The same pace. The same cadence. He had no idea what it was or what was generating it.

"Engineering," he said, contacting her again.

"Sheriff Duke?"

"Caroline. Is my wife still there?"

"No, Sheriff. She said she would finish the report from home. Oh. She was hoping to surprise you."

He considered whether or not to mention the sound to Caroline. He decided against it. Maybe the tapping was normal, and then he would just get her worried for nothing. He would tell Natalia about it when he got home, and if she wanted to come back and check it out, then that's what they would do.

"Should I send out an emergency call to her, Sheriff?" Caroline asked.

"No. No need. I'll talk to her at home. Thank you, Caroline."

"Of course, Sheriff."

Hayden disconnected. He stayed for a few more minutes, but he didn't hear the tapping again. If something was broken, he figured it would have continued indefinitely. The noise was probably typical, and Nat would laugh at him for worrying about it.

He smiled. That was fine with him. He was dead tired, and already two hours past the end of his shift. Things had been a little strange today, but not completely out of the ordinary.

It could wait until tomorrow.

5

HAYDEN PAUSED WHEN HE REACHED THE TOP FLOOR OF THE block, giving himself a few seconds to catch his breath before he headed to his cube. The lift was broken again, jammed between level twelve and thirteen, offline for the third time already this year. He was sure Natalia would have someone over to get it fixed by the time he woke up, but that hadn't helped his already tired legs now.

There was nothing to be done about it. The lifts were seizing more and more often, and Engineering had a whole team dedicated to running repairs. Usually, that meant pulling parts from a lesser-used lift, installing them on the next lift, and then bringing the broken piece back to the shop to machine it back into working order. The problem was that you could only machine something so many times before the integrity was gone and you needed a new piece.

And they didn't have any new pieces.

There were four blocks in Metro that didn't have functional lifts. Some reorganization had gotten the sixteen hundred cubes inside them assigned to the younger residents, those that were more capable of making the hike of up to eighteen floors.

As Hayden marched down the long corridor to his cube, he realized that one of those buildings was Block Twenty-four. The one where Francis lived.

"Good morning, Sheriff."

Hayden shifted his head back to a cube on his left. The door had swung open. A woman only a few years his senior was halfway out of it, heading to work.

"Doctor Hun," Hayden said. "It's still good night for me. I haven't been home yet."

She smiled. "I figured, after the turb. I was placed on standby. Thankfully there were no injuries, that last one was a beast."

"Tell me about it. We did get a Code Blue."

"Any damage?"

"Nothing too bad."

"That's good to hear. Have a great night, Sheriff. Tell Natalia I said hello."

"Will do."

She started down the corridor.

"Hey, Lin," Hayden said, getting her attention. "The lift's jammed. You're going to have to walk it."

She smiled halfheartedly, making sure not to show too much displeasure in front of him. "Thanks for the update."

He nodded to her before turning back and finishing the walk to his cube. They had one of the corner units, double the size of a normal cube with an extra window out to Metro. The Sheriff's Station was in sight of their apartment, as were a pair of the clothing exchanges and the largest farm in the city. It would mostly be dark this time of night, the non-essential lighting shut down to conserve power. Nobody knew for sure how long the energy generation on the Pilgrim would last, but they all agreed they never wanted it to run out.

Hayden stopped again at the door to the cube, straightening his jacket and shirt to make himself more presentable. Then he put his wrist to the scanner there, the embedded tag unlocking the door and allowing him to enter.

Natalia was in the back of the cube in the kitchen.

He smelled steak.

"I think I just died and went to Heaven," he said as she turned around.

Not only did he smell steak, but she was wearing a dress he hadn't seen before, something fresh from the exchange. It was black and red, with long sleeves and a cut that hugged her frame before tapering out at the thighs.

"I know you had a hard day," she said. "We had one steak ration left for the month."

"I thought we were saving it until we had a pair?"

He walked back through the cube, past the living area to the kitchen. Their bedroom was on the left, a smaller bedroom and a bathroom on the right. The door to the smaller bedroom was closed and had been that way for almost a year now. Winning the lottery had been exhilarating.

What came after had been the complete opposite.

The cube's decor was similar to most of the residents' living quarters - a merged collection of knick-knacks and furniture that had been handed down, traded, and exchanged multiple times over the generations. None of it matched, but that made it more cozy.

He met Natalia there, putting his arms around her and giving her a warm kiss.

"You earned it, Sheriff," she said, putting her hand on his cheek. The lightness in her voice hardened for a moment.

"Besides, once the Governor catches up to you, we might not get another steak ration for a while."

"He was that mad?" Hayden asked, shrugging out of his coat.

Natalia turned back to the cooker, opening the door to retrieve the steak, the smell wafting out and making Hayden's mouth water all over again. He knew from the PASS that they had real steak back on Earth, made from real meat that came from real animals. Their version was grown on the farm from stem cells and was supposedly more pure and better tasting than the real thing.

"You know the Governor," Natalia said. "Besides, Code Blues are serious business, Hayden. Any one of them could be life or death. What if the gravity generators had failed?"

"I would have known if the gravity generators failed," Hayden replied, smiling. "I'd say you're mad at me, too, but you did make me a steak."

"I trust you," Natalia said. "If you thought the trouble in the strands was more important, then I believe it was."

"I wish I could say you were right. I heard a shout that sounded like somebody was being attacked. It turns out some lughead from Block Twenty-four was bumping one of Sarah's johns for a hit of his own."

Natalia dropped the square of steak on a plate and carried it over to their small table, placing it down on his usual side. He took his position there, picking up a knife and fork.

"As mad as Malcolm may be with me, he's probably thrilled with you and your team for getting the trouble fixed so quickly."

Natalia joined him at the opposite seat, smiling. "He is. More than I even expected."

"Oh? How so?"

"Eat your steak."

Hayden smiled. Natalia knew something. He could see it in her eyes. The slight wrinkle of her lids and the hint of a smile on her face. What had the Governor said to her?

He stabbed the block, cutting it and taking a bite, keeping his eyes on his wife. She was teasing him. Toying with him. It had been a while since he had seen that look on her face. The last time was-

He swallowed the steak. "It's delicious," he said. "It always is."

"I'm glad you like it," she said.

"I was having a bad night. I didn't think there was anything that could make it this much better so quickly." He paused, playing with his expression. "I have a feeling there might be more to come."

She laughed. "That's what I get for marrying a Sheriff. I can't keep anything from you for more than ten seconds."

He laughed with her, his eyes scanning the room, and heading back to the closed bedroom door on the right. He noticed the handle was slightly smudged, the pattern too large for her small hands.

He looked back at her.

She was still smiling. She had noticed him noticing the door.

"He was here, wasn't he?" Hayden said. "The Governor."

"He was," she admitted.

He took another bite of the steak while she beamed. He knew this game. He was happy to be playing it. He chewed slowly, watching her, waiting for her to burst.

She didn't. She stayed quiet. Hayden swallowed, and then picked up his napkin and wiped his lips.

"Are you going to confess, my love, or do I need to interrogate you?"

He stood up. So did she. As she did, she reached into a

pocket on the side of the dress and withdrew a piece of paper.

"The Governor said the Pilgrim needs more Engineers like me," she said, pausing for a few seconds. "And more Sheriffs like you."

"Lousy, no good Sheriffs who don't respond to Code Blues?"

"Passionate, capable Sheriffs who care about the people of Metro."

"He said that?"

"No. He only said the Engineers part, but I believe the rest."

Hayden's eyes shifted to the paper. They both knew what it was. She didn't have to say.

"Are you sure you want to do this again?" he asked.

"More than anything."

"It's a risk."

"Every second on this ship is a risk."

"I just don't want to see you hurt like that again."

"Nothing's guaranteed, Hayden. But if you aren't willing to risk pain, you'll never get what you want."

He could feel the tears in his eyes. He could see the same in hers. There were two ways to legally have a child in Metro. Win the lottery, or be given a pass by the Governor for exceptional service to the city.

Hayden moved to his wife, wrapping her in a tight embrace, the tears falling more freely. They had been one of the lucky couples to win the lottery, only to have their hearts broken when the pregnancy didn't take.

And now they had their second chance.

"I love you," he said.

"I love you, too," she replied.

"Then what are we waiting for?"

She laughed again. "What about your steak?"

"Who needs steak?"

He took her hand, and they walked together to the bedroom, the steak, and the tapping he had heard in Section C, forgotten.

6

"Good afternoon, Sheriff," Deputy Wilson said as Hayden pushed open the door to the Law Station.

There was a time when the windowed steel block had slid open on its own accord, but the parts from the mechanism had been salvaged for something else a long time ago, leaving entrants to rely on personal strength to shove it aside. Hayden and his team joked that it was the door that kept them in shape.

"Wilson," Hayden said, a big smile on his face. "How's Metro this morning?"

"All quiet, sir," Wilson said. She was a big woman, tall and powerful, a frightening proposition in a scuffle. Fortunately, he had never needed to fight with her. "Well, except for our guest in temporary holding. She's been whining to be released all morning."

"Sarah?"

"Yes, sir. She promised she would come back for questioning, but she wanted to check on her mother."

Hayden shook his head. He wasn't going to let Sarah get

him down. Not today. For as tough as the night before had seemed, it was the best he had experienced in a long time.

"Is Bradshaw in yet?"

"In and gone," Wilson said. "He went to check on a complaint from Block Twelve."

"I assume it's nothing serious?"

"No, sir."

Hayden didn't ask for more. He trusted his deputies to do what they needed to do, and he didn't need to know about every minor call unless it became more than a minor call.

"I'm going to head into Room B," Hayden said. "Can you deliver Sarah there, and escort Francis to Room A?"

"Of course, Sheriff."

"Thank you."

Wilson stood, abandoning the frontmost desk in the Station, bypassing Hayden on her way to the temporary cells. There were more cells on the third and fourth floors, a small penitentiary for more serious offenses, mainly related to gambling, drugs, and alcohol. It didn't matter how limited the resources in Metro were; it seemed that stuff always found a way to proliferate.

Hayden headed into Room B. It was a small space, barely larger than the bedroom he had spent the morning cleaning with Natalia, both of them eager to make a fresh start with the second chance the Governor had given them. There had been a lot of emotions involved with letting go of the past, and they agreed it would never be forgotten. But they had to move on.

He settled into one of the two chairs in the room. They were positioned to face one another, leaving only a short distance between him and his subject. A table rested to his left. There were already two glasses of water on it.

The door opened a few seconds later. Sarah Kaine entered, with Wilson right behind her. His deputy towered over the girl, making her look even smaller. Her hair was haggard, her posture deflated.

"Have a seat," Hayden said, motioning to the other chair.

"Sheriff Duke," Sarah said, not making a move to sit. "I don't have anything to say. I mean, I just met Francis last night. I didn't know his name until you did."

"The Sheriff asked you to sit, Sarah," Wilson said.

She looked back. "Please. I need to get home."

"Sarah," Hayden said. "You'll get home faster if you sit and answer my questions."

"Are you going to arrest me again?"

"No," Hayden said. "But I need you to tell me what happened last night, in your own words."

She hesitated, and then scampered to the chair and sat.

"Go ahead," he said.

She bit her lip and nodded. "Okay, so you already know about my mother."

"Skip ahead to the part where you picked up the john," Hayden said.

"Right. So I was walking the main split, heading back to my place. This guy comes up to me, and he says, "Hey, are you looking to trade?" And I say, "I'm looking for a med chit, skillet."

She lowered her voice when she spoke the john's part, acting out the scene with her hands.

"Skillet?" Hayden said.

"It's a haircut. Shaved on one side, choppy on the other."

"How'd this guy know you were looking to serve? You were wearing long pants and a baggy shirt."

"I dunno. Word gets around, you know? Probably heard I did a trick for a friend or something. Anyways, he was like, "I've got a chit. Come on." And he pulls me into the strand. Hmm, come to think of it now, he did look nervous. His head kept going back and forth like this." Her eyes darted around the room, her head turning back and forth. Hayden had to keep himself from laughing.

"He knew someone was following him," he said. "He was hoping he could lose them in the strand."

"I guess. We went in, and I was like, 'This is far enough.' Because I was nervous about going in, you know. You Laws always seem to know when I go into the strands. But he said, 'No, we have to go deeper. I know a place nobody will catch us.' Then we stopped at that control panel, and he entered the code. It opened up, and he shoved me inside. The first turb hit right after that, but we're used to the turbs, so whatever, right? Only the big guy, Francis, caught up to him before he could close the door. He had a knife, and he tried to grab him, but the skillet knocked it from his hand and took off. The door closed, and I thought I was safe, but then I heard him putting in the code, and it opened again."

"They both knew the code?"

"Yeah. Why?"

"Only a few people are supposed to know the codes to the maintenance boxes. Francis isn't one of them."

"Oh. Well, he did. But then I guess he heard you coming because he came at me, told me to pull off my shirt and pants and all that."

"He didn't do it?"

"Nope. Neither of them did. They never touched me, which I thought was weird."

Hayden thought back. When Francis had attacked him, his pants were up and closed. He shook his head. He should have noticed that. Careless.

He stood up. Sarah followed suit.

"Does that mean I can go?" she asked.

"If they didn't touch you, and they solicited you, then you didn't do anything illegal. Unless he gave you the chit?"

"No, he didn't, the bastard."

"You're free to go, Sarah. Thank you for your cooperation."

She nodded, turning back to the door. Wilson stepped aside to let her leave.

"How would two kids find out the codes for the maintenance boxes?" Wilson asked. "And why were they chasing one another?"

"I don't know," Hayden replied. "I think I'm going to find out."

7

HAYDEN CROSSED THE HALLWAY TO ROOM B. FRANCIS WAS already inside, sitting calmly in the chair with his back to the door. He didn't move when Hayden entered, keeping his eyes forward. His whole attitude was in stark contrast to Sarah. Either he was a kid who didn't think he had done anything wrong or he was a kid with something to hide.

Hayden figured it was the latter.

He sat in the chair opposite Francis. He didn't speak right away. Francis stared back at him, arms at his sides, breathing slow and steady.

"I realized last night that Block Twenty-four is one of the buildings without a lift," Hayden said. "What floor do you live on?"

"Six," Francis said. "The scan should have told you that."

It was the first time he had spoken. His voice was deeper than Hayden expected. He sounded older than he appeared to be. Maybe he wasn't a kid after all?

"I didn't remember. It was a long night."

Francis didn't respond.

"Are you always this quiet?"

Francis shrugged.

"I'll cut to the heart of it," Hayden said. "Sarah already told me about the other guy and the fact that neither one of you laid a hand on her. Obviously, that's left me a little confused. One, who is the other guy? Two, why were you chasing him? Three, how did you get the code to the maintenance box? And four, where did you get the knife?"

Francis stared at him again.

"If I went to search your cube, what would I find?" Hayden asked. He watched Francis' face for a reaction. He noticed a slight twitch in the man's eye. "Something you don't want me to find? I'll tell you what; you answer my questions, I won't search your place. How does that sound?"

Francis breathed out. "Fine."

Hayden smiled. "Good. Start at question one and work your way through."

"Are you sure you want the answers, Sheriff?" Francis asked.

"It's my job to ask them, so why wouldn't I?"

"There's an old saying. Ignorance is bliss."

"I know it. I've never found that to be true. I prefer 'ignorance is for the stupid.'"

Francis almost cracked a smile.

"The PASS is damaged, Sheriff."

"I'm aware."

"How did it get that way?"

"I don't know. It happened a long time ago. I thought I was asking the questions?"

"The answers to your questions are meaningless without context. I'll say this again, Sheriff Duke. Some things that are better off forgotten. Once you remember one thing, it's never enough. You always want to know if there's something else you're missing."

"Is there?"

"I don't know yet. But maybe it's better to be stupid."

"Is that a veiled threat? You did attack me."

"To avoid this situation. More for your sake than for mine."

"Why do you say that?"

"Do you know how long the Pilgrim has been out here, Sheriff?"

"No. I don't even know where here is."

"Me neither. But I do know the answer to my prior question. Three-hundred ninety-six years."

Hayden felt his heart skip a little faster. "What?"

Francis nodded solemnly. "Do you know how long we were supposed to be out here, Sheriff?"

Hayden shook his head.

"The Pilgrim was designed for a three hundred year duty cycle."

Hayden's brow creased. His body was suddenly cold.

"That's right," Francis said, noticing his body language. "We're almost a century past the maximum expected lifespan of the ship. And we still haven't gotten where we were going."

"How do you know this?" Hayden asked, forcing himself to regain his composure. He was the Sheriff here. "The PASS doesn't have that data."

"The data was corrupted. We have ways to filter it."

"We?"

"The guy I was chasing. He helped me figure out how to scrub the corrupted data."

"He's an Engineer?"

"No. Just a curious resident, like me." Francis sighed. "He was coming to the Station, to you, believe it or not, to tell you what we knew. I was trying to stop him. I told him it was too soon. That we hadn't learned enough. That it wasn't safe."

"You think I would do something to you to keep you from talking?"

"That one fact could cause mass panic in Metro. So, yeah."

Hayden took a deep breath. He knew Francis was right. He was already starting to feel panicked. Not that it was news to him that the ship was breaking down, but knowing how long overdue it was?

"I told you ignorance was bliss," Francis said.

The door to the room opened, and Wilson ducked her head in. "Sheriff, I'm sorry to interrupt you, but Governor Malcolm is in your office. He wants to talk to you. Immediately." She said the last word in a mimic of the Governor's deep voice.

Hayden felt a different panic hit him. The Governor was mad enough about the Code Blue to come down to the Station as soon as he started his shift? He forced himself to calm. Malcolm had still given Natalia the birth ticket. He couldn't be that upset.

"Will you wait here?" Hayden asked.

Francis nodded, falling silent again. His eyes were pleading, suggesting that Hayden keep his mouth shut about what he had learned.

He had already decided he wasn't going to mention Francis to the Governor. Not yet. He needed more time to understand all of this, a lot more time before he was going to carry it up the line.

Hayden left the room, heading to the back of the Station where his office was located. The door was already open, and he could see Governor Malcolm in his chair, feet up on the desk. He was short and thin, dressed in a dark blue one-piece, with a badge of office over his chest so everyone would know who he was.

"Governor," Hayden said, entering the room. He reached back to pull the door closed before the Governor asked.

"Hayden," Governor Malcolm replied without changing his position. "You already closed the door. Why don't you have a seat?"

"I'll stand," Hayden said.

He had known Malcolm for a long time. He knew the Governor liked to take advantage of his position to lord over the residents of Metro, especially his direct subordinates.

He wasn't going to give him that satisfaction, and he knew Malcolm wouldn't expect him to.

Malcolm smiled. He had a row of crooked but bright white teeth. Medical could have straightened them for him, but for some reason, he didn't want them to.

"Have it your way, Sheriff." He paused. "I stopped by your cube last night."

Hayden nodded. "Natalia told me."

"Of course, she did."

"I don't know what to say."

"Say thank you, Sheriff."

"Thank you, Governor."

"You're welcome. But I'm sure you know, I didn't do it for you."

"The Code Blue-"

"The Code Blue is not optional, Hayden," Malcolm shouted, dropping his feet to the floor. "This city is on the razor's edge of life and death. From outside the Pilgrim, and from inside. We can't control the external forces, but we have total control over critical life support systems. Failing to adequately address any problem with those systems, no matter how small, puts the lives of everyone in Metro at risk."

Hayden could feel the heat on his face. He knew Malcolm had come to chew him out. He knew he deserved it. He knew he shouldn't try to defend himself, but he couldn't help it.

"Natalia had everything under control," he said.

"As always," Malcolm replied, still angry. "Your wife is definitely your better half, Sheriff. She's one of the best Engineers the Pilgrim's ever had. That's why I gave you the birth ticket. I want another one just like her. This ship needs another one just like her. I can only hope they get the right mix of DNA."

Hayden clenched his hand into a fist. That one stung. He had to stay calm.

"I had a situation in the strands," Hayden said. "Someone was in trouble."

"Someone? Singular? Did you just miss the part where I said you put every single person on this ship's life at risk?"

"I didn't. Natalia-"

"This time, Sheriff. She saved your ass this time. Or you got lucky it was the waste system and not the damned atmospherics. I'm responsible for everyone on this ship. I'm responsible for keeping it all running smoothly, even as more and more of it breaks down every day. You make the wrong prioritization once; it's my job to make sure you don't ever, ever, ever do it again. Are we clear, Hayden?"

Hayden clenched his jaw and nodded. "Yes, Governor."

The anger faded from the Governor as if it had been an act the entire time. He smiled widely, the same smile he had ridden to his election. "Good. Because I don't want Natalia to have to find a new man to help her make a baby."

The remark gave Hayden a fresh chill. There were very few offenses that led to capital punishment, and as far as he knew only six people had been put to death in the entire time the Pilgrim had been in space. That the Governor was suggesting what he had done was one of those offenses drove home how big of an error in judgment he had made.

"Yes, Governor," he said.

"So what happened last night in the strands?" Malcolm

asked. "Your wife told me you had Sarah Kaine and some guy from Block Twenty-four locked up over it?"

Hayden stared at the Governor without speaking right away. How much should he tell him?

"I did."

"Past tense?"

"I released Sarah right before you arrived."

"With another stern warning that she'll ignore?"

"I can't put her in lockup because she wants to take care of her mother."

"That woman needs to die," Malcolm said. "I know it sounds bad, but it's the truth."

"I know. I told her as much. A little more gently."

"You're much more diplomatic than I am, Hayden."

"I sure as hell hope that isn't true, Governor."

"I'm done yelling at you. You can call me Malcolm again." He laughed. "So, what about this other suspect? You let him go yet?"

Hayden hesitated. Malcolm wouldn't question him if he said he had, and it would make it easier to get to the bottom of the whole thing. If the Governor decided to talk to Francis personally, it might shut him down altogether. At the same time, he didn't want to risk putting himself on Malcolm's bad side again, especially not right now.

"I thought that was an easy question," Malcolm said.

Hayden opened his mouth to answer.

Something hit the Pilgrim.

Hard.

8

THE SHOCK WAS SUDDEN AND VIOLENT, THE FORCE ENOUGH that it traveled through the ship in an instant, creating a shockwave that knocked both Hayden and the Governor off their feet, and spilled the items on Hayden's desk to the floor. A whine and pop from the superstructure came with it, so loud that it left their ears ringing as they hit the ground.

"What the hell?" Malcolm said, staying down as the turbulence caused the ship to reverberate with smaller aftershocks.

"I don't know," Hayden replied.

Normally, big turbs like that were preceded and followed by smaller waves. This one had come out of nowhere.

"We'd better check in with Engineering," Malcolm said.

The ship shook again, a smaller turb this time.

Hayden tapped his badge with his chin. "Engineering."

It took a few seconds for someone to pick up, but that didn't surprise him. He could picture the control room and the chaos within as the Engineers scrambled to identify damage to the systems.

"Sheriff Duke," Mae said.

"Is everyone there okay?" Hayden asked.

"Yes, Sheriff," she replied. "We're all fine."

"Mae, this is the Governor," Malcolm said. Not that he needed to announce himself like that. She knew his voice well enough to recognize him.

"Governor Malcolm," Mae said. "We're all okay. No critical damage showing on our displays."

"Do you have any idea what the hell caused that?"

"Do we ever, Governor? I've never felt one come on so strong out of nowhere like that."

"Me neither. We've got the all clear on life support?"

"Yes, Governor."

"Mae, is Natalia there?" Hayden asked.

"No, Sheriff. She was out near Section C, checking on one of the power inputs near the secure zone. I can radio her for you?"

"That's all right," Hayden replied. "I'll contact her myself."

"Thank you, Mae," Malcolm said. He motioned for Hayden to cut the connection. "I'm going to head out into the street to check on the residents and make sure they all stay calm. Normally I wouldn't worry, but this is outside the norm."

"Do you want me to come with you?"

"There's no need. Take care of your business, Hayden. I'll take care of mine." He put his hand out for balance as the Pilgrim shuddered slightly, the turbs diminishing. "You can start by cleaning up this mess." He smiled. "You're a slob, Sheriff."

Hayden smiled with him. He only had a few items on his desk. His hat, an old photograph of a dog that had been passed down through Natalia's family, and a printout of the last sonogram Medical had done before the miscarriage. All three were on the floor.

"Sheriff."

Deputy Wilson opened the door, sticking her head in. "I'm sorry to interrupt, but we've got a small problem, sir."

"What is it, Deputy?" Hayden asked.

"It's Francis, sir," she said. "He's gone."

"What?" Hayden said.

"He took off after the first turb hit. I couldn't get to him in time."

"Who's Francis?" Malcolm asked.

"The person of interest I was questioning," Hayden said. "From Block Twenty-four."

Malcolm laughed. "He ran off? Where's he going to go?"

Hayden didn't say it, but he knew Francis had something at his cube that he wanted to hide. Maybe he had gone to hide it.

"Wilson," Malcolm said. "Send Bradshaw and Hicks to Block Twenty-four, whatever his cube number is."

"Yes, Governor."

Wilson disappeared. Malcolm headed for the door, putting his hand on Hayden's shoulder on the way out. "Why would he run, Sheriff?"

Hayden didn't want to tell him anything. He had to tell him something. "I think he found a way to hack the codes on the maintenance boxes, and he left evidence exposed in his cube."

Malcolm's eyes lowered slightly. "Maybe you should get over there, too? That's a serious offense."

"Yes, sir," Hayden said.

He bent down to grab his hat, and then followed the Governor out into the split. There were more residents out there than usual, but they didn't seem too concerned about the turbs.

"I want him back at the Station immediately, Sheriff," Malcolm said. "I'm sorry I yelled at you in there. If this guy has access to the maintenance boxes, you may have saved the whole city."

"You were right to ream me out," Hayden said. "But thank you."

Malcolm nodded and headed off toward a group of residents. Hayden turned to look down the length of the split. Law used to have transports to carry them across Metro in a hurry, but like many other things they had been broken down for parts years ago.

The Station door and the lack of transportation. That's what was keeping his middle from spreading a little too far beyond his pants.

He started to run.

Residents moved aside for him, accustomed to the Law running through the splits to one place or another. Some of them shouted greetings as he passed. A few urged him on and offered motivation. He ignored it all, focusing on his pace and breathing. He had to cross over a kilometer, and he had to do it without falling too far behind Francis.

He was almost halfway when his badge beeped an incoming transmission.

"Hayden," Natalia said, in a voice that brought him to a quick stop.

She sounded terrified.

"Nat, what's wrong?" he asked, breathing heavily.

"Hayden. I. I was. I was in the corridor near Section C. Near. Near an access door." She paused. He was about to ask her what was wrong again. "There's a body here, Hayden. A man."

"A body?"

His pulse was already quick, but somehow it found another speed. There hadn't been a murder in Metro in all the time he had been Sheriff. It just didn't happen. Not here.

"He's. His blood is everywhere. I don't know. I don't see a wound. He's dead."

She was scared and out of sorts. He hated to hear her like that. But there was nothing he could do. Not immediately. Malcolm had sent him after Francis. If he were going on his own, he would turn around, but he couldn't. Not now.

"Okay. Nat, it's okay. I know you're scared. I know it's shocking. Please try to calm down. Governor Malcolm sent me to Block Twenty-four. I have to stop in there, and then I'll come to you, okay?"

"Hayden," she said, short of breath. "You don't. You don't understand. He's dead."

"Nat, it's okay. I do understand. You found a body. Trust me; it isn't going anywhere. You don't have to stay with it. Head back to Control. I'll meet you there as soon as I can."

"Damn it, Hayden," she said, finding some strength in her voice. "This isn't just a body. It. It. The clothes."

She paused again before spitting out the most chilling words he had ever heard.

"He isn't one of ours. He isn't from Metro."

9

Hayden didn't know how to respond. His heart was racing. His mind was racing faster, her words echoing within. Not one of ours? How could that be?

"Nat, I want you to go back to Control, okay? I want you to go back to Control right now."

"Okay."

"I'll be there as fast as I can. I'll meet you there. Okay?"

"Yes. Just hurry. I don't like this at all."

"Me neither. I'm on my way. I need to disconnect to tell Bradshaw I'm changing direction."

"Okay. I'll see you soon."

"Definitely."

"Hayden?"

"What is it?"

"I love you."

"I love you, too."

Hayden dropped the transmission and then tapped on the badge again. He also started walking back in the opposite direction. Back toward Engineering. "Deputy Bradshaw."

"That you, Sheriff Duke?" Josh said.

"Affirmative. What's your status, Josh?"

"I'm inside the Block Twenty-four stairwell, humping my way up to the sixth floor. What's up?"

"The Governor asked me to head over that way, but I got a call from Natalia. She found something unexpected in the maintenance corridors."

He wasn't about to tell the Deputy what that something unexpected was. There was no point getting him involved when there was nothing he could do.

"It better be important, Sheriff," Josh said.

"It is. Keep an eye out for Francis, bring him back to the Station. And lock down his apartment. I don't want anyone touching anything in there."

"Yes, sir."

Hayden disconnected. He wanted to contact the Governor, but he didn't wear a comm badge. He said anyone who needed him that bad would be able to find him.

Hayden didn't need him that bad.

"Natalia Duke," he said.

The badge beeped as it connected.

"Nat," he said. "I'm on my way to Control."

He waited a few seconds for her to answer.

She didn't.

"Nat?"

He waited a second time.

Still no answer.

"Natalia?"

He grabbed his badge, unclipping it from his collar and bringing it to his face. The indicator light said their badges were connected.

"Natalia?" he said again, louder this time.

She still didn't respond.

He had felt cold before. Now he was truly panicked. He

clutched the comm, breaking into a sprint, heading in the direction of Engineering.

"Natalia!" he repeated.

Nothing.

He tapped the badge to disconnect.

"Engineering," he said, his breath heavy.

He couldn't think. Couldn't focus. Couldn't concentrate.

"Sheriff Duke?" Mae said.

"Mae, did Natalia make it back to Control yet?" He said it breathlessly, a mix of fear and exertion.

"No, Sheriff," Mae said. "Are you okay?"

"No, I'm not. Nat isn't answering her comm."

"What? How could that be?"

"I don't know."

"She was in Section C. I'll go and look for her."

"No," Hayden said. "Stay in Control. I'm on my way."

Only now did he remember the tapping he had heard in Section C. How could he have forgotten it? Maybe it wasn't nothing after all.

He disconnected again. "Natalia Duke," he said, contacting her badge. It beeped when it connected. "Nat, please tell me you're there."

She didn't answer. Again.

Damn it, damn it, damn it, damn it.

He felt the tears spring to his eyes. He felt the rush of desperate adrenaline. He picked up the pace, sprinting hard through the split, reaching Metro Park South. He raced through the park, the residents there turning their heads to watch him.

He made it to the access hatch, breathing heavily, a cold sweat dripping from his brow as he tried to type in the code, fumbling twice before getting it right. It slid aside, and he ran in, retracing his steps from the night before, when it had been him in Section C, examining the waste system.

Why was she out there by herself? What could have happened to her? He kept trying to raise her on her transceiver, but she didn't answer. Was she hurt? Was she dead? What the hell happened?

He charged through the maintenance corridors, back to Section C.

"Nat," he cried out, his voice echoing in the empty passages. "Nat, where are you?"

She didn't answer.

The secure hatch was where? He tried to remember the map from the night before. It wasn't far from where he had checked the waste system. He wiped the moisture from his eyes, reaching for his gun and pulling it from his hip. If anyone had hurt Natalia, he was going to do more than stun them.

He would kill them with his bare hands if he had to, law be damned.

He reached the end of the corridor, turning to the right to face the secured hatch. It wasn't like the other hatches inside Metro's perimeter. It was heavy and thick and had a line of yellow and black stripes along the outer edge. There was no control panel on this side. No way to open it.

He looked to the area ahead of it. There was blood on the floor, a thick smear that covered the metal surface. Something was resting the blood.

Natalia's transceiver.

He ran over to it. Knelt down. He was barely holding himself together. His eyes ran. His lip quivered. There was so much blood. But no body. She said there had been a body. Whose blood was he standing in?

He followed the smear to the hatch. It disappeared below it in a line.

"Naaaaattttt," he shouted at the top of his lungs, his voice echoing in the corridor. "No! Damn it!"

He walked to the hatch. He bent down. There. A handprint in the blood. Only the fingers were sticking out through the hatch, as if they had reached under from the other side. The fingers were small. A woman's hand? Was it Natalia? Was this her blood?

He felt along the bottom, trying to find a seam, desperate to find a way to open it. He scraped his fingers along the floor, breaking a nail on the intersection of steel, shoving his fingers forward to get beneath.

He couldn't. Of course, he couldn't. There was no way to open the door. They had tried. He was sure they had tried at some point in the last. What? Almost four hundred years? Francis' words came back and hit him in the gut like a sucker punch.

"Ignorance is bliss, Sheriff."

No. It wasn't. Not now. Not ever. Ignorance? What kind of ignorance led to this? Natalia was missing. There was a trail of blood from this side of the secure hatch to the other. Someone was out there, where no one should have been. Someone may have taken his wife.

Who?

"Natalia," he shouted. "Nat!"

No answer. He didn't expect one. Not anymore.

He continued to scratch at the hatch. There was no way through. Not like this.

He had to make a choice. Fall apart or figure it out.

He wasn't about to abandon her.

He would figure it out. He knew where to start. He knew who knew how to open locked hatches.

He had to get back to Block Twenty-four.

10

HE RAN BACK THROUGH THE MAINTENANCE CORRIDORS. HIS heart was pounding, his breath ragged. With every step, he felt like he couldn't take another one. His body didn't want to support him. His mind didn't want to stay strong.

She was gone. His love. His life.

How could that be possible?

They weren't alone on the Pilgrim. That much was obvious. Not unless someone in Metro was playing some kind of sick joke. Could it be Francis? No, he wouldn't have had time. The Governor? Was he that mad at him that he would do something like that?

He didn't know what to think. What to believe. That door had been sealed for four hundred years. It hadn't opened when they were supposed to arrive wherever they were headed, why in the universe would it have opened now? And why did whatever was on the other side take Natalia? Clearly, they wouldn't have been expecting to find someone there. Was it because she had found the body? Were they trying to hide something?

It seemed everyone was trying to hide something.

He reached the main corridor that passed Control. Mae was there, heading in his direction.

"Sheriff," she said, concerned when she saw his red face and sweaty brow. "Did you find Natalia?"

"No," he said, the word coming out more violently than he intended. He didn't slow as he reached her.

"Sheriff?" she said. She turned to watch him run past, and then made her way back into Control.

"Deputy Bradshaw," Hayden said, tapping his badge.

He could barely get the words out; his body was working so hard. He knew he should have stayed on top of his daily runs, to make sure he would be ready for anything. He had let himself slip. He had gotten too comfortable. All the Sheriffs did as they aged. Hell, that was one of the perks of being the Sheriff. But they didn't have to deal with what he was dealing with. The turbs had only started ten years earlier. Everything had been so much more peaceful before that.

Bradshaw didn't respond. Why?

"Bradshaw," he said again.

This didn't make any sense. He glanced down at the badge, realizing it hadn't beeped. The connection wasn't made. The indicator was still red. Something was wrong with the transceivers. It figured if anything were going to break right now, it would be that.

He reached Metro South Park. He had to stop then, leaning over from his waist, holding his hands on his thighs and gulping for air. There was no time to stop. No time to breathe. Natalia was in trouble, and every second counted.

His heart thudded in his chest. Sweat dripped off his head. His mouth was dry. His body shook. He looked up at Metro. The blocks came within a half-dozen meters of the membrane at the top, just far enough away that nobody could damage it and defeat the illusion of a sky. The brightest light was active, drenching the city in sunlight, moving slowly across the drape as the day progressed.

He sprinted again, running across the grass to the edge of Metro, reaching Block One. He thundered down the split, streaking along the porous pavement, crossing one block after another. Five. Eight. Eleven.

He tried Bradshaw again, but his transceiver still wouldn't connect. He needed his damn Deputies, and he couldn't reach them. It was as if fate had decided to screw him, and good. His life had been too perfect. Too easy. He needed some hardship. Some adversity. To hell with adversity. He needed his wife.

Block Fifteen. Block Eighteen. He was getting into the more dilapidated portion of the city, where the younger residents and the secondary service citizens were housed - the jobs that weren't deemed critical to the survival of the city. Cleaners and patchers, clothing renovators and creatives.

There were hundreds of small, individual roles to fill in Metro, each one originally intended to prepare them for life on their new world, slowly adapted to keep the city from falling apart. They were shifting what they had forward, keeping the place operational from Engineering back. The deeper blocks down to the last one, Thirty, were in the worst shape.

Hayden reached Block Twenty-four, slowing as he approached the sliding door that would grant him entry. Only this one didn't slide anymore. It was permanently open, a wedge of metal keeping its weight from pulling it closed. Deputy Hicks was standing just inside, gun in hand.

"Hicks," Hayden coughed, trying to catch his breath again. His legs were on fire. So were his lungs.

"Sheriff?" Hicks said, looking at him, his eyebrows creasing at the sight. "What the hell happened to you, Sheriff?"

He ignored the question. There was no time to explain. "Where's Bradshaw? Where's Francis?"

"Francis?"

"The suspect we were chasing here."

Hicks made a face Hayden couldn't read. Confusion? Fear? There was something about it he didn't like.

"Uh. Sheriff, I don't know how to tell you this, but, well."

"Spit it out, Hicks."

"The suspect is dead."

Hayden didn't think he could have been taken by surprise again. Not after what had just happened. He was wrong.

"What?"

"Bradshaw is on his way to Medical with lacerations on his arms and face. Aahro is securing the scene."

"You're saying the suspect attacked Bradshaw?" Hayden said.

"Yes, sir," Hicks replied. "Came at him with a homemade knife. Told him he would rather kill him than let him have it."

"Have what?"

"I don't know, sir. I got here too late. You'll have to ask Bradshaw or Aahro."

"The cube is secure?"

"Yes, sir."

He needed to get up there, to see what it was Francis had been protecting. He had been willing to die to try to keep it from their hands, and Hayden was certain it had something to do with what Francis and the friend had discovered. Maybe it was a device that could open doors? He needed that more than anything right now.

"I'm heading up," Hayden said.

"Yes, sir," Hicks replied.

Hayden entered the Block. As he passed Hicks, he noticed the deputy's badge indicator was green. He had a connection.

"Sir?" Hicks said.

"What is it?"

"Is that blood on your pants?"

Hayden looked down. Some of the blood had been picked up by the cuff, and some had splattered as he ran through it. He did his best not to think that it was Natalia's blood. That it belonged to the body she had found. He had to believe that, or he wouldn't be able to keep going.

He looked Hicks in the eye and then continued to the stairwell without responding.

The stairs were dim. More than half the lights were out and unable to be replaced. The tile on the floor was old and cracked, more worn than the rest from years of added traffic. Hayden hardly noticed as he climbed to the sixth floor, moving as fast as his body would allow. He still felt the chill in his nerves, the panic in his head and heart. He was holding it tight, barely keeping it under control. He needed to stay level-headed and solve the problem. That was the only way he was going to see his wife again.

The sixth floor was quiet, the residents there all moved from the floor while Law completed their investigation. Deputy Innis was guarding the stairwell when Hayden arrived, and he moved aside immediately to allow him through.

"Sheriff," Innis said. "Are you okay?"

Hayden nodded. "I just came from Engineering."

Innis whistled. "That's a long haul, Sheriff."

"Tell me about it. It damn near killed me."

Innis laughed. Hayden continued down the corridor. Francis' cube was easy to spot. The door was open, and blood had been thrown out onto the walls and floor.

"Geez," Hayden said without thinking.

"They made a damn mess," Innis said, overhearing him. "That asshole nearly killed Bradshaw."

"He went to Medical," Hayden said. "Under his own power?"

"No, they came and got him."

Medical was the only office that still had use of a transport. The powered gurney wasn't fast, but the hospital was situated right in the center of Metro, keeping it within ten minutes of any location in the city.

Hayden turned back to the cube. He moved to the doorway, looking in.

The cube was a mess, which was saying a lot. Nobody in Metro had all that much, to the point that when a living space was disorganized, it still didn't look cluttered. Beyond the blood stains and marks that had made it to the walls and covered the floors, the amount of crap the kid had collected was both impressive and frightening.

There were scraps of metal in one corner. Broken pieces of lighting fixtures, tiles from the floor, chips of synthcrete and a stack of cloth that would have gotten him arrested on the spot if they had known it was there; cloth that was now ruined with blood.

There was also more furniture than any single cube should have. Beyond a table and one chair for a single adult, beyond the fold up bed in the wall of the smaller cube, Francis had collected three more tables, six more chairs, and had somehow also gotten his hands on a display like the ones they had in Engineering. His place was stuffed to the brim, with only a narrow corridor to pass from the entrance to the bedroom, kitchen, bathroom, and the different piles of materials.

"How the hell did he manage this?" Hayden said.

Deputy Aarho was on her knees next to the table with the display on it, bent over a broken shard of green plastic with silver etchings in it. She turned her head back to look at him, surprised to hear this voice. She shifted her position to face him better.

"Sheriff Duke," she said. "I didn't know you were on your way down."

"My badge isn't working right," Hayden said. "What is that?"

"This?" she said, pointing at the plastic. "Is a circuit board."

"Okay," he replied. Natalia had spoken about them before, but he didn't know that's what they looked like. "What was it for?"

"I don't know yet. It's broken."

"I can see that. I don't suppose that's what Francis was trying to keep Bradshaw away from?"

She nodded. "How did you know?"

Hayden did everything he could to keep his face straight, despite his sudden internal despair. "Lucky guess."

"The more important question is, where did he get it?"

"Where did he get any of this stuff? No, I want to know what it did. How it worked."

And who the hell might be able to fix it if it could help him find Natalia.

"Who cares?" Aahro said.

"A man died to keep this out of Law's hands," Hayden growled. "Bradshaw is with Medical. What was he so desperate to protect and why? Those are important questions, Deputy."

Aahro's face flushed. "I. I'm sorry, Sheriff."

Hayden scanned the room again. Why would a man who lived alone have so many tables and chairs?

He knew about the one friend, even if he didn't know anything about him except that he had a weird haircut. Were the others who were with him on this?

"Did you find anything that might give us an indication of who he liked to hang out with, or places he liked to go?"

"No, Sheriff. I know this place looks like a disaster, but our perp was very careful to keep personal items out of the equation. Usually, a cube has at least one or two keepsakes. This guy has all kinds of scraps, but nothing like that."

Because Francis knew what he was doing might get him in trouble. Because he had something to hide. A way to recover some of the data from the PASS that had been lost. A way to hack into maintenance boxes. And now Hayden was pretty sure they weren't alone on the Pilgrim.

He clenched his jaw. And that whatever was out there, it wasn't very friendly.

He reached up, digging his hand into his hair. He needed more, and he needed it fast. Francis was gone. Dead. Killed over keeping the secret. Why had he started to talk only to go that far? Had he known they weren't here by themselves? Or had he only suspected? He hadn't wanted his friend to come to the Station to tell them what he knew. Not until they knew more. Why? What was he afraid of?

Or had his fears already caught up to him? Had he expected he would be silenced for his trouble? His paranoia had gotten him killed.

"Are you okay, Sheriff?" Aarho asked.

He wasn't. Not at all. He had been hoping Francis could help him, but that was out of the question.

"Yeah," he replied. "Gather everything associated with the board and bring it to Engineering. Talk to Mae. See if she can put it back together."

"Mae? What about your wife?"

It took all of his strength not to show her anything. He knew if he let the emotion out he wouldn't be able to put it back in.

"Ask Mae," he said. "Okay, Deputy?"

"Yes, sir."

Hayden left the cube, his knees weak. He made it out into the hallway. His mind was alternating between chaotic reeling and focused determination.

He needed help, and with Natalia gone, there was only one person in Metro who could help him.

11

Hayden found Governor Malcolm back at the Law Station, once again waiting for him in his office.

"Sheriff," Malcolm said as Hayden entered. He was standing. Pacing. He didn't look happy. "Where the hell have you been?"

"Malcolm," Hayden said.

"Don't," Malcolm said. "I gave you a pass on the Code Blue. But now Bradshaw is in critical condition because you never showed up at Block Twenty-four. You never even radioed in to let anyone know you weren't going to be there."

"I contacted Bradshaw," Hayden said. "Will you listen-"

"Bradshaw isn't awake to corroborate that, and besides, why would he confront that kid alone? He was a big boy."

"I know he is; he jumped me in the strands."

"He jumped you? And you didn't have him locked down upstairs?"

"He was trying to escape. I didn't think he was dangerous."

"You didn't think at all, did you, Hayden? Damn it. We've

got an injured Law Officer. We've got a dead citizen. And you were nowhere to be found."

"My badge isn't responding," Hayden said. "I don't know why. Malcolm, I -"

"I don't want to hear it. Not now."

"You're going to hear it, damn it!" Hayden shouted. "You need to fucking hear it! Natalia is gone. Something took her."

Malcolm froze. The fight washed out of him in an instant. He stared at Hayden, who was shaking from the admission. The emotions were so close to coming out. The fear. The pain. He could barely contain it.

"What?"

It was all the Governor could manage.

"I said, something took her, Malcolm. She radioed me to tell me she found a body out near Section C. Only it wasn't the body of anyone in Metro. By the time I got there, she was gone."

"Maybe she went back to Engineering?" His voice was hopeful.

"I don't think so. I found this." He opened his hand. Her transceiver was there. It had left deep marks in his palm from being gripped so tightly. "There was blood, Malcolm. A lot of blood. I can only hope it wasn't hers."

"You're saying that-"

"Something took her," Hayden repeated. "Whoever or whatever it was, it came from the other side of the secure access hatch in Section C."

"The hatch?"

"Is sealed again. I don't know how they opened it."

Malcolm sighed heavily. "Who else knows about this?"

"Nobody, yet. I went to Block Twenty-four to find Francis because I know he had access to the maintenance boxes. I thought maybe he would know how to open the hatch. I didn't expect to find him dead."

"That's right; he had the codes to the boxes. He nearly killed Bradshaw to keep him from something."

"A circuit board. He had a display. He had a keyboard. He was working on something. He had discovered something he didn't want us to know about."

"How do we know he didn't open the hatch? How do we know his friends weren't out there? How do we know they didn't take your wife?"

"She said the body wasn't from Metro."

"It could have been some kid wearing a style she hasn't seen before. She wouldn't know someone from Block Twenty-four, and she wouldn't expect them to be in the maintenance corridors."

Hayden swallowed hard. He hadn't considered that. Six chairs. It was possible. Was that why Francis had been chasing his friend? Was he planning to rat them out to Law? Had Francis destroyed the board and attacked Bradshaw to protect them? Was anything Francis told him even true?

"I don't," Hayden admitted.

"If somebody was out there, don't you think they would have tried to contact us before now? It's been years. We don't have a control panel on our side. Wouldn't it stand to reason they can open the hatch from theirs?"

"You're right. That sounds more reasonable. But if they took her-"

"Don't think that way. Where's the board?"

"I told Deputy Aarho to bring it to Mae, to see if she could repair it."

"Okay. Good. That's a start." Malcolm lowered his head. "Shit, Hayden. I'm sorry. I don't know what else to say. I'm sorry I yelled at you again. Damn it. I can't imagine what you're feeling right now." He looked him in the eye. "We'll get her back. I promise. I'll get every resource we have on it.

Law, Engineering, even Medical if it will help. Just tell me what you need."

"I don't know, Malcolm," Hayden said. "I don't know what to do. This isn't supposed to happen. Metro isn't supposed to be like this." He could feel the tears welling into his eyes. He couldn't hold himself together much longer.

"You know the kids here, they're getting frustrated with the way stuff is breaking down. Maybe they wanted to find out why we're still out here?"

"So they killed someone and took my wife?"

"She's a Lead Engineer. Maybe they want her to help them figure out what the hell is going on with this ship."

"That's a lot of conjecture."

"Yeah, but it's hopeful conjecture instead of assuming the worst. We weren't meant to be out here forever. Maybe some good can come of this. Hang in there, Hayden. I know that's a lousy thing to say, and I know it doesn't put Natalia back in your arms, but don't give up. Not yet."

He moved forward, taking Hayden in an embrace. Hayden couldn't hold back the tide anymore. He sobbed into Malcolm's shoulder, the tears running freely.

"I don't want to do this without her," he said.

"I know," Malcolm replied. "To be honest, neither do I."

It took Hayden a while to begin to gather himself, his body spent and exhausted. Malcolm stayed with him, comforting him as well as he could. Finally, he drew back.

"I'm going to head up to Engineering to check in with Mae on the board," Malcolm said. "I'm also going to put Aarho and Wilson on trying to figure out who else this Francis Lira might have known, and see if we can locate them in Metro. I want you to go home and try to relax."

"I can't," Hayden said. "I can't go home. Not now."

"Okay. Give me twenty minutes to reach Engineering. I'll

have them send someone to link your ID to my place. You can crash there."

Hayden looked Malcolm in the eye. He had always respected the Governor, but he was surprised by the amount of compassion he was showing. "Thank you."

"It's not all posturing, Sheriff," Malcolm said, smiling. "We all need to take care of one another out here. Hang tight, okay?"

"Yeah."

Malcolm patted him on the shoulder before leaving him alone in his office. Hayden stood there for a moment, looking down at Natalia's transceiver badge. His was broken, but it hadn't even occurred to him to use hers. He wasn't thinking clearly at all. How could he?

His body was spent. Every muscle ached. Malcolm was right. There was a plausible explanation why someone might have wanted her, and it wasn't for anything violent or sexual. He had to stay positive. Mae was a great engineer. She would fix the board, and then they would have some answers. He couldn't assume Natalia was dead. He had to be strong. He had to believe.

He closed his hand on her badge again. He wasn't giving up hope. Not now. Not ever. He was too physically tired to help her like this, and Mae needed time. He couldn't calm himself, not completely, but maybe he could recover some of his strength.

He sat down behind his desk. He had a drawing of Natalia on it, etched on an old scrap of paper by a Creative in Block Sixteen and propped up by a slim piece of bent metal. His eyes landed on it, and he felt his eyes water again. Nothing was going to stop him from finding her.

Nothing.

12

There were perks to being the Governor that went beyond access to cultured steak. One of them was having the largest and nicest cube in Metro.

Only the Governor's home wasn't a cube. It was an entire floor, the top floor of Block One. It was out of place amidst the rest of the cubes, the only such home in the entire city, and while the PASS couldn't tell them why it was the way it was, there was a legend that the original occupant was the man who had designed the Pilgrim and his family.

That meant the Governor's Mansion, as the populace referred to it, wasn't only the largest cube in the city. It was also the most opulent. It had real, ornate furnishings. Plush sofas, a king-sized, thick foam bed, a dining table for twelve, rugs and paintings and even a collection of books. It was one of the most invaluable troves of history stored within the hull of the Generation ship.

And it was all under the control of one man, off-limits to the rest of Metro save those the Governor invited over.

Of course, the position of Governor was an elected one. Every ten years, multiple entrants would vie for the role, putting forth their background and platforms and pushing for why they should take up the most important mantle on the ship. Malcolm had been in Operations before the election eight years ago. Most of the Governors came from there because the department was in charge of keeping Metro running smoothly, coordinating the other departments and being responsible for chits, food and water, housing, and all of the other vital functions. Malcolm had made a name for himself in Operations, coming up with ideas that helped optimize their dwindling resources to stretch them just a little further. He was also a compassionate, kind, and open leader, and in that regard, he deserved the massive cube and the treasure within.

A treasure he had decided to share with Hayden. The tech from Engineering was already gone by the time he arrived at the cube, but when he held his wrist up to the pad the door unlocked, and he pushed it open and stepped in. He froze there, marveling at the grandiosity of it all. The walls were framed with real wood; the ceiling painted with a mural depicting the Pilgrim traveling through the stars. It was chipped and faded and cracked after all of this time, but it was still incredible.

Part of the legend of the First Governor suggested that he had kept a stash of real, original food hidden somewhere in the large wood and marble kitchen that graced the back of the cube, near the full-length windows. Cans of vegetables, sealed packages of sweets, and bottles of alcohol that were impossible to replace. It was a point of pride among Governors not to admit or deny the existence of the treats, and to be considerate of the incoming administration and take only a small share.

Hayden was tempted to ransack the kitchen to find the rumored stash if only to give himself something to occupy his attention. Waiting was painful, and he felt each passing minute as another stab in the gut despite all of his efforts to stay positive. He approached the kitchen, opening a few of the drawers and cabinets to explore the contents, not surprised to find them empty. There were a few nutrition bars in the pantry, along with a few large jugs of water. It was a standard ration for one, even though Malcolm had every right as Governor to take more.

He gave up easily, not finding any comfort in the search. He made his way to one of the four bedrooms in the cube. The bed in it was a single, intended for one of the First Governor's children. Hayden had traced some of the family trees back in the PASS. He knew Wilson was a descendent of someone who was likely a descendent of the First Governor. It didn't mean anything anymore. Not after so much time.

Unlike the beds in the other cubes, it was constructed of wood, the mattress a soft yet supple foam. He laid down on it, feeling his body sink in, his muscles releasing their tension. He reached for Natalia's badge, about to call into Engineering. He stopped himself. They would let him know when they had something, he was sure.

He tried to clear his head. It was impossible. Memories of Natalia flooded it instead. He remembered the first time he had seen her, at one of the regularly organized social gatherings for the singles in Metro. She had been wearing her Engineering uniform, and she had looked so confident and professional in it. He was drawn to that more than her physical appearance, though he had always found her pleasing to look at. The first three times he asked her to dance, she said no. Not in a disinterested way, but he could tell she wanted him to work for it.

So he did.

She had her own inner strength that he admired, an inner strength he hoped was serving her now. He had been so consumed with his worry that he hadn't thought about hers.

Was she worried about him, knowing how he would feel? Was she afraid? Was she planning her escape? Was she trying to convince her captors to let her go?

Giving her a little more credit gave him a little more peace. She was strong. She was smart. She wouldn't let herself be a victim if she could help it. She had handled the loss of their unborn child with such grace and dignity. He was sure she would handle this situation the same.

It was those thoughts that let his body relax, and his mind calm enough that his physical exhaustion took over.

Before he knew it, he was asleep.

For how long?

He wasn't sure.

He woke up when someone shook his shoulder, calling his name.

"Hayden. Hayden."

His eyes opened slowly. Malcolm was leaning over him, his face serious. Wilson and Hicks were standing nearby, also looking morose.

"What's going on?" Hayden asked.

Malcolm backed away. Wilson moved toward him. "I'm sorry, Sheriff," she said.

"Sorry for what?" he asked.

"You're under arrest," she replied. "For the murder of Natalia Duke."

13

HAYDEN'S BROW DROPPED. HE FELT A FLARE OF PAIN IN HIS chest. His eyes locked on Malcolm.

"You found her?" he said, his voice barely able to make it out of him. "You found her body? She's. She's dead?"

He barely noticed Wilson leaning toward him with the cuffs. He hadn't caught up with her words yet.

"No," Malcolm said. "We haven't found her, Hayden. You're the last person that saw her. You have her badge. Where is she?"

His brain caught up. Under arrest? What the hell? His eyes shifted to the incoming cuffs. "Wait. Wilson. Wait. What the hell is this, Malcolm? I told you, someone took her."

Malcolm put up his hand to stop Wilson. "I know what you told me, Hayden. I went to Section C myself to check it out. There was no blood. There was no indication that the secure hatch had been opened. The only thing I have is a Sheriff with blood on his pants in possession of his wife's transceiver, claiming it was someone else. I don't need to tell you how that looks."

"Damn it, Malcolm," Hayden said. "If the blood was gone

they must have cleaned it up. They must have opened the hatch again."

"Who?" Malcolm replied.

"You know who. Francis' friends, maybe? That's what you suggested."

"I'm sorry, Sheriff," Wilson said. "Aarho and I have been on it for the last four hours. We haven't found any evidence of a link between Francis Lira and anyone else. As near as we can tell, he didn't have any friends."

Hayden shook his head. That wasn't true. He knew it wasn't true. Francis had been chasing someone. "No," he said. "That's not right."

"We have to bring you in, Hayden," Malcolm said. "At least until we get to the bottom of this. I'm sorry, but your story doesn't check out."

"You know me, Malcolm. You know I would never hurt Natalia. That's just stupid."

"Put yourself in my position. I can't ignore the facts as they present themselves. I have a responsibility to Metro. Blood on your clothes. Natalia's badge. Come on."

"What about the circuit board?"

"Mae is working on it. She said it's pretty basic, though. At best, it might be able to run a few simple operations. Nothing powerful enough to figure out codes to the maintenance boxes, or to open a secured hatch, especially one without a control panel."

He motioned to Wilson. She started moving toward him with the cuffs again.

"It's better if you come down to the Station so we can talk," Malcolm said.

Hayden's heart was racing. He couldn't believe this. He was being accused of killing his wife? "What's my motive, damn it?"

"I'm hoping you can help me understand that," Malcolm said.

"Put out your hands, Sheriff," Wilson said. "Please?"

Hayden didn't move. Hicks drew his gun, pointing it at him. "Don't make me use this, sir."

"Malcolm," Hayden said, pleading with him. "Don't. She needs us. I'm telling you the truth."

"I want to believe you. I do. I can't take that risk. The safety of this entire city is at stake."

Hayden looked back at Malcolm. The fear faded in an instant, replaced with a sudden, terrifying understanding.

He turned back to Wilson, holding out his wrists. "You're right," he said. "It's okay. I'll come quietly."

Malcolm smiled. "Thank you, Hayden."

Wilson put the cuff on his left wrist. She didn't look happy about doing it.

He wasn't happy about what he had to do, either.

She raised the cuff toward his right wrist. He jerked his hands back, using the momentum to swing the loose side of the cuff into his hand. He gathered his legs at the same time, springing into the off-balance deputy. She was strong, but she was unprepared, and she fell off to the side as he jumped from the bed.

Hicks fired his stunner, the charged round missing wide. He didn't get another shot. Hayden slammed the cuff against the gun, knocking it from Hicks' hand. Hicks tried to grab him, but he caught his punch, using his momentum to turn him to the side, bringing the metal of the cuff up and into Hicks' stomach and knocking the wind out of him.

"Hayden," Malcolm shouted. He had backed away from the fight. He was a politician, not a soldier.

Wilson had recovered and was pulling her weapon from her hip. Hayden reached to his side, drawing his stunner and firing in one smooth motion. The round hit her in the neck, sending a jolt of electricity through her that caused her to convulse and collapse.

"I need backup," Malcolm said. "Governor's Mansion."

Hayden turned to run, making it a few steps before Hicks tackled him, bringing him to the ground.

"There's no point resisting, Sheriff," Hicks said, trying to climb his legs to his back. "There's nowhere to go. We're all trapped in here."

Hayden bucked and kicked, catching Hicks in the chin. The officer fell off, and Hayden scrambled back to his feet.

"I'm not letting you bury me in lockup," he said. He looked back at Malcolm. "You know I didn't hurt her, you two-faced son of a bitch. What else do you already know?"

Malcolm was calm. "There's nowhere to run, Hayden. Nowhere to hide."

"What else do you know!" Hayden screamed, aiming the stunner at him.

Malcolm was silent. He had secrets.

It seemed they all did.

Hayden backed out of the bedroom, turning and running for the door. It opened ahead of him, two more of his deputies filing in.

"Hayden," Aarho said.

He didn't hesitate. Two pulls of the trigger, and both officers were down. He paused beside them, grabbing Aarho's sidearm before fleeing out to the small foyer. The lift was ahead of him, the stairwell to his left.

He approached the lift, putting his wrist to the scanner.

It didn't open, his access already revoked.

"Damn it," Hayden said, breaking toward the stairs.

The door opened, and Hicks came charging through, reaching out to tackle him again. Hayden planted his feet and ducked, backing away, while Hicks crashed into the opposite wall. He put the stunner to his Deputy's head.

"You know I didn't kill her, damn it," he said.

"It doesn't matter what I do or don't know Sheriff," Hicks replied. "I have a job to do."

"So do I. I'm going to find my wife."

He cocked the weapon back, using it to hit Hicks in the temple and knock him to the ground.

"Stay down," Hayden said.

He slipped into the stairwell, taking it three steps at a time. Malcolm was right. They were all right. There was nowhere for him to hide. He was trapped in Metro with them. That had never been a problem before. It was a huge problem now.

It was a good thing he knew the strands better than anyone.

14

Hayden made it out of Block One, barely clearing the building before the reinforcements from Law arrived. They were composed of off-duty deputies, officers that had been home asleep before the Governor had sent out the call. It was the only thing that had slowed them. The only thing that allowed him to escape.

He ducked into the first available strand, running down the narrow alley between the blocks. He had no doubt Law would look for him in here, so he had to put as much distance between them and him as he could.

He kept running, reaching one intersection and turning right, heading to the next. He took that down three strands and made a left, crossed a split and continued on.

To where?

That was the question. Malcolm had turned on him, ready to lock him up and forget about him in order to keep what he knew a secret. He was sure the Governor didn't think he was responsible for Natalia's disappearance, but there was no way in hell he was going to let him tell anyone else that someone had figured out how to get out one of the secured hatches.

Or that someone had figured out how to get in.

He shook his head as he moved. He had taken Malcolm's suggestion and run with it, but the subsequent reaction didn't line up with that idea. It wasn't a bad thing if Francis had opened the hatch. Not really. If they could reach the rest of the ship, maybe they could find out where they were and if they were off course. Maybe they could do something to get themselves back on target. Unless Malcolm was afraid of what the truth might be? Maybe there was no getting back on course. Maybe their fate was die in the middle of the Universe whenever the Pilgrim died.

He didn't believe that. He had seen the look in the Governor's eye. He had heard the tremble in his voice. Malcolm had seen the blood. He had seen the handprint beneath the hatch. He had cleaned it up to keep the whole thing quiet, and more easily turn the focus back toward Hayden.

But there was more to it than that. He was sure of it. He didn't know how much Malcolm knew, but he had a feeling Malcolm knew something.

His simple life had gotten damned complex in a hurry.

He crossed the next split, entering another area of the strands. The lighting was almost completely out in this one, a dim illumination coming from the interior lights of the cubes above. It was hard to see, but he didn't need to see. He had been in the strands a thousand times. He knew the rules. Keep going in a straight line. Stay away from the conduits on the sides. Don't damage anything.

He only saw the lump in the middle of the strand right before his foot got caught on it. He tripped, falling forward, tempted to put his hands out to brace against the impact. He forced himself not to, rolling his shoulder instead. The last thing he needed would be two broken arms. He hit the ground hard, rolling to a stop. He got to his knees, looking back at the lump.

"Shit," he said, standing and walking back to it.

He knelt in front of it, pushing it over. The motion shifted the jacket over the resident's head, revealing the man's dead face. His mouth was open in a silent scream. His neck was sliced so deep the head rolled to the side, nearly detached.

Hayden fought against the sudden nausea. Another body? Another murder? This wasn't Francis' friend at least. This was a different resident.

But who had cut his throat? And why?

He reached to his hip for his scanner, bringing it to the man's wrist. David Chapman, Block Nine. Married. Damn.

He reached up, closing the man's eyes. He tapped Natalia's badge. "Law," he said.

"Sheriff, is that you?" Deputy Chao said.

"Yeah, it's me," Hayden replied. "Did the Governor tell you I might call in?"

"Sheriff, you need to come back to the Station. None of us want anything bad to happen to you. We don't want to chase you."

"I don't want to be chased. But I need to find Natalia, and I can't do that in lockup. I found a body in the strands. I can't give you the exact coordinates for obvious reasons. David Chapman, Block Nine. You need to tell his wife, and then come and look for him."

"Another body?" Chao said.

"What do you mean another body?" Hayden asked.

Chao didn't respond, disconnecting the link instead.

"Sorry, David," Hayden said to the dead man. "Someone should be along to collect you soon."

He rose and continued his sprint through the strands, pausing before the next split to check the area. He had almost reached his destination. Hopefully, Malcolm or Wilson wouldn't think to look for him there. He didn't want to have to shoot her again.

He slipped onto the split, staying tight against the block, grateful there weren't many residents outside. He was too recognizable, especially in his uniform.

He reached Block Ten, entering the lobby and moving to the stairwell.

"Sheriff Duke, are you okay?" a passing resident asked him.

Hayden nodded. "I'm fine. How are you?"

"Well enough. Say, those were some turbs we had earlier today, weren't they?"

"They were," Hayden agreed. "If you'll excuse me." He motioned to the stairwell door.

"Right. See you around, Sheriff."

Hayden entered the stairwell, ascending quickly. He made his way up to the eleventh floor, already starting to feel worn out again as he peered out into the corridor. Empty. He abandoned the stairwell, hurrying to Cube 1141 and knocking on the door.

It swung open.

"Sheriff Duke," Sarah Kaine said. "What are you doing here?" She paused, looking him over. "You look like hell."

"Sarah," Hayden said. "I need your help."

15

"YOU NEED MY HELP?" SARAH SAID. "I ALREADY ANSWERED ALL of your que- hey, Sheriff, why do you have a cuff on your wrist?"

Hayden looked down at his left wrist. The handcuff was still dangling from it. "Can I come in?"

Sarah hesitated, looking back over her shoulder. "Uh. I guess."

He nearly shoved his way past her. "Close the door."

She did. Hayden moved back to her cube's small window, looking down on the strand below. There was no activity there. That didn't mean he was safe, but he would rather take his chances in here for now.

"What's going on?" Sarah said.

"Sarah," a new voice said from the bedroom on the left. An older woman emerged from it. She was thin and pale. She didn't look well. When she saw Hayden, her face twisted into a scowl. "Sheriff Duke. Did you come to arrest my daughter for trying to do the right thing again?"

Hayden would never understand how the woman

thought prostitution was the right thing. Then again, he didn't know if she had done the same in her prime.

"Gene," Hayden said. "I don't have time to argue with you about this right now."

She noticed the cuff on his wrist, her eyebrows crinkling. "Trying some new kink with your wife, Sheriff?" She smiled mockingly. "Come to get a third? She's available if you have a med chit to spare."

It took all of Hayden's will to bite his tongue. Everything about Gene Kaine was repulsive to him. Still... "I need her for something else. But there is a med chit in it for you, Sarah."

Gene's eyes lit up. Sarah was less enthusiastic.

"What. Uh. What do you need me to do?"

"Nothing like that," Hayden said. "What kind of Sheriff would I be?"

"Like your father," Gene said. "That's what kind."

Was she trying to piss him off? "What the hell is that supposed to mean?" he hissed.

"Oh, calm yourself, Sheriff. If you want to pretend your dad was a saint, you go right ahead. You've always seen Metro through your own idealistic filters."

"Mom," Sarah said. "Do we have to do this now?"

"Nope. Sheriff Duke doesn't have time for that. What do you need my sweet Sarah for, Sheriff?"

"I'm not about to share that with you, Gene," Hayden said. "Sarah, shall-"

He stopped speaking as a scream echoed up from the strand. He darted back to the window, looking down. The bulbs below were flickering, showing the alley in flashes of light. A dark shape was moving down the strand, faster than Hayden could believe. A woman was lying on the ground within, blood pouring from her neck.

"Bastard cut her throat," he said absently. "Son of a bitch."

"Oh my," Sarah said, joining him at the window. "That's Jane Freeman. Is she?"

"Don't look," Hayden said, pushing her away. She had been attacked right under his nose.

He looked down at Jane. She was already motionless. Dead. Chao had said there were other bodies. Someone in Metro was on a killing spree? That didn't make sense. Who? The lighting made it hard to tell. Whoever it was, they weren't that large, but they were quick.

Why were they doing it? And why now? Was it a coincidence?

He doubted it.

"What the hell is going on, Sheriff?" Sarah said. She was in tears.

"I don't know yet," Hayden replied. "I told you I need your help. We have to go."

"You aren't bringing my daughter out there," Gene said. "Not when someone's killing people. You're the Sheriff. You should be telling everyone to stay inside."

Hayden glared at her. "Why don't you go out there, Gene?" he said. "Take a stroll in one of the strands? You'd be doing the rest of us a favor."

Gene flinched in reaction to the comment. "Well, I-" She stared at him, her mouth snapping open and closed. "Get out of my cube, Sheriff. Right now."

"Fine," Hayden said. "Sarah, are you coming?"

"She's not coming with you," Gene said.

"Not even for a med chit?" Hayden said, challenging her.

Gene stared at him for a few seconds. He could see the war being waged in her mind, written clearly on her face. She growled under her breath.

"Fine. Sarah, go with the Sheriff."

"I don't want to go out there," Sarah said.

"Sarah, you'll be fine," Hayden said, patting his gun to

remind her he wasn't defenseless. "I'll protect you. Please. I need your help."

She wiped at her eyes. "Jane Freeman is dead," she said. "I could be next."

"You won't be," Hayden said. "I promise."

"You Sheriffs may not be good for much," Gene said. "But you can take care of yourselves. I know that. Sarah, do you want your mommy to die?"

"No, but-"

"Then go with him."

"Mom," Sarah said.

"When are you going to grow up, Sarah?" Gene said. "You're two years away from marriage. That means you have two years before you're useless. Do you want to waste them hiding in my panties?"

Hayden clenched his fist. He didn't know how much more of Gene he could take. Everyone knew she was a piece of work, but now he saw what kind.

"Sarah," he said calmly. "I won't let anything happen to you. This is important. The most important thing you'll ever do."

She looked at him, then at Gene, and then back at him. "Okay, Sheriff," she said.

"Thank you," Hayden said.

He glanced out the window one more time, looking down at Jane Freeman. A Law Officer was standing over her. Who was that? He squinted his eyes to try to get a clearer view. Not Wilson. Not Chao. By the size of them, it was probably Lahish. She had gotten there quickly.

Maybe too quickly.

"We need to go," he said. "Now."

Someone knocked on the door.

16

"Shit," Hayden said.

He started toward the bedroom, putting himself right in front of Gene. The woman was tiny, her size not helped by the disease ravaging her body. Anyone sane would have gone to Medical for palliative years ago. The woman was anything but sane.

"I'm not here," he said, staring into her eyes.

She looked amused. "No? Why not? Are you in some sort of trouble, Sheriff?"

"Two med chits," Hayden said. "But keep your mouth shut about me."

The knock came again.

"If you're in trouble, how do I know you can deliver?"

"You have my word."

"Is it worth anything? I might be able to wring a guaranteed chit out of whoever's on the other side of the door. Another Law Officer, if I had to guess. Not so kinky after all, are you Sheriff?"

"How about this, Gene," Hayden said. "You give me up; I

put a stunner into your head. Do you think you'll survive that in your condition?"

"You wouldn't dare."

"I killed a man once," Hayden said. "It's one of the hardest things I've ever had to live with. But I've learned to live with it. Do you follow?"

She made an ugly face and then stepped aside. He vanished into the bedroom. There wasn't anywhere to hide, so he closed the door and positioned himself behind it.

Sarah opened the door to the cube.

"Can I help you?" she said.

"Miss Kaine," the visitor said.

Hayden recognized the voice. Hicks. Damn it.

"Deputy Leland Hicks," Hicks said. "Sheriff's Office."

"I know you're Law," Sarah said. "You don't have to announce it. You're wearing a uniform."

Hayden cracked a small smile. Sarah had thrown her snark at him more than once, too.

"Right," Hicks said. "Sarah, I don't suppose Sheriff Duke has been here?"

"Why would Sheriff Duke come here?" Gene snapped. "He let Sarah go. He said she didn't break any laws this time."

"We're trying to get Sheriff Duke to come back to the Station," Hicks said. "We need to talk to him about the disappearance of his wife, Natalia. We tried to pick him up at home, but-"

"I'll ask you again, Deputy," Gene said. "Why would he come here?"

Hicks was slow to answer. "Well, ma'am, he arrested your daughter last night, and-"

"He arrested her, Deputy. That's what you Laws do, isn't it? You arrest people for trying to make ends meet. He didn't buy anything from her. He isn't having an affair. If his wife is missing, it's probably because she got bored with him. Why don't you go do something useful for a change?"

Hayden's smile grew a little bigger. Gene Kaine was a psychotic bitch, but at the moment she was using it to his advantage.

"I'm sorry, ma'am," Hicks said. "I'm just doing my job. Do you mind if I come in and take a look around?"

"Is there something wrong with your brain, Deputy Hicks?" Gene said. "I told you, he isn't here. He hasn't been here. Why are you wasting time here, anyway? Are you aware there's a dead girl in the strand down there? Why don't you go find whoever cut her throat?"

Hayden winced at the words, knowing it was the wrong thing for her to say.

"How do you know her throat was cut, ma'am?" Hicks said.

"What do you mean?" Gene asked, suddenly defensive.

"I'm guessing the lighting isn't all that good up here. How do you know her throat was cut. What did you see?"

"I didn't see anything."

"Are you sure?"

"I'm sure. I heard a scream, that's all. When I looked, she was down there, dead."

"But you know it was her throat?"

"It's just a guess, Deputy. What does it matter?"

"Can I come in?" Hicks asked.

"No," Gene said. "Answer my question."

"I need you to answer my question, ma'am," Hicks said. "What exactly did you see? You can talk to me here, or we can talk at the Station."

"Leave her alone," Sarah said. "Can't you see she's sick?"

"Did you see anything, Miss Kaine?" Hicks asked.

"Yes," Sarah said. "From the bedroom window."

"Sarah!" Gene said.

Hayden cursed under his breath. Was Sarah going to sell him out? He hadn't expected that.

"Can you show me, Miss Kaine?" Hicks asked.

"Of course, Deputy."

"No, she can not," Gene said. "This is my cube."

"It's my cube, too," Sarah said.

"She's right, ma'am. She's over eighteen, which means she has full rights to the cube."

"Sarah, I'm going to beat your ass silly over this. I don't want some nosy deputy snooping around my bedroom."

"Too bad," Sarah said. "Come on in, Deputy."

Hayden could hear them moving through the cube. He slipped sideways, slowly withdrawing his stunner from its holster as they neared. The door opened, just enough that they could enter but not enough to push against him or reveal he was behind it. Was it intentional?

"I was in here," Sarah said. "Getting dressed."

"You get dressed in your mother's bedroom?" Hicks asked.

"We share the bed sometimes," Sarah said. "Mommy gets cold because of her condition, and I try to keep her warm."

"Oh. Uh. Okay."

Hicks sounded disgusted. Hayden didn't blame him. He hoped what she said wasn't true.

"I was right here, looking out the window into the strand. Come see, Deputy."

Hayden shifted to peer around the door. Hicks was beside Sarah, looking down into the strand. She glanced over at him and winked.

"I saw someone with her," Sarah continued. "A man. He was shorter than average. I saw. I saw."

"It's okay, Miss Kaine," Hicks said. "Take it slow."

Sarah started to sob again. "I knew Jane," she said. "She was a good person." She fell into Hicks' chest, crying.

"Miss Kaine," Hicks said. "It's okay, Miss Kaine."

"She's dead," Sarah said.

Hayden couldn't believe Sarah had it in her to be so manipulative. Then again, she was her mother's daughter. He slipped around the door behind them and out into the living area.

"Have her meet me on the fourth floor," Hayden whispered to Gene.

"How do you know I won't turn you in as soon as you're gone?"

"Because I'll only be on the fourth floor." He eyed her threateningly. Her pale face managed to find a lighter shade.

"You owe me two chits," she said.

"You'll get them when I find Natalia. I swear."

"What happened to your wife, Sheriff?" She sounded genuinely concerned.

"I don't know," he replied, his voice cracking. "That's why I need Sarah's help."

"Fourth floor," Gene repeated. "Get out of here."

Hayden slipped out of the door and into the hallway. It was empty. Law didn't have enough officers to be everywhere at once, and the increasing body count was sure to be putting pressure on their resources.

"Miss Kaine," he heard Hicks say. "Can you describe the man you saw? Anything can help."

"It was hard to see-"

Hayden hurried away from the cube, back to the stairwell. He went down two floors, staying hidden while he waited.

He heard the stairwell door open a few minutes later. He kept his gun ready, crouching near the door facing the risers. He heard the feet coming down, boots echoing on the metal grating, but the steps were too light to be Hicks'.

"Don't shoot, Sheriff," Sarah said, turning the corner and seeing him there.

Hayden lowered the stunner. "Sarah. Is Hicks gone?"

She smiled. "Yup."

"Thank you."

"I didn't do it for you, Sheriff. I did it for the chits."

Hayden holstered the stunner, releasing a light sight. Of course, she did. He felt a twinge of sympathy for her. He couldn't imagine what it must be like to be so mistreated she didn't even know it.

He wished he could do more for her, but only one thing mattered now.

"You'll get them. All I need you to do is come down to the southern blocks with me and help me find the guy who propositioned you last night. The one you called Skillet."

"Are you really running from your own Law?" Sarah asked.

"Not by choice," Hayden replied. "It's a long story, and you're better off not to get too involved."

"Pozz that, Sheriff."

"Pozz?"

She smiled. "You don't know any modern slang, do you? Pozz, like, I agree, or I understand. That sort of thing."

"Pozz that."

She smiled. "Exactly."

"Skillet," he repeated. "Southern blocks. We'll take the strands as much as we can."

"What about the murdering creep?" she asked, trembling slightly at the idea of going into the strands.

"If he shows up, I'll take care of him."

"Do you think he knows what happened to your wife?"

"If he does, he'll talk," Hayden replied, voice sharp. "I'll do whatever it takes."

"I'm glad I'm not on your bad side, Sheriff."

17

It was difficult, but not impossible, to travel from the north end of Metro to the south staying mostly to the strands. They had to cross the splits when moving between block quads, leaving Hayden exposed eight times as they traveled back toward Francis' cube and the buildings around it.

Having Sarah with him during those crossings was massively helpful at first, as she provided a lookout while he skirted the shadows and dashed across the wider lanes to the closest strands. The deeper south they went, the harder it started to become. Malcolm had guessed he would be heading that way, though it was unclear if the Governor had determined whether it was to disappear or to find someone who knew Francis.

Malcolm knew the truth, at least part of it, whatever that truth happened to be. He wanted to bury any suggestion that there could be anything outside of Metro's walls. He wanted to suppress the notion that the hatches beyond the perimeter could be opened and that they might have some semblance of control over their destiny.

Hayden understood why, to an extent. To prevent panic. To keep the residents under control. To protect them. That was the Governor's job. That had been his job, too. But what was he trying to protect them from?

"There's a Law Officer two strands down," Sarah said, returning to him from a quick walk down the split. "I can distract him for you."

"There are too many people out here," Hayden said, noticing a lot of younger residents walking the split, all of them headed east.

"They won't bother you, Sheriff," Sarah said. "They're heading to the Dox."

"Dox?"

"It's a club," she said. "A meeting place for singles. You're married; you must have been to one before?"

"The Dox is new? I haven't kept up with the Socialization Office's efforts."

She paled. "Oh. I probably shouldn't have said anything. The Dox isn't sanctioned."

"Meaning it's an illegal gathering?"

"Technically."

"There's nothing technical about it." He shook his head. "How come I didn't know about this?"

"When was the last time you came this far south before today, Sheriff?"

"I have Deputies assigned to the southern blocks."

"Fresh recruits, right?" Sarah said. "Maybe they've been keeping secrets from you."

"It seems like everyone's keeping secrets around here."

"Welcome to Metro, Sheriff," Sarah said. "Pozz?"

He nodded. Maybe Gene was right. Maybe he had seen the city through his own filters for too long. "Pozz. There's an Exchange in the same direction. I could use a change of clothes."

He pulled on his collar. He still stood out way too much in the dirty uniform. He wasn't sure his deputies would even recognize him in street clothes. He hardly ever wore them.

"I don't have anything to exchange," Sarah said. "Unless you want me to go naked? Besides, they'll know I'm not married. I can't pick up men's clothes."

"Tell them you're making a run for me," Hayden said.

"At a southern Exchange?"

"The fact that it's unexpected will make them less suspicious, not more."

"The transaction will show up in the daily reports. What if the Governor sees it?"

"How do you know about the daily reports?"

"Mom was in Administration," Sarah said. "I'm going into Admin, too."

"Right. Yes, he'll probably see it, but that won't be for at least six hours. I don't intend to be idle for very long."

She sighed. "Okay, Sheriff. Hang tight here. I'll be right back."

She wandered off in the direction of the Exchange, leaving Hayden to wait. He hated standing around in the shadows of the strands, leaning on someone else to help him. He hated leaving Natalia's fate in the hands of a nineteen-year-old prostitute.

That wasn't fair. Sarah was a good kid. Her mother was the monster.

Besides, what other options did he have?

Like the rest of the residents of Metro, none.

Hayden faded further back into the strand when a Law Officer passed the corner. Deputy Shanks. He was a large, dark-skinned, muscular officer. Fresh out of training and eager to make a name for himself. He turned his head to peer into the strand, forcing Hayden to squeeze himself under one of the conduits next to a non-operational light.

He could see the man's small eyes tracking along the strand.

Could Shanks see him? He should have gone with Sarah's suggestion. Let her distract him. She was probably good at that.

He stared at the Deputy, lowering himself further to the ground. It was still damp from last night's precipitation, the porous synthetic stone floor slowly collecting and filtering the water before returning it back to the elementals. It soaked through his shirt to his chest, making him cold. He didn't dare move, even if Shanks had spotted him. If he wasn't careful, he could rupture the conduits and create a major problem for the blocks around him.

A dozen heartbeats passed. Shanks' eyes were locked on the strand, the Deputy barely bothering to blink. Then he took a cautious step forward, reaching for his sidearm. He tapped his chin on his badge.

"Lahish, this is Shanks," he said. Hayden could hear his deep voice across the distance even though he was whispering. "I'm at Twenty-two dash fifteen dash one. Can you sweep across from dash five, real slow?"

It was an odd request, and if Shanks did see him, it was an unnecessary one, especially considering the other activity in Metro. They were shorthanded as it was, and the big man certainly wouldn't need help subduing him.

Then again, maybe he would.

"I'm on my way," Lahish replied. "Entering the strand now, coming your direction."

Lahish must have been nearby, sweeping the entrances to the strands. Shanks started moving, entering the strand. He took slow, deliberate steps, as if he was trying to stay as quiet as he could.

One step. Two. Three. He drew his stunner from its holster. His eyes stayed locked forward, and he leveled the weapon, clutching it in his right hand and balancing it with his left. Four steps. Five. Six. He reached Hayden, standing beside him. It was clear he wasn't the target of his attention.

Hayden turned his head, trying to see. Shanks stepped past him. He could hear Lahish's footsteps a little further off.

He wasn't sure what happened next, even though he was looking right at it. The darkness of a dead light against the intersecting block moved, shooting forward toward Shank, taking him by surprise. He cried out, firing his stunner and hitting something ahead of him. The attacker shrieked loudly, an ugly sound, before pouncing on the Deputy.

He saw a pair of long, black blades reach out and clutch at Shanks' shoulders, tearing deep into the flesh as it used him to springboard off and dart away, seemingly unslowed by the stunning round. Shank roared in pain, falling to his knees as the dark shape vanished down the connecting strand.

"Shank," Lahish said, reaching him. Blood was pouring from both his arms.

Hayden shifted, pulling himself out of his hiding place hand over hand along the ground. Lahish saw him, walking over to him.

"Sheriff?" the Deputy said.

Hayden cleared the delicate utility system, rolling over and looking up at Lahish. "Deputy," he said. Lahish pointed his stunner at him. Hayden held out his hand. "Help me up."

"Sir?"

"Damn it, Deputy. Shanks is injured, and whoever just cut him like that is getting away. You know whoever is killing people is more dangerous than I am. Help me up."

Lahish didn't hesitate. He grabbed Hayden's hand, pulling him to his feet.

"Get Shanks to Medical," Hayden said. "I'm going after him."

He didn't wait for a reply. He started running again,

following the dark shape down the strand. He could only hope Sarah was smart enough not to wander far from the block.

He raced through the strands, just barely able to make out the dark form ahead of him, dressed all in black and nearly disappearing whenever they crossed a dead portion of the alley's lighting. The target reached the intersection first, turning left and vanishing. Hayden pushed himself a little harder, forcing as much effort from his legs as he could get. He made it to the intersection, turning to look. The dark shape vanished to the right.

Hayden didn't follow. He knew the layout of these strands, even if he hadn't walked them in years. They didn't change. They would never change. He kept going forward, finally taking a second to wonder what he was doing. Shanks had hit his quarry with a stunner, and they had barely flinched. What was he going to do, shoot them again before it was his throat that got cut?

It didn't matter. If there was even the smallest chance catching up might help him find Natalia, then he had to catch up. He couldn't beat them in a foot race, but unless the dark shape was Bradshaw, there was no way they could navigate the strands as efficiently.

He crossed one junction to the next, taking a seemingly circuitous route between the blocks. He slowed as he neared the last of the intersections, drawing his stunner and dropping to a knee.

He didn't hear anything coming. He barely had time to react to the perpetrator as they whipped around the corner, coming right at him. He squeezed the trigger, firing three rounds into the dark shape, watching in horror as the electric discharge illuminated it.

A sharp hiss sounded as the target leaped sideways, catching the edge of a block and lifting itself upward. Hayden stared at it, still in shock as long, dark claws dug into the synthcrete and carried it away.

His heart was racing, struggling to make sense of what he had just seen. It was nothing human; he was sure of that much. It had come from the other side of the secure hatch. He was sure of that, too.

It had gotten into Metro, and it was slaughtering the residents with impunity. He had fired three stunners into it, and it didn't seem to care.

That wasn't the worst part.

What if there were more of the things on the other side of the hatch?

Was this thing his proof that Natalia was dead?

He slumped on his knees, lowering his head into his hands. Did Malcolm know what was out there? Did he know Natalia was gone and he couldn't get her back? Was that why he needed someone to blame for her disappearance?

The creature was killing people, but it wasn't eating them. It was leaving them where they died, moving on without a second thought or a moment of hesitation. Was it killing for sport, or did it have another reason?

It didn't matter.

He pushed himself up, holstering his weapon again. He refused to believe that Natalia was gone. Not until he saw her body. He didn't and wouldn't accept it. He was going to find a way to the other side. He was going to find her.

One way or another.

18

It took Hayden nearly twenty minutes to circle back to where he had left Sarah. He played it extra safe; concerned Malcolm might leave one of the deputies to keep an eye on the area. Maybe the Governor would have if Shanks hadn't been hurt, but he was losing Law Officers at a quickening pace.

That Malcolm might be hoping the monster had killed him was tough for Hayden to swallow. They had never been friends, but they had a mutual respect for one another and a shared appreciation for Natalia.

How quickly things had changed.

Sarah was standing at the corner of the strand when he arrived. She was chatting quietly with a short, blonde haired young woman. He couldn't hear their conversation, but they broke it off within a couple of minutes, and she secreted back into the strand to search for him.

She gave a curt wave when she saw him. "What the hell is going on, Sheriff?" she asked. "I leave you alone for five minutes, and when I come back there's a Deputy leading another out of the strands covered in blood, and you're nowhere to be seen."

"It wasn't me," Hayden said. "It was the thing that's been attacking the residents."

"What do you mean, thing?" Sarah said. "A really ugly guy?"

Hayden wasn't sure if he should tell her what he had seen. The Governor wouldn't want him to. Malcolm was trying to keep it secret, and for good reason. If the people realized there was a demon hunting them, there was no telling what kind of chaos it might cause. Then again, the people had a right to know they were being hunted. They had a right to protect themselves.

As if they could.

"Something like that," Hayden said. "Do you have the clothes?"

She was holding a bag in her hand. She thrust it out to him. "You need it. You're soaked, and you smell."

They backed further into the strand, moving behind the block, near where Shanks had been attacked.

"What does he look like?" Sarah asked as Hayden began unbuttoning his shirt.

"Who?"

"The killer."

"I thought you saw him from your bedroom window?"

Hayden unhooked his belt and lowered it to the ground. Then he pulled off his shirt, followed by his undershirt. He didn't want to get the new clothes wet, so he stripped himself naked before opening the bag, hoping that no one was looking down from their windows.

"Your wife must be happy," Sarah said, looking at him.

He knew she was staring. He didn't have the energy to care, and besides, he didn't understand what she meant. He pulled a new pair of underwear out of the bag.

"If you have time, I can give you a little bonus," she said. "No extra charge."

He slid the underwear on, grateful to be dry again. "Sarah, you're better than that."

"My Mom says women in our position have to get by any way we can. It's not a question of better or worse. It's a question of using our assets to the fullest. But I like you, Sheriff. You've always treated me with kindness. Not all of my customers have. I don't mind doing you a favor."

"I do," Hayden said. "You use your assets for her gain. You cheapen yourself and diminish your self-worth to take care of a woman who only cares about herself."

"She's my Mom. What else am I supposed to do?"

"She's a blood-sucking leech," Hayden said, pulling on a fresh pair of pants. They were tighter than he would have liked, the cut more in line with current style and less considerate of his functional needs. "Do you think any of the men in Metro are going to marry you, knowing what you've done with your life?"

"Mom says she found a husband. She used her body to get what she wanted, too. Did you know that, Sheriff?"

"I suspected, but I'm not surprised. Your father was a Cleaner, Sarah. An ex-con. She married one of her customers because she won the lottery and wanted someone to take care of her when she passed age."

He pulled the shirt on. It was faded blue, the threads barely holding together. Everything had been exchanged and re-woven so often it was all starting to fall apart.

"That's not a nice thing to say, Sheriff," Sarah said. She looked hurt.

"I'm sorry, Sarah," Hayden replied. "My point is, you don't have to be what your mother tells you to be. You don't have to be her servant."

"Whose servant am I, then?"

"Nobody's. You can be your own person."

She laughed. "You know what a line of bullshit that is, don't you Sheriff?"

"What do you mean?"

"There aren't many choices on the Pilgrim. The city has needs, and everything is organized and prescribed to fill them. You said before I could get pregnant without a ticket, and maybe I could, but what I do is one of the city's needs, whether you like it or not. So are the dark markets, so are the illegal trades."

"Did your mother tell you that?"

She shrugged. "Most of it. But I believe it. That there aren't many real choices. Your father was Sheriff, wasn't he?"

"Yes. And his father. The Dukes have been in Law for as far back as the PASS has records."

"My point, exactly."

"I chose to become a Law Officer. I had to take the aptitude tests. I had to pass training."

"But you were predisposed to it. You had a way in through your family."

"And now I'm wanted for killing my wife," Hayden said. "There's no such thing as fate, Sarah. You can be whatever you want to be."

"What if I want to be a prostitute? What if I like it?"

"Do you?"

She was silent for a few seconds, and then she shook her head. "Not really, but my Mom." Her voice trailed off.

"What were you talking to that other girl about?" Hayden asked, changing the subject. He had tried, but the damage was done.

"I was asking her about Skillet," she said. "If she's seen him around."

"And?"

She smiled. "She thinks she saw him heading into the

Dox. It could be the wrong guy, the skillet's pretty popular right now, but it's better than nothing, isn't it Sheriff?"

Hayden bent down to pull on the boots she had picked for him. "It is. How did you know my size?"

She shrugged. "You're about the same height as my Dad was."

They were a good fit. He reached for his belt. It didn't make sense to ditch the uniform only to keep the utilities. He took the stunner from it and left everything else. He looked at his wrist. He still needed to get the cuff off it.

He shoved the stunner into his pants. "I guess we're going into the Dox."

"You're kind of old for it."

"Do you think I'll be recognized?"

"Nope. You look good in cazzie, Sheriff."

"Thanks, I think."

Sarah smiled. "You're welcome." She paused. "So, the killer. Did you get him?"

"I tried. He got away."

"From you? He must have been fast."

Hayden could still see the creature scaling the block in his mind. "He was more than fast."

19

Sarah had called the Dox a club, but it wasn't really. The gathering place was unsanctioned, meaning it had been created illegally by the residents and was operating out of one of the blocks. Twenty-two in this case. Only two strands away from Francis' cube.

During the day, it didn't exist at all. The three floors of cubes were their typical homesteads for a number of residents, nearly all of them single and between eighteen and twenty-five years old. They were the future of Metro, the next generation in a long line of pilgrims.

Hayden didn't see much hope for the future in them. Not if the Dox was any indication of their ability to maintain Metro. Then again, there might not be anything to maintain if Law couldn't get the creature under control. Their weapons were ineffective against it, leaving him unconvinced that they could.

Hayden got more than his share of looks as he entered Block Twenty-two with Sarah. Not only because of his age but also who he was with. It seemed her reputation had already been made downtown, and not in a good way. They stared at her, pointing as she passed by, pointing at him as well. They didn't recognize him as Sheriff Duke. They didn't know him at all. He was thankful for that.

The narrow hallways between cubes were crowded with people, talking and laughing, many of them with cups in their hands, filled with a liquid he could smell was some kind of alcohol. There was music coming from one of the rooms; a passed down relic of technology blasting out ancient tunes that echoed in the hall. Other cubes had been set up for trade, small merchant stations bartering chits from one resident to another and taking a small cut of the deal. There were items for sale, too. Clothing, mainly, cheated from the Exchange and collected into scraps that could be traded for other clothing, keepsakes, chits, or services.

They stopped by each of the open cubes, making their way past the other citizens in search of Skillet. They came across a couple of kids with the same haircut, but not the one they were looking for.

"He might be upstairs," Sarah said. "The really illegal stuff is on the third floor, so they have longer to stash it if the Law shows up."

Hayden raised an eyebrow.

"The other Law," she said.

"What kind of really illegal stuff are we talking about?" he asked.

"I probably shouldn't tell you."

"What am I going to do? I have more important things to worry about."

"You're going to see it anyway." She hesitated before speaking. "I know a girl with a cube on the third floor. We've worked together a couple of times."

"What do you mean?"

"We did this routine together. Nothing too over the top. Got a handful of nits to split."

Hayden was surprised her face started turning red. Maybe their conversation hadn't been as useless as he thought.

"Nits?"

She pointed to a small beaded bracelet on one of the girls' wrists. "You should have come down here more if you wanted to stay on top of things."

"I was trusting my deputies to report this stuff."

"You told me that. I think you trusted them a little too much."

He was starting to think he had trusted almost everyone a little too much. Everyone except Natalia.

"I hope I can trust you."

"Keep your promise to my Mom, and you have no problems with me, Sheriff."

A few of the residents glanced over when she said it.

"Shh," Hayden said.

Sarah smiled. "Sorry. I'll call you Dezz instead."

"Dezz?"

She laughed, leading him to the stairwell. It was more crowded than the hallways.

"At least they're in here and not the strands," Hayden said.

"Especially now," Sarah agreed.

They bypassed the second floor, heading to the third. They moved out onto a much quieter landing. A man was waiting there, easily two heads taller than him and in much better physical shape. He had a large homemade knife tucked into his belt.

"Two nits to get in," he said.

"Dezz," Sarah said, looking at Hayden. "Can you take care of this?"

Was she kidding?

"You didn't bring any nits?" he asked.

She shook her head. "I didn't think I would need them."

"You have the nits or not?" the man asked. "If not, fezz off."

Hayden was starting to see a pattern with the way the newest generation was making up or changing words.

"I need to get in there," Hayden said.

"And I need a nice screw. Too bad."

"I can help you with that," Sarah said. "If you let us in."

"Sarah," Hayden said. He wasn't about to let her sell herself for access.

"Oh yeah?" the big man asked. "Full deal for two nits?"

"One time offer," she replied. "It's no big thing, Dezz. I do it all the time. You know that."

Hayden glanced back at her. It was a big deal to him. He was angry at himself for being so blind to everything that was going on downtown. The Dox shouldn't even exist. His father had always told him that Law didn't have the resources to cover everything that could happen in a city the size of Metro, and he would have to pick his battles. It had only been getting worse over the years as deputies retired out and nobody replaced them. Still, he felt responsible.

He also felt powerless to stop it. Maybe if he could get Natalia back. Maybe if he could smooth things over with Malcolm, they could make some positive changes. For now? It didn't matter.

For now, he wasn't even the Sheriff.

He was a fugitive, and normal rules didn't apply. The sooner he accepted that the better off he would be.

"You have a deal," the big man said. He thrust a big finger at Hayden. "You go in." He reached out to take Sarah's arm. "You and me have a date."

Hayden made his decision, reaching out and grabbing the big man's meaty arm, using what he had learned in training to pull the man off-balance, throwing a well-placed elbow into his gut and knocking the wind out of him.

The man doubled over, while Hayden grabbed the knife from his belt. It was better quality than the one Francis carried, with a leather grip and a twenty-centimeter blade. He didn't know if the thing he had seen had a tough hide or not, but if he encountered it again, it would be a good tool to find out.

The big man straightened, prepared to lunge.

"Don't," Hayden said, leveling the knife at him.

"What the fezz is this?"

"I need access, and I'm not giving you the girl to get it," Hayden said. "You can drop the issue and stand there like a good boy, or I can stick you with this."

The man stared at him. He was angry, but he also knew he was defeated.

"Whatever, sprocket. Can I have the blade back when you leave?"

"No," Hayden said. He could guess what sprocket was slang for. "I'm keeping it. These things are illegal you know?"

The man laughed. "Yeah. How else are we supposed to keep order down here? Four Law Officers for ten blocks? It's a joke. I paid twenty nits for that. You can't just take it from me."

"I already did. I'll tell you what, you give me the name and location of the guy you bought it from, and I'll give it back to you when I leave, pozz?"

"Easy deal. Hector is in 315, right down the hall."

Hayden nodded. He was hoping the dealer was here.

"Thank you."

"Rezz out, behemoth," Sarah said.

The big man smiled, his posture relaxing. "Who the fezz are you, anyway? You're a little old to be single."

"None of your business," Hayden said.

"Fair deal."

They started down the hallway. Hayden heard the man behind them announcing the toll to two more newcomers. They passed a few of the cubes, stopping at the open doors and looking in. The first was selling the alcohol he had seen the kids drinking below, in big makeshift containers to be redistributed lower down. The next was offering something they called 'fairy dust,' a powder he assumed was a narcotic of some kind.

"How do they know how to make this stuff?" Hayden asked. He had been a kid once, too, but he had never been exposed to any of this. As a Sheriff's son, why would he be?

"They don't directly," Sarah said. "They get it from someone else."

"Who?"

"He calls himself the Source. Nobody knows who he is or where he gets the stuff. Most people don't care. They're too busy enjoying it."

Could the drugs and alcohol be made and sustained with what they had in Metro? Or was this so-called Source getting it from somewhere else?

Like beyond the secured hatches.

The passed by Leyla's cube. Her door was open, and she had a decent crowd inside her place. She had some scratchy, flat music player blaring some kind of upbeat instrumental, and by the time they crossed over she was nearly finished with her show, all of her clothing distributed into the group. Hayden only got a glimpse of her through the gathering, a small, slender girl who should have been doing anything else with her time. He felt another pang of guilt at the situation, and he forced it aside. Guilt wouldn't help him now.

They reached Cube 315. It was a dim room guarded on the inside by a pair of kids almost as big as the guy at the stairwell. They were both carrying knives of their own, and their attention fell immediately to the blade in Hayden's hand.

"Where'd you get the poker?" one of them said.

"That looks like Gary's," the other said.

"I traded him for it," Hayden said.

"Oh?"

"I need to speak to Hector."

"You looking to deal?"

"Pozz that."

"You got nits?"

Hayden nodded, hoping they wouldn't ask for evidence. They didn't. They moved aside, letting him in.

The main living area was clean, still arranged for daily use. Hayden glanced over at the bedroom. He could see it had been transformed, the walls occupied by sharp utensils of various shapes and sizes. A table had been set up in the doorway, and a heavyset man was positioned behind it.

This had to be Hector.

"Come in, my friend. Come in," he said, getting to his feet and smiling. "Sarah, you brought me a guest?"

"Hey, Hector," Sarah said.

"You know him?" Hayden whispered.

"We've done a few deals. He's got a lot of nits." Her face reddened slightly. "Hector, this is Dezz."

"A pleasure, my friend," Hector said. "A true pleasure. You've got nits, I've got protection."

Hayden walked over to the table, still eyeing the product on the walls. Gary's poker was high-end compared to most of it, but his attention settled on a blade in the back, hanging over the dealer's head. It wasn't homemade, that much was obvious. At least forty-five centimeters long, curved on one side with a jagged point near the center of the other, with a metal guard and a leather-wrapped handle. He had never seen anything so violently beautiful before.

"You like her, I can tell," Hector said. "That one's my treasure. I put her up just for display, to show her off."

"Where'd you get it?" Hayden asked.

"She's been in my family since they boarded the Pilgrim," Hector said. "They used to keep her in a box so Law wouldn't take her, but we aren't afraid of Law around here. She's got a sheath, too." He leaned over to pick it up. It was a hard material with an artistically etched design. "She's priceless. It's about respect, you know?"

"She's incredible," Hayden agreed. The poker had a chance of being useful against the creature. The blade? He might even be able to kill it, or any others like it. "I want it."

"I told you, sprocket, she ain't for sale. You want to deal, take a look at anything else I've got. Something to match that poker there, maybe? I see Gary traded with you."

"You could say that," Hayden said, reaching behind his back. "Those were some turbs we had earlier."

"Oh, man, that was crezz. One of the worst in my lifetime. I thought the whole ship was going to snap open. One leak, that's all it takes, you know? One leak and we all die. Live in the moment. That's what my pops always said. Live in the moment because every moment might be your last. This is all there is, am I right, Dezz? We're traveling, but we ain't got a destination."

"It's good advice," Hayden agreed.

He pulled his stunner, swinging it around and pointing it at Hector's head.

"What the fezz is this?" Hector said, surprised by the weapon. "You stole a fezzing stunner from Law? Are you crezz, sprocket?"

The two guards saw him holding the weapon, and they

started toward him. He turned quickly, firing a pair of rounds that caught the kids in their chests. They shook slightly as the charges knocked them to the ground.

Hayden spun back. Hector had a blade in his hand, and he slashed at Hayden's shoulder. Hayden swung his poker defensively, his trained reflexes the only thing that kept him from being sliced. He knocked the knife away, returning the stunner to Hector.

"Don't," he said. "Drop it."

Hector dropped the knife. "I don't get it, sprocket? What do you think you're going to accomplish by messing with me?"

"I'm living in the moment," Hayden said. "Now give me the blade. I need it."

Hector looked pained at the idea. "You can't get away with this. You have to know that, right? The Source won't take Baby for trade. She's too well known."

"I don't give a fezz about the Source or about you," Hayden said. "I'm not worried about your reprisal."

"You should be, sprocket."

"Where do you think a man gets a stunner, sprocket?" Sarah said. "You have no idea who you're talking to. This is Sheriff Duke."

Hayden could have killed Sarah for opening her mouth.

"Sheriff Duke?" Hector said. "Oh fezz me on a fezzing gear shaft. You're breaking a few laws with this action, ain't you, Sheriff?"

"Are you going to report me?" Hayden asked. "I'd love to read it."

Hector stared at him in silence.

"The blade," Hayden repeated. "You've got five seconds before I use this on you."

He only had one round left. He didn't want to waste it on this kid.

Hector stepped back to the wall and lifted the weapon from it. He held it by the handle.

"Don't get any stupid ideas," Hayden said.

Hector returned, putting the weapon he called Baby in its sheath and then putting it down on the table. "She's been in my family a long time, Sheriff. What do you need it for?"

Hayden put Gary's poker on the table and picked up the real blade. It felt much better in his grip. "Believe it or not, I intend to use it."

"What do you mean?"

"You know a guy about this high?" Sarah asked. "Skillet cut, pale, skinny sprocket?"

"You're looking for Jonas? Why?"

"That's my business," Hayden said. "You know where to find him?"

"He's upstairs. Cube 430. You gotta have serious nits to get up there."

"I don't," Hayden said. He slipped the stunner back into his pants. "I'll return Baby to you when I'm done with her. Make sure Gary gets that back. You could be doing a lot more to help everyone in Metro, you know."

"What's the point, Sheriff?" Hector said. "Metro is fezzed. We're all fezzed. Everyone knows it. We're just trying to get as much as we can out of it before we all vaporize or suffocate, or whatever kills us. We're almost a century past our arrival date, did you know that?"

"So I heard," Hayden said. "Did you know Francis?"

Hector put up his hands. "I heard what happened to him. Cube 430, Sheriff. I don't want to get involved in that shit."

"Is there anything specific you want to tell me?"

"The PASS lies, Sheriff."

"What does that mean?"

"Ask Jonas."

That's exactly what he intended to do.

"Sarah, let's go."

She nodded, waving at Hector. "See you around, sprocket. Thanks for the sharpy."

Hector glowered at her but didn't say another word as they left.

20

"I have a bad feeling about all of this," Sarah said as they reached the stairwell again.

Gary had noticed Baby in Hayden's hand and hadn't bothered to ask him about his own makeshift weapon, allowing them both to pass without a word.

"Did you have to antagonize him?" Hayden said. "For that matter, did you have to tell him who I am? You're supposed to be helping me."

"I am helping you, Sheriff," Sarah insisted. "You would have had a lot more trouble if Hector thought you were just some crezz sprocket instead of the Sheriff of Metro. Believe me."

She was probably right. He was out of his element down here. There was so much going on in Metro that he hadn't known about. Judging by Hector's comment, there was a lot going on in Metro that nobody knew about.

"Okay, I believe you," Hayden said.

Sarah smiled. "I'm a good girl, aren't I, Sheriff?"

He cringed to hear her speak like that. "You're not a girl, you're a woman, and you're helping me out a ton. Don't let people talk down to you. Not me, not your mother. Not anybody."

She looked at him like she was going to cry. She didn't say anything.

They reached the next floor. There was no guard at the door here. There was no gathering. The level was quiet, the doors all closed. He could hear the light strain of Leyla's music coming up through the floor, but otherwise there was no evidence anything out of the ordinary was happening in the Block.

They made their way to Cube 430. Hayden put his ear against the door to listen. A light hum and occasional tapping. Someone was inside. Jonas?

He knocked on the door.

The tapping stopped. He heard motion in the cube like a mad scramble. The hum silenced. Then he heard footsteps approaching.

"Stand here," he said to Sarah, positioning her in front of the door.

She did as he asked, acting like she had been the one to knock. He pulled his stunner, standing to the side.

The door opened a couple of inches. A big blue eye peered out through it.

"You?" Jonas said. "How did you find me?"

"You owe me a chit," Sarah said.

"What?" Jonas replied. "We didn't do anything."

"It's not my fault that other sprocket showed up. You owe me, and I came to collect."

"Get out of here. It's not safe."

"Give me my chit and I'll rezz out, but not before then."

"Forget it."

Hayden took that as his cue. He shoved the front of the stunner into the doorway, jamming it as Jonas tried to slam it closed. Sarah stepped aside, and he shoved into it, knocking the other man back and storming into the room.

"What the hell is this?" Jonas said. "Sheriff Duke? Shit. Don't kill me. Please. Don't kill me."

Hayden kept the stunner trained on him. "Sarah, can you close the door?"

"Yes, sir," Sarah said, shutting the door behind them.

"Don't kill me," Jonas repeated. "Please."

"Why would I kill you?" Hayden said.

"They killed Francis. They killed Saul. Fezz, I'm next."

Hayden lowered the stunner. "What are you talking about?"

"Law. They killed my friends. Shit. Francis told me not to go to you. I didn't listen. I would have if he hadn't stopped me. Now he's dead, and it's your fault."

He had tears in his eyes. He was a skinny kid, a little hunched, in clothes that hadn't been changed in a few days.

"Francis attacked them," Hayden said. "He came at Deputy Bradshaw with a knife."

"That's crezz," Jonas said. "Franco wouldn't do that. He only carried the knife to threaten. He'd never use it on anybody, especially Law."

"He jumped me in the strands. He sure seemed like he wanted to hurt me."

"With his fists, maybe. Not with a blade. I don't know what you heard, Sheriff, but if they say Francis stabbed anyone, it's a lie."

A lie? Why would Hicks lie to him? That didn't make sense. "Who's Saul?"

"A friend. A dead friend. They got him, too."

"Who did?"

"I don't know. Someone from Law. That's what I heard. They went into his Block, and when they came out, he was dead."

"That can't be."

"I heard it from good sources, Sheriff. Why don't you know about it?"

Hayden couldn't answer that question. He should have. There was only one person with the authority to go around him with his deputies.

The Governor.

Was he having Francis and his friends systematically killed because of what they knew? Because they could open the maintenance boxes?

Were his officers really going along with it?

"I'm not with Law anymore," Hayden said. "They're after me, too."

"Why?" Jonas asked, looking confused and relieved at the same time.

"Something took my wife. Something from beyond the Metro perimeter. He's trying to pin it on me. He's trying to keep it a secret."

"Who?"

"Governor Malcolm."

Jonas shook his head, his expression sullen. "I knew it. Damn it. I can't believe we were right about this."

"Right about what?"

Jonas raised his head, looking him in the eye. "You know about the PASS, right Sheriff? The corruption?"

"Everyone knows about the PASS," Hayden said. "So much of our history lost."

"No. That's wrong."

"What do you mean?"

"It wasn't lost, Sheriff. It was deleted. Erased. Intentionally."

21

HAYDEN WANTED TO FEEL SHOCKED, BUT AFTER WHAT HE HAD been experiencing since the turbs, he found it difficult to be surprised.

"Why?" he asked.

"Why was it deleted?" Jonas said. "I don't know the exact reason. But I'm pretty confident that they wanted us to forget where we came from. They wanted us to forget where we were going."

"Or that we might never arrive?" Hayden said.

"Yes," Jonas agreed. "That, too."

"Does Law know you're here?"

"No. I'm not stupid. This isn't my assigned cube. I moved everything out when Francis didn't come back last night."

"The Governor told me they hadn't figured out who Francis' friends were," Hayden said, remembering the conversation. "They took one of his circuit boards to Engineering."

He looked past Jonas. He didn't see any of the same kinds of equipment they had found in Francis' cube in this one. He didn't see whatever had been making the humming sound.

Of course, if Jonas was afraid Law was looking for him, and they probably were, he wouldn't leave his stuff out in the open.

"It was a binary filter," Jonas said. "A basic tool to scrub the data from the PASS."

"Meaning?"

"I should probably go back to the beginning," Jonas said. "But I'm not sure if I can trust you."

"You can trust him," Sarah said. "His wife is missing."

"And someone came into Metro through the secure hatch where she vanished," Hayden said, fighting the emotions that wanted to pour out. It was hard for him to think about. He wasn't ready to tell them what he had seen wasn't a human but some kind of demon. "They've been killing people in the strands."

"Oh, fezz," Jonas said. "I'm sorry, Sheriff. We've both lost people we cared about since yesterday."

"And my question is, why?" Hayden said. "What's happening on the Pilgrim?"

"I don't know, exactly. All I know is that Law is willing to kill to keep what little we discovered quiet."

"And charge me with murder." Hayden sighed. "Okay, Jonas. Start at the beginning."

Jonas nodded and motioned them to a small table in the corner of the room. It only had two chairs, so he stood while Sarah and Hayden took them.

"You know the PASS is public. Open to all. And there are a few terminals around Metro that let us access the main database."

"Yes," Hayden said. "There's a terminal in the Law Station."

"Okay, so I knew Francis since we were eight years old. We both grew up in Block Seventeen. He was always the brain and the brawn, big and smart. He wanted to be an

Engineer more than anything. We used to go into the strands together, and he would play with the maintenance boxes. He tried to open them, so he could see how everything worked. I was always the lookout, and we had to run away from Law ten, fifteen times over the years.

"This went on for ten years. He never cracked the access codes, but we also never got caught. Anyway, Francis applied for Engineer training. So did I. He was accepted into the program. I wasn't. But Francis was the kind of guy; he was loyal to a fault. He refused to go in without me, even when I told him he was making a huge mistake. I wanted to see him become an Engineer. I was certain he would excel and become a lead one day. But he insisted. He declined the invite, and decided to get into Cleaning instead."

Cleaning was the lowest level occupation on the Pilgrim. It seemed a terrible fit for the man if he was as intelligent as Jonas claimed.

"He didn't only want to clean," Hayden said.

"No. He had managed to open up one of the conduits near Block Thirty without anyone noticing. He started taking things from it. Bits and pieces of wires, scraps of metal. He showed me how to pirate the stuff, too. He said as long as nothing stopped working, nobody would notice, and he was right. He also started getting more and more curious about the state of the Pilgrim. When we were kids, we would access the PASS a couple of times a week. He started dragging me to the nearest terminal every day. I would watch while he ran all of these queries. History of the Pilgrim. The Pilgrim's launch. The Pilgrim's destination. He had compiled a list of queries that the PASS returned as lost or corrupt. He showed me how all of them linked together, and how all of them were obscuring critical information about the ship's mission, its age, its speed, its vector. Stuff that wouldn't be obvious on the surface, but if you questioned it hard enough it became pretty obvious."

He paused, going over to the door and putting his ear against it. Satisfied, he returned to them.

"He said that if the data had been corrupted like the system claimed, it would have been more random. He had been talking to some of the Engineering students, and they said data was stored wherever there were available bits, with pointers that told the system where to find them. It shouldn't have lost everything related to a specific subject."

"Which is what led him to believe the data was deleted?" Hayden asked.

"Yes. He was sure of it. So he started talking to a couple of others. Saul and Neila."

"You said Saul is dead. What about Neila?"

"I don't know. I haven't heard from her in a few days."

"The four of you started working to prove his theory?"

"Yes. It took almost a year, but we managed to hack the PASS terminal and get to the source code. He was able to print the raw storage data to the terminal display. Do you know what he found?"

"Evidence?"

"Damning evidence, in the form of a pattern. An algorithm."

"Algorithm?"

"A set of rules followed by a process. In this case to alter the bits in the PASS storage unit. It was too perfect to be an accident."

"So someone deleted it. Who? Why? When?"

"All good questions, Sheriff. It took Francis almost another year to break the algorithm. Once he had, he made the filter. But it's low power. Slow. And even though the data was related it was still removed at random. We had to filter the entire storage system to get the bits and pieces we wanted. But in learning how the PASS worked, we also learned how some of the networked systems in Metro worked."

"The maintenances boxes?"

"For one, yes. We had the codes. We were hoping to pillage them for more processors, to speed up our work. We didn't get the chance."

"What about the secure hatches?"

"That's where it gets interesting. Well, one of the places where it gets interesting. We got into Metro's network, and do you know what we found?"

"I can't even guess."

"Another network. One internal to the city, and one external."

"You mean-"

"The Pilgrim has a network managing the critical systems, propulsion for instance, and it has a direct connection to the Metro network. I'm not saying if you have access to one you can see everything on the other because you can't. Every node on the external network is protected, and figuring out the keys has been a long process. But, we did get into one of the nodes."

He stopped, checking the door again before heading into the bathroom. There was a shifting sound as he moved some things around, and then he emerged with a board similar to the one Aahro had shown him and a small display. He put them both on the table, running a wire from the device to the cube's power supply.

The board had a fan attached to it, and it hummed as Jonas turned the device on. Within a few seconds, some text appeared on the display, and a red beam came on, projecting a keyboard to the surface of the table.

"It's easier for me to show you than to tell you," Jonas said. "We only got access to the outside network last week, and this is what made me want to come and talk to you. But Francis was convinced that was a bad idea. He said there was no way someone had deleted data from the PASS and someone in Law or Org or Engineering didn't know about it. He was worried there were protocols in place to deal with breaches."

"Not any protocols I was aware of," Hayden said. "The Governor is a different story."

"Apparently." He tapped on the tabletop, on the projected surface. The characters flew along the display. A window opened, showing a black box. "Are you ready for this, Sheriff? It's going to blow your shit. If the Governor knew we had this, I think he'd raze this entire Block."

Hayden looked at Jonas. The man was determined, and angry. His best friends were dead because of this.

"Go ahead," Hayden said.

Jonas tapped the keyboard. The dark box turned into an image. A corridor similar to the maintenance passages. Alone, it would have been unimpressive.

But the corridor wasn't empty. It was grainy, but it was obvious. A skeleton was slumped against the wall, long hair flowing over its shoulder. A woman, then. She was wearing a jumpsuit, not unlike the one the Governor wore. She had a patch on her chest, under an insignia. "Hoskins." The middle of the jumpsuit was torn, the material darker there. Stained.

Hayden felt his heart start thumping in his chest. He had already learned that there was more life on the other side of Metro's perimeter, but this?

"Geez," Sarah said. "This means that-"

"We weren't alone on the Pilgrim," Jonas said. "Not always."

Hayden stared at the insignia. It matched the logo on the screen for the PASS.

"It's more than that," he said. "The Pilgrim wasn't always

autonomous. She had a crew. A real, live crew. This woman was a member of it."

"That's what we think."

"Something killed her."

"We believe that, too. We were hoping whatever did that was dead. It's been a long time."

The cuts looked familiar, but the location was wrong. The demon had always gone for the throat.

"It isn't dead," Hayden said. "Or they aren't dead. I don't know. Something took my wife. And something is wandering around Metro."

"Something?" Sarah said. "I thought you said it was a man?"

"I lied," Hayden said. "What I saw, it wasn't a man. I hit it with three stunners, and it reacted by climbing to the top of one of the blocks. It had claws. I saw them."

"It could be the same thing that killed Hoskins," Jonas said.

"It could," Hayden agreed.

"Geez," Sarah said, frightened. "What the hell is this? What the hell? Seriously, Sheriff. You're telling me there are monsters on the Pilgrim? You're telling me the crew is all dead? Are we even supposed to be locked out of the rest of the ship?"

Hayden was surprised she asked that. He was starting to wonder the same thing.

"You said the secure hatch opened, Sheriff?" Jonas said. He was staying impressively calm and reasonable, more like an Engineer than a Cleaner.

"During the last turbs. My wife, Natalia radioed me and told me she found a body, and it wasn't one of ours. By the time I got to her position, the hatch was closed, and she was gone. There was a bloody handprint under it. Maybe it was hers. I hope to the Universe it wasn't. The Governor, he cleaned it all up. He made it disappear so nobody would know. I came to you because I need you to help me open the hatch. I need to get out there."

"I don't think you want to go out there, Sheriff," Sarah said. "Not if there are monsters out there."

"They took my wife."

"How do you know she isn't dead?"

"She isn't dead," Hayden snapped, so violently Sarah flinched like she had been hit. "She isn't dead," he repeated more quietly. "I'm sorry, Sarah. I can't accept that. I won't. Why do you think I took Hector's knife?"

"Sheriff, if you can get out there," Jonas said, pausing. "If we can get out there, maybe we can find out what happened. Maybe we can find out where we are, or how we got knocked off course. Maybe we can do something about it."

"Are you crezz?" Sarah said. "You can't go out there, either of you. You'll die."

"There's no 'we,'" Hayden said. "I'm going alone. Assuming we can find a way to open the hatch."

"What about the Governor?" Sarah continued. "He's desperate to keep this a secret. Why? He has to have a reason. Maybe a good reason."

"There's no good reason for killing people," Jonas said.

"How do you know?" Sarah countered.

"Sarah," Hayden said.

"No. I'm sorry, Sheriff. You said, don't let anyone talk down to you, so you should listen to me. Maybe what Governor Malcolm knows that we don't is worth killing over? Maybe he deleted the data, or one of the Governors before him did it. Maybe some things should be remembered, but there are some things that should stay forgotten."

Hayden stared at her. He couldn't deny that she had a point, but he also didn't care. "My wife is out there, which means I'm going to do anything I have to to get out there." He looked at Jonas. "Can you open the hatch?"

Jonas shook his head. "No. The camera was the only thing we were able to get access to. Every system has a different code. We weren't sure the hatches could be opened, but I guess you have proof that they can."

"Unfortunately, that proof is running around Metro killing people," Hayden said.

"I'm telling you, Sheriff," Sarah said. "Don't go out there. Don't try to open the hatch. What if you can't close it again? What if you let more of those things in?"

"We need to find a way to open the hatch first, or it doesn't matter either way. Jonas, can it be done?"

Jonas shrugged. "I don't know, Sheriff. We were working on it for a long time. The camera was our first and only breakthrough, and look what happened since. Plus, the Governor knows we've been hacking the PASS now. He's going to have all of the terminals guarded."

"But can it be done?" Hayden repeated. "Is it possible? Yes or no?"

"Yes. It's possible. Clearly, the hatch is functional. There has to be a control system for it."

"You need a terminal?"

"Yes. I can plug my rig into it and run the root system. But I don't have a way to figure out which connector is the hatch, and even if I did, I don't have a way to get the right access code except by trial and error. It could take weeks."

"We don't have weeks," Hayden said.

"I know. I want to do it, Sheriff. I really do. But we weren't ready for this. We weren't close to ready. Franco was right about that. I should have listened to him, maybe none of this would have happened. Maybe he would still be alive."

"Natalia would be gone, and I would have no idea how to

get to her," Hayden said. "I thought you could help me, but maybe you can't."

He leaned back in the chair. He wasn't ready to accept that there was nothing he could do. He wasn't ready to give up. There had to be a way through that damn hatch.

"Maybe the Governor knows how to open it?" Sarah said. "I mean, it's not like he'd admit it if he did."

"Somebody deleted the data," Jonas said. "It's possible they made a copy first?"

"Somebody like the Pilgrim's designer?" Hayden asked.

"Could be."

"Have you heard the rumors about the Governor's secret stash?"

"I thought that was food?" Sarah said.

"What if it isn't?" Hayden replied. "What if it has to do with this? Maybe he has access after all? He'd never use it. Not if his position dictates he keep the truth silent at all costs."

"What is the truth, Sheriff?" Sarah said. "When it comes down to it?"

"My best guess? When the Pilgrim launched, there was a human crew guiding her. Only something happened, and the ship was boarded by these demon creatures. They killed the crew, but not before they sealed the city to protect the people inside. Instead of delivering these creatures to a new world, they put the ship off course and left us drifting."

Sarah shook, her chill visible. "You think they knew we were going to die out here?"

"Eventually, yes."

Hayden didn't like it either, but it was what it was.

"And the Governor is going along with this?"

"He wants to keep the residents of Metro alive for as long as he can," Hayden said. "I think you're right. He believes he's doing the right thing, and I can't argue that he isn't. But my loyalty is to Natalia first."

"No, I wasn't right," Sarah said. "My life is a lie. Your life is a lie. We're all going on for what? An end that's sure to come if we just sit here and do nothing? Having babies so those babies can die when the power fails, or the atmospherics break, or when more of the monsters get in? Fezz that, Sheriff. I want you to get your wife back. I want to know the truth."

"What about your mother?" Hayden asked. Her reaction was almost a complete reversal from her previous attitude.

"Fezz her, too. It's not her decision. I'm an adult."

"So," Jonas said. "Where do we start?"

22

"THIS WASN'T WHAT I HAD IN MIND, SHERIFF," JONAS SAID.

"You aren't safe up here. Not for long. As soon as the Governor decides finding you is the top priority, this place is going to get raided and shut down."

"But the Source pays off the deputies. They can't renege on that."

"They'll have to if it means staying out of lockup. Nobody can turn a blind eye forever."

Jonas shoved the homemade computer into a large satchel along with a few of his other possessions.

"Who does this cube belong to, anyway?" Sarah asked.

"My girlfriend. She's downstairs."

"It's not Leyla, is it?"

"No. I'm not going to plan a future with a whore."

Sarah's face tensed, but she didn't reply.

"What can you tell me about the Source?" Hayden asked. "I never heard that name before today."

"He keeps a low profile. Nobody knows who he is, and word on the street is to only bring him up when in certain company. Everybody around here is so afraid of him; nobody dares fezz it up."

"Why are they afraid?"

"He makes people disappear, and Law never seems to notice."

"He's also supplying you with drugs and alcohol," Hayden said. "Where does he get it?"

"Who knows? Could be he already hacked the system and can open the hatches. Maybe he goes outside the perimeter? But I've heard there are chemicals in some of the systems that can be used to make stuff. Siphon it from the conduits, a tiny bit at a time. Engineering won't notice. Law won't notice. It's not a new thing, but it is cyclical."

"You mean previous generations have done the same thing?"

"Yeah. It all gets passed down word of mouth. We don't have anything to write on down here. The recycled paper gets prioritized to the top end. So do the functional tablets. But I'm sure you knew that."

He had never given it much thought. The Law Office was always stocked. He had been living his entire life in a bubble within Metro, never venturing too far beyond it.

"The way they tell it, sometimes there's more illicit activity, sometimes less. But it's always come from the Source."

"Like the sprocket is immortal?" Sarah said.

"More like he's having kids that carry on the tradition." He closed and buttoned the satchel. "I'm ready, but I still think this is a bad idea."

"Do you have a better one?" Hayden asked.

"No."

"Come on."

Hayden led them out of the cube and into the hallway. They were approaching the stairwell when he heard the familiar strain of the ship's skeleton.

"Turbs," he said, putting his hand against the wall.

The ship shuddered, the sudden pressure vibrating it. It wasn't too bad this time, and they managed to stay on their feet.

Hayden kept walking, entering the stairwell and descending. The others inside had paused during the first turb, but only for a moment. They were acclimated to them.

The ship shook again, a little harder this time. Sarah almost fell down the steps, but Hayden grabbed her wrist, keeping her upright.

"Thanks, Dezz," she said, careful in the company of others.

He nodded. They made it to the second-floor landing. The turbs were getting stronger, and the third hit the Pilgrim pretty hard. They all fell to their knees to keep from tumbling around.

"Bad timing," Hayden said.

At the same time, he heard a loud clang from outside. It came from above deck. It sounded like it was right next to the Block.

"What was that?" Sarah asked.

"I don't know," Hayden replied.

There were no windows in the stairwell. No way to look outside.

The quaking subsided for a moment. They stood and started down the steps again.

A fourth turb hit. This one was the strongest of them all.

Hayden heard a soft hiss, and then the stairwell beneath them was engulfed in a gout of flame.

He didn't think. He reacted by grabbing Sarah and throwing her behind him, smothering her body with his as the fire exploded through the doorway and climbed upward with the air. He heard the screams from further below, the cries of pain and agony as the explosion rocked the Block, shaking everything as hard as the turb. His eyes watered from the heat, and he could feel it licking at his back.

The fire vanished almost as quickly as it came, the heat subsiding. Hayden jumped to his feet, looking down on Sarah. She was alive and alert, her eyes watering like his. Jonas was beside her, facedown on the steps. He started to get up.

"Shit. Kylie." He turned his head to the base of the stairs, his face distraught.

"What the hell was that?" she asked in a small voice.

"I think one of the conduits ruptured," he said. "Do you remember Block Eight?"

He looked at the base of the stairwell. The fire had claimed a dozen kids, leaving their bodies naked and burned and motionless. He could still sense heat from below. The Block was on fire.

"Up," he said, reaching out and grabbing Sarah's hand. "We need to go up. Quickly."

They started to ascend. More of the residents in the Block were moving out onto the stairwell. Gary, Hector, and his two guards were among them.

"Sheriff?" Hector said. His bravado was gone. He was just a scared kid, trying to find his way out.

"Up," Hayden said. "Come on."

They climbed as quickly as they could. The smoke was starting to pour into the stairwell, rising with them. Residents were moving out onto the stairwell, trying to come down, slowing the progress as the others directed them upward.

"Cover your mouths," Hayden said. "Try not to breathe in the smoke."

"Where are we going?" Hector asked. "Sheriff, the rooftops are locked. We'll die in here."

"I can open it," Hayden replied.

The building shook again as another turb hit, causing a number of them to scream. It was smaller than the last, the shaking beginning to subside.

The damage had already been done.

The air was getting thicker with every passing second, the smoke increasing as the fire expanded upward into the floors above. Block Eight had been left a bent mess of slagged metal framework within thirty minutes, the flames eating through the unprotected innards of the space. Hayden understood the loss. Hundreds of years of hand-me-down mementos and keepsakes were being lost, burned and gone forever. Entire family histories. Not to mention essential resources they could never get back.

More and more of the residents were coughing. A few of them started to fall, their lungs overcome by the smoke. It was hard for him to pass them by, to keep moving without stopping to help them. But there was no help. If they didn't keep going, they were all going to die.

The first of the residents reached the door, pulling on it to try to make it open.

"Move out of the way," Hector shouted. His friends took up the call, getting the people in front of them to clear a space for Hayden. Sarah and Jonas followed him through it, all the way up to the top.

His lungs hurt. His legs burned. He could barely breathe. He knew they all probably felt the same way. Even once they were outside, they wouldn't have much time.

He made it to the control panel, quickly entering his access code. The panel flashed a message it him in red:

"Code Invalid."

What?

"They locked you out," Jonas said beside him. "Don't worry; I know the master code. It can't be locked out or changed."

He tapped on the panel. The light turned green, and the door clicked. He pushed it open, letting the circulating air in and the smoke out. The scrubbers would clean the atmosphere in time, but the collected debris was going to reduce their efficiency even further.

They poured out onto the rooftop, nearly five hundred in all. It was a small amount for an entire Block. Much too small. Hayden was left hoping a lot of the residents hadn't been in their cubes. That they were anywhere else.

"Now what?" Hector asked.

"Cross over to Block Twenty-one," Hayden said.

"How?"

"You'll have to jump."

"What?" Gary said beside him. "It's over two meters."

"We don't have a choice," Hayden said. "Try to jump or die in the fire."

"I can't do it," Hector said. "I'm terrified of heights." He moved to the edge and looked over. "No way."

Hayden didn't know what else to do. Some of them weren't going to make it, that much was assured. But most of them would. More than would have survived the flames that were climbing the Block.

"Sarah, follow me," Hayden said.

"Sheriff?" she replied. "I can't do it."

"Yes, you can. I'm an old man, and I can do it. Watch."

He backed up a few steps and ran toward the edge. He pushed off as he reached it, his legs screaming as he found himself in the air, flying 60 meters off the deck. His body began to slow, the rooftop of Block Twenty-one drawing near.

He hit the other side a half-meter in, tucking his shoulder and rolling on it to his feet, careful not to drop Baby. He faced Block Twenty-two, waving to them.

"It's easy. Come on."

Emboldened by his jump, Sarah backed up and charged forward, making the leap. He caught her as she landed, keeping her from taking the same tumble he had. Jonas followed right after, and Hayden caught him, too.

Their success signaled the rest of the residents to follow, lining up along the rooftop to leap. The first round turned to help the others, catching them as they came in.

Then Hayden heard a scream, and a thud as the first of them missed the jump. Someone on his side cried out and started to sob. The pace of the crossing slowed. But the flames were rising higher, and the smoke was getting thicker. Emergency systems triggered the elemental generators to start dumping massive amounts of water like a giant sprinkler. They were all drenched within seconds, but it wasn't enough to kill the progression. The flames emerged from the stairwell at the remaining residents' backs.

"Come on," Hayden shouted. "You can make it. Come on."

The others followed his lead, shouting across, holding out their arms to beckon the remaining people to make the leap.

Hayden heard another scream. Then another.

Only they didn't come from in front of him.

He spun around, looking for the source. He saw the two bodies on the ground first, blood pouring from their necks. His eyes shifted upward, into the darkness of the creature standing on the opposite side of the rooftop.

His left hand gripped the sheath of his newly acquired blade. His right hand took the handle. The demon seemed to recognize him as the one who had shot it. It ignored the others, lowering itself and charging.

He slipped the blade from its case, holding it in front of him.

"Come on then, you son of a bitch," he said.

23

THE DEMON RUSHED TOWARD HIM, SMALL FEET SLAPPING HARD on the rooftop, claws scratching against the surface. It held its arms out wide, flexing the claws there, which were still dripping with its other victims' blood.

Hayden was getting a better look at it now. It was almost as tall as he was but much thinner, its body composed of a narrow musculature with thin muscle and dark, leathery flesh resting on top. It had a smallish head, tiny black eyes, and a snout filled with rows of sharp teeth. It wasn't clear how intelligent the thing was, charging right at him while he held the blade, but it was apparent it knew who he was and that it was pissed at him.

He waited for it, crouching slightly as it approached. Its mouth opened, but it didn't make a sound, coming at him in silence. When it was four meters away, it jumped, leaving the ground and arcing toward him, its speed increasing from the maneuver.

The people around him were screaming in terror. He didn't budge, holding Baby tight and judging the creature's speed.

He swung the weapon, sweeping it in an uppercut across his body as the demon came in. The weapon caught it in the shoulder, the force knocking it aside as the blade dug into its flesh. It hissed as black blood splattered from the wound, sliding sideways, using its claws to stop its momentum and turn back in his direction. It dove at him before he could recover, slashing up at his neck.

He threw himself backward, the daggers passing close enough that he could smell the blood on its fingertips. He put himself off-balance, stumbling away as the creature pounced again.

He raised the blade, catching its claws on the flat more by accident and luck than anything else. The creature's weight against it pushed him back more, and he fell to the ground, Baby dropping from his hand.

It hissed a second time, opening its jaw wide as it loomed over him, lifting a foot toward his chest.

Hayden heard a grunt, and the demon made another hissing sound, twisting back. Gary's poker was sticking out of its back, buried twelve centimeters deep. Hayden saw past the thing to where Sarah stood, frozen after delivering the blow.

He reached out for Baby, finding the grip and picking it up, swinging it toward the demon. It hopped away before he could hit it, powerful legs carrying it to Sarah. She barely had time to scream as the creature's claws whipped across her neck, cutting deep into her throat. She fell to her knees, clutching at the wound while her life bled out in front of him.

He got to his feet, lunging at the demon. It knew he was coming and it spun back, slashing Baby and bringing it toward the ground with one hand, slashing at him with the other. He ducked low, feeling the air as the claws went over his head. He pulled his stunner from his pants at the same time, bringing it up and sticking it in the monster's open mouth.

"Resist this," he said, pulling the trigger.

The final charged round sank into the demon's mouth, lighting up its insides. The electric burst passed over to Hayden, sending a jolt through his system and knocking him away.

He stayed down, trying to regain his senses. The shouts had died out, replaced with sobbing and murmurs. Two meters away, Block Twenty-two was completely engulfed, the entire structure going up in flame.

His body was numb, and the parts that weren't numb were burning from fresh exhaustion. Sarah. He had seen the wound before she collapsed.

He knew she wasn't going to get up again. He let out a soft sigh of anguish. She was too damn young. She was just starting to understand her worth. Damn it.

He moved slowly, gathering his arms and legs. Everything was tingling. A pair of shoes stopped ahead of his face. He looked up. Gary was standing over him.

Hayden didn't know if the big man was going to help him up or take Baby and leave. He got his answer a moment later when Gary reached past him, picking up the blade.

"Hector didn't make the jump," Gary said. "This is mine now."

"I need it," Hayden said.

"Go fezz yourself," Gary said.

Hayden watched him turn and move for the stairwell. He noticed the demon was still on the rooftop, laying face down. A few of the residents were standing over it, examining it with fear in their eyes.

A larger group moved to intercept Gary, blocking his path.

"What do you think you're doing?" Jonas said, leading the group.

"This is mine. I'm taking it."

"No, you aren't. The Sheriff wants it."

"I don't give a shit about the Sheriff. He got Hector killed."

"He saved the life of everyone on this rooftop. That's more than anyone else would have done."

"Get out of my way," Gary insisted.

"Hand it over, and we will."

Gary considered them for a moment. Then he dropped Baby on the rooftop. "I don't need it anyway."

Hayden struggled to his feet, looking over at the burning building. The fire was beginning to die out, the combination of water and lack of fuel starting to win the fight. If they followed procedure, Engineering would be there any minute now, if they weren't there already. He had read the report on the Block Eight fire. He knew what the outcome would be. A reduction in population for starters. Tighter rationing, stricter controls.

What about the outcome of killing a monster in the city?

Hayden limped slowly to where Sarah's body was resting. He knelt beside her, forcing himself to look at her lifeless face. She had died to protect him. He wasn't going to let her courage be for nothing.

He returned to his feet, putting his attention back on the creature, approaching it slowly. A few of the residents filed in behind him as if he could protect them if it decided to get up again. Even if he had been holding the blade, he wasn't sure he had the strength.

He looked down at it. He nudged it with his foot. It was surprisingly light. He turned it over, hearing the gasps as its face became visible once more. Its eyes were open, staring up at the membrane not far above them. He was disgusted by it all over again. It was a real monster, a true demon.

"What is that thing?" one of the residents said behind him.

"Where did it come from?" another asked.

He was tempted to tell them. So tempted. He could have destroyed all of Malcolm's efforts in an instant. But what would the point of that be? These people had suffered enough already tonight. But how was he supposed to lie about it? What was he supposed to say it was?

"We need to go, Sheriff," Jonas said. "Law is on the splits, and they'll be coming up here as soon as they figure out some of us jumped the gap."

He was holding Baby. Hayden stuck out his hand. Jonas hesitated a moment, and then passed the blade to him.

He stood over the creature. He thought about what he was going to do for a few seconds. Then he raised the blade over his head, taking it in a two-hand grip. He knelt slightly, bringing it down on the demon's neck and severing its head.

The residents around him drew back. He bent down, grabbing the head by the sides and tucking it under his arm. Then he put his foot against the body, rolling it toward the edge.

"What are you doing, Sheriff?" Jonas asked.

"Destroying the evidence."

"Why?"

"Because Metro doesn't need this," he replied. "We have enough monsters in this town already."

He kicked the headless corpse. It tumbled off the side, falling out far enough that it landed in the burning Block, vanishing in the smoke.

"I'm going to Block Twenty to make my way down," Hayden said. "Are you with me?"

Jonas nodded. He looked like he wanted to cry. "My girlfriend was in there. She's dead, isn't she Sheriff? Fezz the turbs. Fezz this whole damn ship."

Hayden put his hand on Jonas' shoulder. "I'm starting to feel the same way. But the turbs weren't responsible for the fire."

"They weren't?"

"I don't think so. Look down there, Jonas. Where the hell is Engineering? Why isn't anyone doing anything to stop it, or to save anyone? Where is Law? Where is Medical? Where is Emergency Response?"

Hayden was getting angrier with each observation. He couldn't believe it would go this far, this fast.

"Do you really think-"

Hayden turned to the few hundred residents who had made it across. He took a deep breath, preparing to shout. To tell them to stay quiet, and forget what they had seen.

He didn't get the chance.

A whirring sound rose from the split behind them, a plural buzzing off the edge of the Block.

A moment later, a trio of drones appeared over the corner. They were two meters long and featured a pair of long cylinders reaching from either side of a short nose.

Hayden had never seen drones like these before. They were larger than Law's inoperable machines. Where had they come from?

The twin cylinders on each began to belch fire.

The people on the rooftop started to die.

24

"MOVE!" HAYDEN SHOUTED, GRABBING JONAS' SHOULDER AND pulling him away.

The flashes from the front of the drones were constant, the rain of death overwhelming. Hayden had never seen anything like it. He had never heard of anything like it. Not from the PASS, not from the stories handed down by the older generations. These weapons weren't firing stunner rounds. He didn't know what they were firing, but they were murderous.

The residents on the rooftop screamed, most of them trying to run for the stairwell door. One of the drones broke away from the others, circling the rooftop to cut them off. The people were caught in the crossfire, hit with something and knocked down or simply cut to pieces.

Hayden put his eyes forward again. They were nearing the edge of the block and would have to make a second leap. Could the drones see him? Would they follow? He didn't know. It didn't matter. He had to escape.

Malcolm had gone off the deep end. He was willing to

slaughter every single one of the people on the rooftop to keep them from saying anything about the demon. Who was piloting the drones? Who was pulling the trigger? His deputies? He couldn't believe they would be so cold and inhuman.

He heard the whine of one of the drones closing in behind them, and the rhythmic thwap thwap thwap of the weapons it carried. The rooftop behind him began spitting up shards of synthcrete, raising a cloud of dust. He had Baby in his left hand, the demon head tucked beneath his arm, his right hand pulling Jonas along. He didn't know if anyone else had run, or if they had made it from this Block to another.

"Jump," he shouted, letting Jonas go as they neared the edge.

He pushed off, once more going airborne across the gap, passing over the strand below. He could see Jonas jump out of the corner of his eye.

He hit the other side, his foot nearly sliding off the edge. He tumbled, losing the demon head as he rolled to a stop facing the ledge.

Jonas landed more smoothly than him, his legs flexing slightly. He didn't lose his footing, rushing forward to regain his balance. The drone wasn't far behind.

Hayden forced himself up. He rushed to the head, lifting it and joining Jonas in a sprint for the stairwell. He could still hear the other drones firing on the rooftop of Block Twenty-two, but there were no screams now. He risked a quick glance back. Not a single resident was left standing.

The third drone took a wide route around the rooftop, clearly tracking them but not firing. They made it to the stairwell door, forced to come to a stop while Jonas entered the master code.

The drone swooped around, dropping directly behind

them. Hayden turned, staring at the front of it. He heard the door click behind him, and then Jonas turned, too.

Why wasn't it shooting?

He didn't wait to find out. He threw himself backward, through the door. Jonas didn't hesitate to follow, and they charged into the stairwell, tripping on the steps and falling to the sixteenth floor. An instant later the guns on the machine opened up, tearing the stairwell door to pieces and dropping fragments of synthcrete on top of them.

"Get up," Hayden said, to himself as much as Jonas.

It was easier said than done. He didn't want to get up. His body was done. His mind was struggling to process everything it had witnessed. It had barely been ten hours since he had woken up beside Natalia, turned over and kissed her face before sliding out of bed and making his way to the shower. She had joined him there a few minutes later, washing his back as he washed hers. Holding her close in the warm afterglow of their evening together and the promise of a second chance to have a child of their own.

It was gone. All gone. Natalia. The baby. His life would never be the same. Metro would never be the same.

Or maybe it would. Maybe it would go on as it had been going on for almost four centuries. Maybe everything he had witnessed would die in the slow and steady progression of time.

Covered up.

Buried.

Forgotten.

He had read about the fire in Block Eight. The report said it was an accident. Was it?

He got up, gathering himself. Jonas made it to his feet beside him. They started down the stairwell, one step at a time.

"Sheriff, this-" Jonas' voice trailed off. He was struggling to comprehend. To understand.

"It's not safe here," Hayden said.

Not for him. Not for Jonas. It never would be. Not ever again.

Not unless he could figure out what had happened to the Pilgrim and somehow make it right.

Not unless he could free the people of Metro from their prison in the massive hold, and give them safe and unfettered access to the rest of the ship.

Not unless he could expose what the Governor had done to keep them quiet.

"We need to get through the hatch," Hayden said. "We have to get to the other side. It's the only way we survive."

"There are monsters out there."

"There are monsters in here. Worse than these." He held up the demon's head.

"I can't open the hatch, Sheriff. I need a terminal and time."

"I'm not sure you need to crack it."

"What do you mean?"

"You theorized that the Governor might know the truth about the Pilgrim, or at least have access to information we don't. If that's true, we'll find it in his Mansion."

Jonas froze. "You want to go to the Governor's Mansion?"

Hayden nodded. "We might be wrong. There might be nothing to find there. But I don't think so."

"How are we going to get in?"

"The Mansion's access panel is on Metro's network, isn't it?"

Jonas nodded.

"And you have the master code, don't you?"

He nodded again.

Hayden held Baby up in front of him. Some of the

demon's black blood had dried to the edge. He hoped he wouldn't have to use it again, especially against his own deputies. But if he had to choose between going after Natalia and killing them?

He was going to kill them.

"You open the doors. I'll worry about the rest."

25

It was easier to get out of Block Twenty than Hayden expected.

With the master code, it didn't matter if the Governor ordered Engineering to cut off access to the lifts, which were functional here. Jonas simply overrode the lockout, opening the doors and carrying them to the bottom floor. If Law was in the building, they had been sent up the stairwell, not realizing that they were able to defeat the security protocols.

The lift doors opened on the second floor of the Block. Hayden moved out first, scanning the area carefully before motioning Jonas to follow. They made their way down the corridor to the row of cubes adjacent to the strand that ran between Block Twenty and Block Nineteen. They were both soaking wet, dirty and scraped from their fall down the steps. Jonas had managed to hold onto his satchel, but he had said he was worried the computer inside had been damaged.

They knocked on the door of each of the cubes, moving out of sight while they waited for an answer. They repeated the effort four times until no one responded. Then Jonas used the master code to open the apartment to them, allowing them inside.

Hayden headed straight to the bedroom, opening the drawers to the wardrobe and rifling through the clothes. They were lucky to find a man lived here. The clothes would be a little big on Jonas, a little small on him, but they were better than what they had. Both stripped and changed in a hurry, leaving Hayden in a tight shirt that accented his gut and a pair of worn pants with holes in both knees. He also grabbed a second shirt to wrap the demon head in.

Then they returned to the living area. Hayden looked out at the strand, only a few meters below them. It was clear. He looked up, searching for the drones. They seemed to be gone. He took Baby and started slamming the bottom of the grip against the window.

The glass was designed to be resistant to impact, but it couldn't hold out forever. By the twentieth blow a spiderweb of cracks had formed along the surface, and by the thirtieth, the pane finally surrendered. It didn't shatter. Rather, the outer edge had bent enough that he was able to grab it and pull it inside.

He climbed through the empty pane, hanging from the edge and then dropping down into the strand. Jonas dropped his satchel down and followed, coming into the strand beside him.

"We make a good team, Sheriff," Jonas said.

"Let's keep it up," Hayden replied. "This way."

"Sheriff Duke! Don't move!"

He heard the voice at the end of the strand. He rotated his head, finding Aarho standing at the intersection of the split, aiming her stunner at him.

"They took Natalia, Deputy," he shouted back at her. "I'm not stopping for you or anybody."

She tilted her head, tapping her chin against her badge.

"Sheriff?" Jonas said.

"Follow me. Don't look back."

Hayden broke away from Aarho. Jonas broke with him. She fired the stunner, two rounds, but they went wide, hitting the wall beside them.

He broke through an intersection, turned right and dashed across a split. He heard shouting as he crossed it, glanced over and saw another Deputy drawing their stunner. He didn't notice who it was before passing into the next strand.

He turned left and then right, staying within the maze. He knew the strands better than anyone.

"Wait," Jonas said as they passed a maintenance box. "In here."

"We need to get to the Mansion," Hayden said.

"We'll never make it like this."

Jonas had already stopped and was keying in the code for the box. It opened, and they both ducked inside.

"What are you thinking?" Hayden whispered.

"Listen for them. Take them by surprise and grab their stunners. I know you don't want to hurt them."

Hayden smirked. The kid was right. "Okay."

They waited in the box. He was thankful for the chance to catch his breath as he kept his head against the hatch, listening for the deputies.

"Aarho, this is Chao. Do you see them?"

"Negative. I think he lost us."

Hayden heard the muffled sound of the transceiver through the hatch. He handed Baby to Jonas. Then he tapped the inner panel to open the door.

Aarho spun as it slid aside, but he dove out at her the same way Francis had lunged at him. He grabbed her by the waist, tackling her and bringing her to the ground.

Her face twisted, and she threw a punch at him. He

turned his face aside, letting it strike him on the side of the head before pushing against her shoulders, using his greater strength to hold her down.

She tried to shout. He braced her arms with his elbows and put his hand over her mouth.

"I don't want to hurt you Cyn," he said. "Please don't make me."

She kept squirming beneath him, trying to dislodge him, but he was bigger and stronger. He held her down.

"Get off her, Sheriff," Chao said, coming up behind him. "Now."

Damn it. Hayden glanced back. Chao was still a few meters behind him. He looked ahead. Aarho's stunner had fallen behind her, only a long reach away.

"Why don't either of you understand?" he said. "All I want to do is find my wife."

"Why don't you understand, Sheriff? You've put the entire city in danger."

"I have? I'm not the one killing innocent people."

"They were infected. Just like you've been infected."

Is that what Malcolm was telling them? Had he convinced them the creature carried some kind of disease?

"The crew of the Pilgrim lost control," Hayden said. "Those things killed them."

"It's our duty to protect the people of Metro from all threats. We aren't supposed to like it. We're just supposed to do it."

"What if there's another way? What if we can get beyond the perimeter and put the Pilgrim back on course?"

"There's nothing beyond the perimeter," Chao said. "Only infection and death. If Natalia did go out there, she's dead, Hayden."

"No. I don't accept that."

"It doesn't matter. It doesn't change anything."

Hayden felt his body begin to shake. He couldn't accept it. Not now. Infection? It was a lie. Another damn lie. His eyes tracked back to Aarho's stunner.

"Get up. I don't want to use this on you. Please don't make me."

He tried to remember Chao's marksmanship scores. If he recalled correctly, they were middling at best.

He dove forward, reaching for the stunner. Chao fired, too cautiously, the round hitting the ground a good twenty centimeters from his head.

He grabbed the stunner, rolling over to his knees as Chao fired again. He heard the slug whip past his ear at the same time he returned fire. One pull. Two. Both rounds hit their marks, causing the deputy to shudder and drop.

His marksmanship scores had been top of the class. There were reasons he was the Sheriff.

"Jonas, let's go," he said, grabbing Chao's stunner and both of their badges.

The kid emerged from the box, glancing at the two downed officers. "We might really have a chance to do this."

"Come on."

He tucked the two stunners into his pants and started down the strand again.

26

It took nearly an hour to reach Block One. The other Law Officers had found Aarho and Chao by then and disabled their badges, but not before Hayden had gotten a decent picture of where each of the deputies had been assigned.

They weren't anywhere near the Governor's Mansion. Maybe they figured the last place he would go would be the lion's den? Or maybe they just didn't have enough Law left to cover everything? Bradshaw was down. Shanks was down. Aarho and Chao were down. That left Wilson, Hicks, Lahish, and six other deputies to cover all of Metro. It wasn't enough at the best of times.

And these were hardly the best of times.

They monitored the split for a few minutes. The area was quieter than normal, but that didn't surprise him. The fire at Block Twenty-two in conjunction with the turbs had probably driven them into their cubes. Or what if Engineering had called a Code Blue? Would Malcolm have left deputies off the call to keep an eye out for him, despite the shit he had given Hayden earlier?

It was a perfect storm.

"How do we know what we're looking for in there?" Jonas asked.

"I'm hoping you'll know when you see the place," Hayden replied. "I already looked in the kitchen for the secret food stash." He shook his head, feeling stupid about it now. "I didn't find anything."

"Pozz that," Jonas said. "Do you know if the Governor has a terminal in there?"

"I'm sure he does."

"It will probably be close to there, but out of sight."

"Roger," Hayden said. "Let's go."

They hurried across the split, keeping the pace quick without breaking stride. They made it to the entrance, the sliding door opening before they reached it. The lobby was as empty as the streets. They reached the lift, and when it opened, they ducked in and hit the button for the sixteenth floor.

Hayden drew the twin stunners from his pants, ready for anything when they reached the top.

The lift slowed to a halt. The doors slid aside. The small foyer was empty.

"Nobody home," Jonas said.

Hayden nodded. He wanted to believe they were having a bit of good luck after all of the lousy, but he didn't trust it. What if the whole thing was a trap? What if they were waiting for them to go inside, and then they would be cut off and surrounded? The possibility existed, whether he liked it or not.

They approached the door. Jonas keyed in the master code, and it unlocked with a click. He smiled at Hayden, who stayed ready for anything as it moved out of their way.

He entered the Mansion the way he had been trained, sweeping the large room with his weapons before deciding it was clear. He continued to the hallway, past the bedrooms, checking each. All clear.

He reached the end of the corridor and the master bedroom. This one was locked.

"Jonas," he said, calling him over.

Jonas entered the code. The door opened. They moved into the room.

Hayden swept through it, into the bathroom. The place was empty.

"I didn't see a terminal," Jonas said.

"There has to be one," Hayden replied.

They walked back through the Mansion, covering the entire floor. There was no PASS terminal. There wasn't even a desk.

"It doesn't make sense," Hayden said.

Jonas eyed the room. He held up his hand, tracing the outline from the front door.

"What are you doing?" Hayden asked.

"Hold on, Sheriff."

He walked back through the Mansion, tracing it. He stopped when got to the end.

"There's a hidden room in here."

"Are you sure?"

"Yes. All of the blocks are laid out the same. Every cube. Every floor. There are some slight variations with corner units, but they're all identical to one another. Except for this specific part of this specific building. It's missing a space." He walked toward one of the walls. "Right about here."

He reached up and knocked on the wall. It sounded hollow.

Hayden smiled. "You're a genius."

"Just observant."

"I'm going to guess what we're looking for is there. How do we get in?"

"There has to be a secret panel or something," Jonas said. "Feel along the wall."

They both did, running their hands along the surface. It took a couple of minutes before Hayden found it, his fingertips brushing against the slightest change in the surface. A blue projection appeared on top of the wall. A keypad.

Jonas typed in the master code.

The wall clicked and swung outward.

There was no room behind it.

There was a lift instead.

"Where do you think it goes?" Jonas asked.

Hayden stepped into it. Jonas joined him there a moment later. The wall swung closed again. There were no buttons on the lift, though it was nearly identical to those in the blocks. It only made two stops, and Hayden knew it couldn't go up.

"Down," he replied.

They started to descend.

27

THE LIFT CAME TO A STOP. THE DOORS SLID OPEN, REVEALING a short, sterile hallway ahead of them. It was as vacant as the rest.

"Where are we?" Jonas asked.

"We have to be under the Block. Below the deck."

Hayden couldn't believe it. He had always thought there was no below the deck. How had they put a lift inside the Governor's Mansion and kept it secret for all of these years?

Misdirection. Distraction. Everyone was thinking about the food the Governor might have in his quarters, not a secret passage to somewhere else.

There was a hatch at the end of the hallway. It was protected by another access panel, opened easily with the master code. It slid aside, revealing another long corridor that seemed to stretch forever.

"It must run the entire length of Metro," Hayden said. He couldn't see the end of it from where they were standing. "It could take hours to find anything useful down here."

His heart began to sink. The discovery was incredible, but time had never been on his side.

"The most useful stuff needs to be close," Jonas said. "The Governor isn't going to be running under metro every time he needs something."

"That depends on what's down here, doesn't it?"

"A terminal? It has to be close."

There was a door a few meters from where they were standing. It was sitting slightly open, as though the last person in it had forgotten to pull it shut and it didn't have the velocity to catch. They moved to it, pushing it open and looking inside.

The room was small; the walls surrounded with cabinets. Hayden pulled one open, finding hundreds of pages of files inside. From the yellowing of the paper and the smell, it was all very old.

He lifted one of the files out. It was a personnel record, stamped with the eagle icon. "Amanda Bennett," he said softly, reading the first page. "She was the ship's navigator. Thirty-four years old. Married. Two kids."

"It's fascinating," Jonas said, standing by the door. "But not helpful."

Hayden dropped the file and closed the cabinet. "You're right."

They left the room. There was another across from it on the right. They opened it and looked in. This one was filled with books. At least two or three hundred. Hayden looked them over. They appeared to be manuals and guides for different systems on the ship.

"Engineering sure could use these," Hayden said. "Why are they being hidden down here?"

They left that room, glancing quickly into the next few rooms and continuing down the corridor. They started to hear a soft hum as they moved, coming from a corridor that branched away to the left. Hayden started following the noise, traveling another three hundred meters before pausing at a door. The noise was coming from behind it. He pushed it open.

The room had a small device in it, attached to a series of tubes that were connected to what appeared to be a large barrel of liquid. Dozens of other barrels were resting against the wall, along with a number of smaller containers.

"What is it?" Jonas asked.

"I don't know," Hayden replied. He went to one of the barrels and opened it, leaning down to smell. He shook his head. "Son of a bitch."

"What?"

"Alcohol," Hayden said.

"Are you sure?"

He nodded.

"But that would mean-"

"The Governor is also the Source." Hayden paused, trying to understand the implication. The Governor was giving the youth of the Pilgrim drugs and alcohol? Why?

He already knew the answer. Control. All of it was about control. To keep the population from learning the truth about the Pilgrim.

"We need to keep moving," Hayden said. "Let's head back to the central corridor."

"Pozz that," Jonas said.

Hayden walked quickly back to the center corridor, stopping when he reached the intersection.

"What is it?" Jonas asked.

"If we go that way, it should put us below the Law Station."

"So?"

"Those drones that killed the people on the roof. I've never seen anything like them before. They had to come from somewhere."

"How could they come from Law if you've never seen them before?"

"Not from Law. From beneath Law. The Station has a garage in the back corner where we used to keep the transports and drones before they all either broke down or got scavenged for parts."

"I've seen the doors to it on the east side of the Station."

"Yes. The garage is empty now. It has been since my father was Sheriff. But what if the floor opens?"

"What would make you think that?"

"Metro isn't what I thought it was. I don't think it's what any of us think it is. Not exactly. The fact that this place exists down here? I don't believe the Station is where it is by accident. I've always thought it would have made more sense to be in the middle of the city near Medical instead of so far uptown. Unless it had another reason to be there."

He started down the passage without waiting for Jonas. He broke into a run. He had to know if he was right about this. He had to know if his hunch was good.

There were a few more intersections along the way, but he had a good spatial understanding of Metro and was able to navigate below it to get where he wanted to go. The corridor ended in a large, secured door, again opened easily with the master code.

The door slid aside.

He had expected he would find a few drones. Some fresh equipment for the Governor to use in the event of an emergency. What he saw stole his breath away, rendering him static and speechless as he stared into the space.

There were drones. He had been right about that. Nine more of the machines like the ones that had killed so many people on top of Block Twenty-two. They were suspended in a pair of racks that sat on the left side of the large room.

Beside them rested three lines of armored machines, ten

meters tall and vaguely humanoid, with thick legs and arms than ended in barrels for weapons instead of hands. There were a dozen in all, and behind them cages to climb to the top where a cockpit was visible, along with some machinery to load large cases of ammunition into the rear.

On the other side, armored vehicles of some kind, low to the ground, wide and angry looking, with three mounted turrets on the top of each, and again more support equipment nearby.

Beyond them, another contingent of drones. These were smaller than the first set, more like the machines that had once patrolled Metro's strands.

There was other equipment, too. Random machines and carts and ordnance that Hayden couldn't identify. It was all arranged neatly in the space, organized around a square in the center of the room that was clearly a platform. A simple terminal rested at the edge of the platform, offering controls to work it.

"Sheriff, look at that," Jonas said after a period of stunned silence.

Hayden followed his point past the armored vehicles, to the wall of the room. There were lockers spread along it, at least three or four hundred of them. Hayden crossed the room to one of them, noting the name on the front, "Jackson," before pulling it open.

A uniform hung inside. It was semi-rigid, with plates along the chest and the top of the legs. An eagle icon was emblazoned over the breast with the letters 'USSF,' whatever that meant. There was a shelf above it, and a helmet sat there. It had a dark visor and the same logo and inscription as the uniform.

Next to that was a secondary locker within the locker, still closed. Hayden flipped the latch and pulled it open, revealing a different treasure inside.

A rifle, the length of his arm and as sleek as anything he had ever seen, with a small top barrel, a larger secondary barrel, and two different types of magazines hanging from the body. It had a bulge on top of it that looked like a display of some kind, and a small switch to turn it on and off. More magazines rested in a neat pile beneath it, along with a smaller pistol that took a lower caliber round.

"This looks like military equipment, Sheriff," Jonas said, as Hayden hefted the rifle. It was heavier than he expected, and his tired muscles complained about raising it to a firing position.

Hayden switched the weapon on. A soft buzz and then the display appeared, offering only a reticle on the area ahead of him. A small message on the bottom read "Disconnected."

"According to the PASS, the Pilgrim was a civilian ship," Hayden said. "No military."

But their eyes didn't lie. Not like the PASS did.

He checked the size of the uniform. It looked too big. He went to the locker beside it and clicked it open. It was empty. The soldier, Percy, was out there somewhere. Dead. He tried the next three. One of the was empty. Another had armor designed for a woman. The third was the jackpot. He lifted the uniform out of the locker. It felt like it was made of rubber, and the plates were hard but not too thick.

"What are you doing?" Jonas asked.

"This has to be better than a t-shirt and pants," Hayden replied, figuring out how to put the suit on.

It had a heavy zipper on the front, and he took off his boots and put his feet in and started zipping, slipping his arms in and bringing it over his chest. When the zipper reached the top, the small box on the back made a soft hissing sound, and the whole thing was pulled in tighter against his body. He thought it would make it harder to move. It made it easier. He grabbed the boots from the locker and slid them on. Then he reached for the helmet. He lowered it onto his head. Something in the back of it clicked as he did, and the visor lit up, filling with text and data. He turned his head in it, watching as different readouts changed. It was too much. He took the helmet off and put it back. He decided he would rather trust his eyes.

He ran his fingers along the name patch on the body armor. "Williams." Then he returned to Jackson's locker and reached for the rifle again. He wanted to sling the weapon over his shoulder, but it didn't have a strap. Did he have to carry it? He looked down, noticing a small indentation on the hip of the uniform for the smaller pistol, as well as a pair of extrusions that looked like they would hold the magazines. He took the pistol, placing it on the indentation. Something grabbed it and held it in place. Nice.

He took enough magazines to fill the extrusions. Then he returned his attention to the rifle. It had to go somewhere.

He picked it up again. There was only one place that made sense. He held it by a small handle in the center and reached it to his back. It snapped into place. Satisfied, he picked up Baby and the demon head, pressing the blade to a band that wrapped around the waist of the uniform, happy to find it stayed in place.

"We need to find the terminal," Jonas said.

Hayden nodded. "Check a few of the lockers for yourself, first."

"I don't want a weapon, Sheriff," Jonas said.

"What about armor?"

"I'm not a soldier."

"Suit yourself."

They headed back the way they had come, walking past the armored vehicles. As they did, Hayden noticed a back ramp was extended on one of them, and it was giving off a bit of warmth.

"Jonas, wait," Hayden said.

He approached the ramp. He began to notice a foul smell from inside. He was going to turn away, but something about it begged his attention. He drew the pistol he had just claimed, holding it ready as he climbed the ramp. The inside of the vehicle was small and dark, making it hard to see. He found a switch on the side, and he flipped it.

Half a dozen monitors on either side of the transport flicked on, along with lighting that extended the length of the vehicle. Each monitor was attached to a station of some kind, with individual seats and a control stick on the right arm. All of the seats were empty, but the cushioning was slightly depressed on three of them, showing they hadn't been deserted for long.

One of them had a dark stain on the back and a similar stain on the arm. The wall beside it was damaged as well.

Blood. Splattered away from the seat as if whoever was sitting in it had been shot.

Hayden remembered the drone hovering in front of them. It had them both in its sights, and yet it had waited to fire, giving them the previous seconds they needed to escape.

Someone had refused to shoot him. One of his deputies. Which one? They had saved his life.

Hayden turned away, flipping the switch to power down the vehicle and heading back out into the hold. Jonas was standing by the central terminal.

"I thought it might have PASS access," he said. "It doesn't. It does open a lift up into the garage like you thought. I bet the missing drones are up there."

"Maybe," Hayden said. "They were piloted from here." He didn't mention the blood.

"Sheriff, we could use this lift to get back into the city with one of the vehicles. We could find the Governor, and make him let us out. Or we could show the people what he's been doing. What he's been hiding. You have the creature's head. We can show them the truth. It's what Francis would have wanted."

Hayden stared at Jonas for a few seconds. Then he shook his head.

"No," he replied. "I don't think it is. What the Governor's been doing is horrific, but what's out there? It may be worse. Francis wanted to gather more information, to understand the whole picture before he did anything stupid. Except you were coming to blab to me about all of this and wound up doing the stupid for him."

Jonas winced at his choice of words. "I didn't-"

"The people in Metro are safe right now. As safe as they can be, Governor be damned. We go up there, and then what? He comes at us with those things?" He pointed to the large robots on the other side of the room. "We shoot up the entire damn city? We kill how many more innocent people? No thank you. That's not what this is about. It's about finding my wife. Plain and simple."

"Maybe for you," Jonas said. "For Francis, for me, it was always about finding the truth. The PASS has been lying to us. The Governor's been lying to us. Don't you care about that?"

"Not while Natalia is out there, no."

"He killed hundreds of people. He killed my girl."

And the demon killed Sarah because the Governor was too busy trying to kill him.

"I know. I don't condone it. At all. But what are we going to do? Start a civil war? To what end? If there are more of these demons on the ship, they'll tear the people apart. Now, do you want to keep standing here and arguing, or do you want to help me find a way past the secure hatch? The only way either one of us gets what we want is to get out there."

Jonas stared at him. He looked angry. Sad. Resigned.

"Okay. You're probably right. I was thinking, Sheriff. The PASS mainframe isn't inside Metro. I always assumed it was beyond the perimeter, but what if it's down here? It would make things much easier to delete if you had direct access to the source."

"And much easier to gain access to, I hope," Hayden said.

"Possibly," Jonas said.

"Then let's find it."

28

IT TOOK THEM NEARLY AN HOUR TO FIND THE MAINFRAME. They explored more of the below deck complex than Hayden had ever intended, and he had nearly given up on the idea that the repository of data accessible through the PASS terminals could be found in this part of the ship. The other areas they found on the way had left him angrier and angrier at the Governor, and at Metro's prior Governors. It was obvious Malcolm wasn't the first to learn about this place, nor the first to use it. Each successive head of Metro must have known this area of the ship existed. At least some of the Sheriffs and Deputies must have known, too. Who? How many?

His father?

It wasn't only the military machines, uniforms, and firepower. It was worse than that. They passed an area with a handful of massive storage cylinders, each marked as containing water. They passed a room filled with medicines and medical supplies to handle all kinds of illness and injury. They passed thousands and thousands of small, perma-wrapped packages of food. It was enough resources to put

Metro on a more secure footing, and maybe it would have been used for that if things got bad enough? But Hayden didn't think so.

It was enough resources to fuel an army.

What he didn't understand was why it was all sitting dormant, waiting for a day that might never come. They had enough guns and ammunition to go to war with the demons that had gained control of the Pilgrim. Why weren't they using them? They had enough food and water and sundries to venture out into the rest of the ship, to regain control and maybe put themselves back on the right course. Why didn't they?

There had to be a reason.

They had also passed another hatch, a secured access hatch to an area beyond Metro's perimeter, marked with the same pattern as the hatch in Section C. It didn't have a control panel on their side. It was sealed as tightly as the rest.

"This has to be it," Jonas said, smiling when they entered the room.

To Hayden, it was the least identifiable of any of the rooms they had explored. A series of black cubes rested across a floor of metal grating, wires visible beneath, stretching from one cube to another. Each one had a single blue light that flickered and faded at variable speed.

A single terminal sat at the front of the columns of cubes. Like the other equipment, it bore the eagle logo of the USSF.

Jonas approached the terminal, standing in front of it. He put his satchel on the ground beside it and started typing on the projected keyboard. Hayden stood behind him, looking over his shoulder.

"What are you doing?" he asked.

"Getting access," Jonas replied.

Hayden watched the display. It bore the eagle logo, with the words "USSF. Pilgrim Assistance Service System" below it, along with an area to enter data. Jonas was filling that area now, not with standard text, but with some gibberish Hayden didn't recognize.

"That's access?" he asked.

"It's code," Jonas said. "The programming code the PASS was written in. It's how Francis got to the source in the first place."

The screen changed, showing lines of text and a blinking cursor. Hayden had never seen the screen before.

"Here we go," Jonas said.

He kept typing, more of the code. The PASS Hayden was familiar with had a graphic menu, where users could drill into specific topics, or run queries against what they were looking for. This was like a stripped down version, where everything had to be entered differently. But Jonas seemed to understand it.

"What are you looking for?" Hayden asked.

"Do you remember when I said I thought maybe the missing data had been copied?"

"Yes."

"What if I was wrong? What if it weren't copied, but simply cut off from the terminals?"

"Can that be done?"

"Pozz. It's a much less destructive way to block data. So I'm running one of the queries. You can see it on the mainframe there, the way the lights flash. That's data access."

Hayden looked out at the machines. The lights were all flickering. He couldn't tell the difference from before Jonas accessed the terminal.

"Hah!" Jonas shouted. "I was right!"

Hayden looked back at the screen. There was a list of responses, all assigned to a number.

"Sheriff, look at this," Jonas said, pointing at one of the lines.

"What is it?"

"I'm not sure. I ran a search for the Pilgrim's mission, and this is what came back."

The line in question read:

Mission Log #1

Jonas tapped on it before Hayden could respond. The display changed, showing a video instead. An image of a man with short hair and a white beard, sharply dressed in a military uniform. He had a ton of hardware on his chest, and his name tag read Cpt. Bradshaw.

"Bradshaw?" Hayden said.

"Captain Bradshaw. Captain's Mission Log One. The navigation computers have been set. We've identified a system forty-six light years from home that our people have eighty-six percent confidence contains a habitable planet with a breathable atmosphere. Based on their calculations, we should arrive in approximately three hundred years. Of course, I won't be around to see it, but that's the reason for this log. It's important that future generations have access to everything that occurred on the journey, to keep them from losing hope in the mission. I know the need to move up the timeline has been painful for many of us, especially those selected for the journey. The decision to leave family and friends behind has been difficult for many of us, but at the same time, we have hope in our future and the future of human civilization on other worlds. The Pilgrim is a marvel of modern technology, produced at a speed none believed possible. It only goes to show what we can do when we all stop arguing over the details that don't matter in the end."

Jonas turned to look at Hayden. "Three hundred years, Sheriff. This confirms it. And they moved up the launch. Why?"

"I don't know. Let's not lose sight of why we're here. We

need to access code to the hatch. Any of the hatches. Get me one."

"Okay, let me see."

He typed some more code into the PASS. A few seconds later, it returned a single response:

Mission Log #59

Jonas selected it, and another video started.

"Captain Bradshaw. Captain's Mission Log Fifty-nine."

The Captain was disheveled. His hair hadn't been cut; his beard hadn't been trimmed. His uniform was hanging from his pants. He looked thinner and stressed.

"We thought we could handle the situation," he said. "It's become clear that we were wrong. We brought everything we thought we would need. We thought we could find a way. But this? We can't stop this. We tried. Half our defense forces are dead. Eighty percent of the crew is dead. Lyle's done an amazing job prepping the colony for the years ahead, but the strategy." He shook his head, looking away from the camera. "Outlast them. That's his plan. We have to seal in the colony and stay alive longer than they do. We have to make sure the future generations don't know what happened here. It needs to be forgotten. All of it. Buried for as long as it takes. It's the only way to survive."

Hayden winced as the video output a high whine of gunfire, way too close to the Captain. A soldier in a uniform like the ones Hayden had seen earlier entered the room backward.

"Captain, we have to go."

"I'm coming, Sergeant Hicks," Bradshaw said. He looked at the camera again. "This will be my last recording. It won't be made available to the people of Metro. It can't. Like so much of our history, this too needs to be forgotten."

A creature moved into the doorway in front of Sergeant

Hicks. He fired his weapon, a stream of rounds cutting the demon in half. An instant later, the recording was stopped.

"Damn it," Hayden said. "He didn't say anything about the codes."

Jonas turned his head. "I'll try another search. Give me-"

A single report sounded from behind them. Jonas' head lurched forward, the side of it detonating outward and spreading across the terminal display. He collapsed to the ground, dead.

29

Hayden didn't hesitate, diving past the terminal toward the rows of computers beyond it. He felt a bullet hit his lower back, a soft tap against the tough plate there. A second round hit the ground behind him, nearly striking one of the machines.

"Watch your aim, damn it," he heard Malcolm say. "You damage the PASS, I damage you."

"Sorry, Governor," someone replied. It sounded like Deputy Bradshaw, but wasn't he supposed to be wounded?

Hayden scrambled behind one of the PASS servers, knowing it would keep him safe for now.

"Hayden," Malcolm said. "I see you're helping yourself to equipment that doesn't belong to you. It's fine; you can keep it for now." He paused, waiting for a response, continuing when Hayden didn't say anything. "You were a hard man to find. Which is surprising in a place the size of Metro. But then I thought, if nobody had seen you topside, you probably found your way down here. And when I went home, I could smell something awful in my bedroom and assumed it was you. I'm impressed, Sheriff. Very impressed. I should have given you more credit."

"We don't have to do this, Malcolm," Hayden said. "I just want to go out there. I want to go after her."

"I know you do," he replied. "But that's the whole problem. I know you'll do anything to reach her. I know you won't give up until you get past the perimeter, and I can't let you past the perimeter. You'll put all of Metro at risk."

"How? I killed the one that got in. I took care of your problem. You owe me."

Malcolm laughed. "You made me kill three hundred people, Hayden, not counting this one here. Damn it, Hayden, you made me kill Wilson."

Wilson? What had happened to her? He remembered the blood in the armored vehicle. Damn it.

"I didn't make you do anything. If you had focused your energy on the creature instead of trying to stop me-"

"I knew we could deal with one. If you found a way out and let in the rest? Why the hell do you think they sealed the city in the first place?"

"I watched the mission log. To wait them out. Bad news, Governor. It's been almost four hundred years, and they aren't dead."

"Which means we still have to wait."

"Because that's working so well?"

"The people are safe in here, Hayden."

"Tell that to Jonas. Tell that to Sarah. Tell that to Natalia, you son of a bitch."

"I'm sorry for what happened to your wife. I really am. You know how much I valued her. But I have a responsibility. There are rules to being Governor. Did you know that? You don't just get elected. Once you take office, your whole life changes. You learn things you never wanted to know. You learn about the bogeymen who haunt the corridors beyond Metro, waiting for a chance to get in and start killing again. Every night, you go to bed, and you hope you don't wake up to your worst nightmare. The seals on the secured hatches failing, like the one in Section C. Or worse. The atmospherics breaking down. The gravity generators failing. The reactors running out of plasma. We've got about a hundred years left, and then the Pilgrim is going to run out of power."

"And what makes you think anything is going to change? What makes you think these things will die so that we can get where we're going?"

"Hope, Hayden. I have hope."

"You're an idiot to depend on hope after all this time. You need to take action. Or just let me take action. If I die, I die."

"It doesn't work like that. We have a duty to protect these people. Bradshaw understands that. Hicks understands that. They bought in when I explained the situation. They don't want to hurt you. None of us do. But you need to understand; it's not enough to keep the monsters out of Metro. We need to keep the very idea of monsters out of Metro. You may think hope is stupid, but hope is essential to keep the city running."

"Is it? Then why are you handing out drugs and booze? Why are you corrupting the young instead of leading them?"

"I didn't start that. But there will always be some who don't go along with hope. People who question the status quo. Troublemakers like Francis and his group. It's a less violent alternative to keeping them from making problems."

"How are we protecting them by letting them die? We have guns. We take the fight to the demons. We get them out of our damn ship."

"Don't you think they tried?" Malcolm shouted. "They died, damn it. By the handful. Hundreds of people, their bodies torn apart. They're better killers than we are, plain and simple."

"Maybe you just weren't motivated enough," Hayden replied.

"You think you're so tough?" Malcolm laughed. "I'm almost tempted to let you go. But I took an oath, and I aim to keep it. Don't make things hard."

"I'm going to find a way out, Malcolm. One way or another."

"There is no way out. Not unless a turb shorts the controls and causes it to open temporarily, and that doesn't happen often. Other than that, the only way to access the external network is through my identification implant, and I'm sure as hell not about to let you use it."

"There has to be a master code to transfer the codes to your implant," Hayden said.

"It's encrypted. Only the PASS knows what it is, and there's no way to retrieve it directly. Don't you think the original Governor thought of that? Lyle was a genius. Way ahead of his time. Now, why don't you drop your weapons, stand up, and let Hicks and Bradshaw take you in? I promise I'll make you comfortable. We aren't enemies. Not really. We just see things differently."

"Bradshaw," Hayden said. "I thought you were hurt?"

"A few cuts and bruises, sir," Bradshaw replied. "Medical patched me up, and the Governor needed the extra hands."

"And you believe this bullshit? You didn't have a problem gunning down innocent people?"

"They were infected, sir," Bradshaw said. "Exposed to the xenotrife."

"What do you mean, infected?"

"Diseased," Malcolm said. "They carry a virus. It takes about three months to become fatal, but whoever gets close enough to one is exposed, assuming it doesn't kill them during the interaction."

"Like Shanks and Lahish?" Hayden said.

"And a number of others."

Hayden glanced down at the wrapped head. "What if the xenotrife was already dead?"

"You did me a favor, throwing it into the fire."

Hayden unwrapped the xenotrife's head, grabbing it by the top. He unlatched the pistol from the armor and got to his feet.

His eyes landed on Malcolm first, and then Bradshaw and Hicks. Bradshaw's face was bandaged, but he didn't look that bad. Hicks had a bruise on his face where Hayden had punched him earlier.

"So, you wouldn't want this thing anywhere near you, then?" he asked, calling Malcolm's bluff.

Malcolm's expression was flat for a moment. Then his eyes rose, and he flinched back, taking on a fearful look.

"Hayden. Damn it. Keep that thing away from us."

"Really, Malcolm?" Hayden said. "You really want me to believe this thing is carrying some kind of disease? I get it. You needed to tell my deputies something to get them to kill civilians without feeling like shit for doing it. I understand. You needed an excuse to burn down Block Twenty-two."

"Hayden, I'm not lying to you."

The way he said it was almost convincing. For his sake, or for Bradshaw and Hicks?

"Let's find out," Hayden replied.

He flipped the head toward them.

Malcolm was the first to move, turning and diving toward the door. Bradshaw and Hicks were a little slower.

The reaction left Hayden momentarily stunned. Was Malcolm telling the truth after all?

Nothing had changed.

If he was going to die, he was going to die with Natalia at his side.

He moved out from behind the servers, following the head as it rolled to a stop on the floor. The Governor and his deputies were past the hatch and into the corridor, and Hayden swung out at their backs as they tried to gain some distance from him.

Hicks paused, turning to shoot. Hayden fired first, the unfamiliarity of the weapon causing his first shot to go wide as the kickback took him by surprise. Hicks shot back, the round hitting the armor plating on his chest and giving him a second chance.

He was ready this time. He adjusted his aim and fired. The bullet tore into Hick's leg, tearing through bone and knocking him down. Damn it. He hated to do this.

Bradshaw saw his fellow Deputy fall. He stopped running, facing off with Hayden.

"Sheriff, don't do this," he said.

"I didn't start this, Josh," Hayden said. "The Governor did. All I want is my Natalia back."

"At what cost?"

"At any cost."

Bradshaw pulled the trigger. He was nervous, and his bullet missed.

Hayden's didn't. It hit the Deputy in the shoulder, the wound causing him to drop his gun. Bradshaw cursed as he gripped the injury, falling back against the wall in pain.

"Damn it, Sheriff."

"I'm sorry, Josh," Hayden said, racing past him.

Malcolm was on his own. Unarmed and unprotected. He looked back. Both of his deputies were down and Hayden was approaching behind him.

Hayden watched him try to run. He gave chase with a

fresh lightness in his step, as though the body armor was easing his effort. He was faster than the Governor.

Malcolm realized it, too. He turned and stopped, holding his hands up. "Hayden, wait. Please. Wait."

Hayden slowed. "You know what I want, Malcolm."

"I can't. I would if I could."

"You said your implant could open the hatch. You can open it. You won't."

"You'll kill us all. I'm not lying about the disease. I swear. Go back to the PASS, query the terminal. You'll see."

"Nothing will come in. I'll make sure of that."

Malcolm fell to his knees. "I'm begging you, Hayden. Metro needs a Governor. A smooth succession. There's too much at stake. If you don't care about me, think about the residents."

Hayden kept approaching, each step taking him closer to the Governor. He couldn't help but consider Malcolm's words. He didn't want to be responsible for killing everyone in the city.

"I don't need to kill you," Hayden said. "We can go to the hatch. You open it for me, and then I'm gone."

"It's not that simple."

"Why, damn it?"

"You need the chip to open the hatch. You also need the chip to close it." Malcolm was in tears. Terrified.

"From the other side?"

"Yes. It's only supposed to be used when the ship is clean. That's why it was programmed that way."

Hayden stopped moving. He didn't want to take Malcolm with him. But how else was he going to get through the hatch?

Unless?

"I'm sorry, Malcolm," Hayden said, taking a fresh step toward him. "For all of this. It's not what I want. It's not what either one of us wants, I know. I was happy in Metro. I was happy with Natalia. I can't live without her. I can't die without her, either."

"Hayden, please don't kill me," Malcolm said.

"I'm not going to kill you," Hayden replied. "I'm going to save you from those things. You and all of Metro."

He snapped the pistol back to its spot on his hip, reaching out and grabbing Malcolm's arm, using his strength to push the Governor back against the wall. He reached to his side with his free hand, detaching Baby from his hip.

"Hayden?" Malcolm said.

"I just need you to lend me a hand," Hayden said. He shifted his grip, still holding Malcolm's arm pinned to the wall. With one quick motion, he drove the blade in, chopping through flesh and bone centimeters above the Governor's wrist.

The weapon made it through in one powerful stroke, separating the Governor from his hand. Malcolm cried out in pain, bending over and clutching at the bleeding stump. Hayden reached down, taking the severed appendage.

"You're going to die out there, Hayden," Malcolm cried. "You and your wife. You have no idea what kind of Hell you're in for."

"Maybe not," Hayden said. "But at least we'll be in Hell together. I'm sorry, Malcolm."

He started running, heading for the secure hatch he had passed with Jonas earlier, the sounds of Malcolm's cries fading as he moved away.

He crossed the corridors in a daze, his mind a blur of rage and love and fear and excitement. He hated himself for what he had done and yet he felt no true remorse for doing it. Natalia was out there. She needed him. He had given Malcolm so many chances to help.

He reached the secured hatch, coming to a stop in front

of it. There was no going back. Not now. His love was all that mattered.

He approached the blockade, raising Malcolm's wrist, moving it across the wall beside the door, trying to find the hidden controls.

Like before, a blue light appeared when he located it, scanning the Governor's severed hand. A deep, ominous tone sounded, an echoing clang signaling that the hatch was unlocking.

It started to rise.

30

Hayden didn't wait for the hatch to open completely. He ducked below it to the other side, quickly scanning the corridor beyond. It was lit only by emergency lighting that ran along the center of the ceiling, revealing a hallway that ended in a t-junction a hundred meters away. The air was cooler than inside the perimeter by at least a few degrees and had a damp, stale smell to it that he didn't like.

Once he was sure the immediate area was clear, he turned and put the Governor's hand to the hidden panel. A soft tone indicated the scan was complete, and the hatch started to close.

Almost immediately, Hayden heard movement ahead, scampering footsteps that didn't suggest anything friendly. He dropped the hand to the ground, reaching behind and grabbing the rifle, bringing it up to his face. He had never fired a weapon like this before, and a part of his mind worried that he was going to die because he couldn't aim it.

The xenotrife came around the corner, and he forgot all about his concerns. He looked into the small display with the reticle, quickly lining it up with the creature as it bounded toward him. He planted the stock on his shoulder to keep it steady and squeezed the trigger, feeling the pull of the kick as a dozen rounds sprayed from the weapon and into the demon. It hissed as the rounds entered it, blowing out chunks of its body and leaving it crumpled and motionless on the floor ahead of him.

One down. How many to go?

A second creature came around one side of the junction. Two more from the other. He had been expecting to draw attention, but four in a matter of seconds? Had he made a mistake?

He had to keep them from ducking below the hatch before it closed. It was the only thing that mattered.

He lined the first one up and fired, a more controlled blast this time that sent four rounds into the thing and knocked it down. He shifted his aim to the next, squeezing the trigger. They were closing quickly. Too damn quickly.

He tried to get his reticle on the third, but the two remaining creatures were nearly on top of him. He dropped the rifle to the ground, grabbing the pistol in one hand and Baby in the other. He didn't need as much time to aim the handgun, raising it and pulling the trigger as the two xenotrife lunged for him, bearing their mouthfuls of teeth. The round went right into the mouth and through the head, the first creature falling a half a meter in front of him.

The second made it to him, and he brought Baby around in a hard swing that caught the demon in the mouth. Metal slammed into teeth, breaking through them and tearing into the creature's skull. The demon's mass hit him, but they were so much lighter than a human. He was able to turn with the collision, throwing the thing into the hatch behind him, pulling out Baby and swinging the blade at it again, slashing its leathery skin and tearing a large gaping line across what he thought was its throat.

It too fell to the ground and didn't move.

The hatch finished closing behind him, the clang of the locks sliding into place telling him Metro was safe.

For now at least. Until the turbs caused the hatch to open again. Until something else went wrong that threatened their safety.

It didn't matter now. He only had one thing on his mind. Find Natalia. Once he did? They could figure that part out together.

He didn't pick the rifle up right away. Instead, he retrieved the Governor's hand. The identification implant was a small chip five millimeters or so in diameter, injected into every Metro citizen's wrist at birth, and retrieved from the wrist for reuse upon death. He couldn't risk leaving the chip near the hatch, and he didn't want to carry a severed hand around with him, so he had to get the chip out.

He had a vague idea where it was located, and so he used Baby to slice through the flesh. Then he dug into it with his fingers, pulling apart the skin and muscle until the chip came into view. He took it out, holding it between his thumb and index finger. He needed to keep it somewhere. He considered for a moment, and then tucked it under the armor. He thought about swallowing it, but he didn't know if he would need it to get into other parts of the Pilgrim.

He left the hand behind. He hated that he had been force to cut it off, but Malcolm hadn't left him with a choice. Not getting out of Metro wasn't an option, and these xenotrife or whatever they had decided to call them weren't as tough as he had imagined. He had killed five of them already on his own, and the weapons he had found seemed more than up to the task.

He walked cautiously to the end of the corridor, sweeping the t-junction with the rifle. The area around him was silent, but when he paused he could hear a distant tapping from somewhere else in the ship. He remembered hearing the tapping in Section C before things had all gone wrong. He should have told Natalia about it then. Maybe she would have been more careful going out that way.

He had no idea what the ship looked like beyond the perimeter. He had never seen a map or schematic, and he had no idea where he should go. He had left behind the maze of strands and splits he knew so well for the fresh maze of the Pilgrim, a maze that promised to be less forgiving.

He considered where he was, drawing a mental picture of the corridor in his mind. It was his starting place, regardless of where it began inside the ship, just as the Law Office had been his starting place in Metro. As long as he could keep the lines organized, he could map the passages and corridors and hopefully keep it all clear. It wouldn't help anybody to be wandering the ship forever.

He headed down the left corridor, careful to walk lightly and keep his steps quiet, rifle ready to fire. He continually scanned the area ahead of him, not just directly ahead but the floor and ceiling as well. The floor beneath his feet was a metal grating like the PASS mainframe, and he could see wires running underneath. There were vents on the sides of the passage as well, large enough that he could probably wriggle into them if he removed the armor. He hoped he wouldn't have to remove the armor and go in there. But what if Natalia had decided to hide in a similar shaft?

He stopped beside one of the vents, putting his hand to it. He could feel a draft of air spilling out. He considered taking the cover off and banging his rifle into it, to see if anyone knocked back. There was no way that kind of noise wouldn't attract the xenotrife, and he wasn't ready for a full-on assault by the demons. He needed to be silent and slow despite his desire to hurry and find Natalia. He needed to learn more about the creatures in order to survive. He needed to become the hunter instead of the hunted.

Did he have the skills to do it? He wasn't a soldier. He was a Sheriff. He had some hand-to-hand training and some weapons training, but most of his skillset revolved around solving problems and managing people, and he was alone out here.

Then again, the soldiers who had fought the xenotrife hadn't exactly done an incredible job.

Maybe a Sheriff could succeed where they had failed.

31

It took Hayden nearly an hour to cover half a kilometer of corridors, picking his way slowly through the Pilgrim, before he came across his first body.

Or rather, what was left of it.

He was positioned against the side of the corridor, a soldier in body armor that matched his, time having reduced his to little more than a skeleton. His rifle lay beside an outstretched hand, his helmet across the hallway, his body armor torn in multiple places by multiple sets of claws. The fact that the xenotrife didn't feed on their kills still confused him. What did they eat, if not the meat of the dead? How did they continue to survive on board?

That thought also reminded him that he hadn't brought any food or water with him. Was there any to be found out here? Could he eat the demons, if it came down to that?

He knelt beside the remains, picking up the rifle. It was powered on, but the display was dark. Whatever battery kept it functional, it was dead. He searched the corpse for anything else he might be able to use, noting the name on the chest. Bower. He tried to remember if there were any Bowers in Metro. It was impossible to know everyone. He didn't think so. This man had died before he could carry his generation forward.

He stood and continued forward. The passage was moving in what he would have called north in Metro. That meant he was likely on a deck below the hatch to Section C. He wanted to find a lift or a stairwell or some other way to ascend a level and return to the scene of Natalia's disappearance, in hope there would be a clue to guide him further. He had only come across a pair of doorways so far, and they had both led into empty storage rooms. It seemed odd to Hayden that the ship had spaces that weren't being utilized, but maybe all of the supplies that had once been located in the rooms had been moved to Metro? It made sense that equipment would have been consolidated.

There was no sign of more of the xenotrife so far. He stopped every few steps to listen, and while the tapping had paused and resumed, the clicking of thick feet against the metal surfaces had yet to repeat itself.

He traveled down the corridor, reaching another junction in the passages. He swept the rifle across each, taking his time to ensure nothing was hiding in the shadows cast by the dim emergency lighting. To his left, he noticed another pair of bodies. More soldiers. These had other skeletons on the ground around them, the skulls revealing them as xenotrife. So the soldiers had at least managed to kill some of them. He wasn't sure if that was good or bad. It was obvious they had been overwhelmed.

He had to decide which direction to move. He needed a way to the next deck. He turned a circle in the intersection before noticing a plate on one of the walls. He had seen similar plates inside Engineering, which often contained the section codes and directions to other parts of the ship. This one had been scratched at so thoroughly that if it had ever contained writing, it was illegible now. It had been done intentionally. By who? Why? Were the xenotrife intelligent enough to remove the labels in an effort to confuse the soldiers?

The fact there was a plate at all suggested there was something of value down either of the two corridors. He decided to head past the dead soldiers, figuring they had died in an effort to defend something from the creatures. He paused again to search them. He also paused to examine the xenotrife's remains.

Their skulls were much larger than their bodies, and it became immediately obvious their bones were hollow instead of solid because whatever material was inside had deteriorated away over time. They had four long fingers on each hand with four joints to give them a tighter grip and no apparent thumbs. Their feet were small, but the toes on them were large, again with extra joints for dexterity, spread out for balance. Their midsection was narrow and long, and they had ribs with large gaps between them, important to remember the next time he needed to use Baby.

He couldn't tell from the bones what they used for sustenance, or what other skills they might have. He had seen them climb, and he had seen them hide in darkness. Their frames suggested they might be able to squeeze into small spaces, and possibly even flex their bones. Someone from Medical could probably tell him a lot more about it, but that wasn't a possibility.

He moved beyond them, continuing down the passage, heading in what he decided to call east. Whether that was the port or starboard side of the Pilgrim was still unclear, because he didn't know if Metro's north faced the bow or the stern. He reasoned that there would be multiple access points to the other decks of the ship and that they would be positioned equidistant from one side of the hull inward and across to the other. By heading lateral toward the hull, he should come across a stairwell or lift, or at least an outer corridor that did lead to a way up.

He made it a few hundred meters down the corridor when he heard a sound from somewhere nearby. It wasn't the clacking of claws on metal like before. It was more of a rubbing sound, a whispered hint of movement. His eyes landed on a hatch a few meters ahead. It was hanging open fifteen centimeters or so. Not enough for him to fit through, but possibly large enough for a xenotrife to enter.

He stopped and considered turning around and going back the other way, heading west instead. It would cost him time, and who was to say that direction was any safer? He had to try to slip past the door unnoticed. Was that even possible? He didn't know if the creatures were attracted to sound or smell or sight or all three.

He put the rifle on his back, switching to Baby and the pistol instead. If anything came out of the door as he passed, he wouldn't have time to aim the larger weapon. He crept slowly toward it, drawing nearer. The rubbing sound continued, joined by a hissing noise that he recognized. There were definitely demons in there. He lifted his feet slowly, taking careful, silent steps, ears focused on any changes to the sounds in the room.

He froze when he reached the opening. There was a small amount of light filtering out of the room. He leaned his head forward to look inside. It was a risk, but the more he knew about the creatures, the better. Knowing your enemy was a timeless piece of advice.

He saw the dark, leathery flesh of the xenotrife. Enough of it pressed together that he couldn't identify one creature from another. They were in the center of the room, which had a few metal boxes stacked in the corner he could see. Supplies the Pilgrim's crew hadn't been able to claim. Was there food in there? Water? Something else? There had to be a dozen of the creatures at least, writhing and slithering against one another, creating the rubbing sound he had heard.

A fluid of some kind was running between them, clear and thick and sticky, secreted from some part of the xenotrife and spread along one another's flesh. It seemed to be coating them and making their skin look more hydrated and supple. Were they copulating? Was the fluid their food? He had no idea, but it was disgusting.

He shifted back from the door to continue beyond it.

A heavy, stinking breath wafted across the side of his face.

32

THE CLAWS HIT HIM A MOMENT LATER, CATCHING THE RIFLE and armor plating across his back and sending him lurching forward. His body hit the partially open door hard, bouncing him off it and pushing it open further, disrupting the orgy of whatever taking place inside.

A cacophony of hisses followed, the interruption gaining the xenotrife's attention. Hayden stumbled, desperate to recover, getting his attention on his attacker as a fresh swipe of claws angled for his unprotected neck.

Baby swished through the air, the blade reaching out and smashing into the demon's outstretched hand, cutting easily through its hollow bones and severing the limb. The creature hissed in pain, dropping back a step, its head turning in the direction of the doorway.

The first of the xenotrife emerged. Its head turned to Hayden, small eyes noticing him. Then it changed its focus to the injured demon. It pounced on the creature, and they both fell away in a twisting whirl of dark flesh.

Hayden backed away, knowing the other creatures would join them in seconds. He dropped his weapons to his hips, thankful he didn't need to locate them exactly for them to lock into place. He grabbed the rifle on his back as he continued to retreat. There was a score in the back from the demon's claws, but it hummed when he switched it on.

Two more xenotrife emerged from the room. They were slick with the fluid, which hung from their bodies like lines of spittle. They ignored Hayden, piling onto the creature he had damaged, helping the first end its life.

The others charged into the corridor, one after another, slowed by the substance that joined them together. They hissed and bore their teeth at Hayden, flexing their legs to attack.

He found the secondary trigger on the rifle, assuming it would fire whatever ammunition was in the larger magazine. He squeezed it once, hearing a heavy thunk as a round ball burst out of the hole, hitting one of the demons square in the chest with enough force to knock it back and get embedded in its ribs.

It looked down at the dull grey sphere.

Then it exploded.

The detonation caused a flash of light that blinded Hayden, leaving him unable to see the aftermath of the attack. Instead, he felt the force of the blast catch him and throw him backward. He felt the impact of bones and flesh and blood and slime slapping against his armor and face. He felt the whole corridor vibrate from the shockwave, and he heard the deafening echo of it ripple around him.

He landed on his back. He blinked a few times in an effort to restore his vision, suddenly panicked that it was lost for good. What if he hadn't killed them all? What it more of them were drawn to the immense noise he had created? He rolled over, feeling the floor, crawling along it until he found the wall. He made it to his feet, still blinking. He began to see the blurry shape of the corridor as his eyes started to adjust. Not blind. At least he wasn't blind.

What the hell kind of munition had he fired? He had never seen anything like it before. He imagined that if he used it in the wrong place, he could cause catastrophic damage to the Pilgrim. He needed to be careful how he used it, or if he ever used it again.

His eyes continued to clear. He tried to listen, but his ears were ringing, too. If more of the xenotrife were on their way, he would never be able to stop them from ripping his throat out. He needed to hide.

He stumbled forward, back toward the damage. He cursed as he reached a hot spot on the wall, burning his fingers and pulling his hand back. He wanted to get into the room where they had been, hopeful he could wait in there until his senses returned. The whole scene was a blur of pieces of the creatures, fluids, and scorch marks. He hurried forward, finding the hatch. It was bent half off its hinges and had pieces of shrapnel digging into it. He slipped inside, using the butt of the rifle to shove it closed as far as it would go. The explosion had killed the light in the room, leaving him with only the weapon's display for illumination. He quickly shut it off, settling into the dark.

Stupid. He had been stupid, getting too caught up in watching the creatures and losing awareness of his surroundings. It had almost cost him his life. He was lucky it had hit him in the back, instead of going for his neck. But was it luck? The creatures seemed smarter than that. They knew where to aim to get between the armor and the helmets the soldiers wore. It seemed almost like it wanted to fight him face to face.

And the way the others had attacked it when it was injured. What did that mean? They didn't suffer weakness among them. Or maybe they were in competition? Territorial? Did they feel more threatened by another of their kind than they did by him? And what had they been doing in here?

He reached up to his face, feeling the sticky substance on it. He scraped at it, pulling it away. It smelled sweet, as though it was made of sugar. He wiped it on the armor, cleaning off his face. He hoped it wasn't some kind of reproductive fluid.

He leaned back, keeping his eyes open. The white light of his blindness was fading, sparkles of it bursting across his retina in slowing, less dense patterns. The room was nearly pitch black, with only a sliver of light making it in from beyond the damaged door.

He waited.

Ten minutes passed. Twenty. His ears recovered. So did his eyes. He could see the metal crates against the wall, a line of nearly fifty of them. He could see the center of the floor where the xenotrife had been gathered. A pile of goop had been placed there, nearly a meter high. There were small, clear bulbs within it, with dark blotches at the centers.

He turned on the rifle to add more light from the display, adjusting it to shine into the mass. He drew back at the sight of the tiny xenotrife shifting within the gel. Babies. He had stumbled across a nest.

He felt nauseous. He was tempted to destroy the nest, but it was obvious these creatures were nowhere near ready to do him harm, and he didn't want to draw any more attention to himself. He returned his attention to the crates, approaching a stack and pulling one from the top, placing it on the floor. He put the rifle on his back and used Baby to leverage open the lid.

It was filled with small, wrapped squares. Each one had an eagle logo on it, and the letters M-R-E beneath. He picked one up and tore it open, giving it a sniff. His body told him it was food, so he took a bite. It was dry and chewy, but not bad. He downed it, and then took a few more, replacing one of the larger magazines in the extrusions on his armor for the sustenance. He was sure he wouldn't need that many of the explosive spheres anyway.

He gave himself a few more minutes to recover, and then returned to the hatch, moving slowly back into the corridor. He could see the full extent of the mess he had made now, and it caused him to almost lose the ration he had just downed. At the same time, he was proud of himself.

Hayden seventeen, demons zero.

33

He was lucky. The path remained clear as he crossed the width of the Pilgrim, finally arriving at the end of a long corridor and the closed doors of a between-decks lift. He was afraid the noise of the explosion would have brought a mass of the demons to him, but it seemed the opposite was true. Did the creatures have experience with the spherical rounds? Did they know to stay away? Or were they more like hunters, playing a game with him and letting him think he was doing well?

Whatever it was, he was grateful to cover some ground without having to fight for his life, and when he reached the lift doors, he sighed audibly, feeling as though Natalia was that much closer to his reach.

He put his hand on the control panel, tapping it to order the elevator inside to his deck, whichever deck it was.

He was only partially surprised when the panel didn't respond. Maybe it had been functional once. It was dead now. He would need to find the stairs. He didn't mind. It was a minor setback compared to the events he had already survived.

He made his way past the lift, reaching another intersection. He went a dozen meters along it before identifying the emergency stairwell by a faded plate on the floor nearby. Most of the writing had been scratched off, but the red background was a strong clue.

He pushed the door open slowly, leading with the muzzle of the rifle, and sweeping up and down as he entered. The stairs were dark, darker than the corridors, and bathed in an eerie green light. Each section of risers ended at a small platform and ninety-degree turn, wrapping around one another in a dull metal grating that didn't leave much clearance over his head. There was a corpse on the steps beside him. Not a soldier this time. A crew member in a USSF uniform, their head lolled to the side, throat slashed. The name on the chest was Lao.

There was blood on the stairwell wall behind Lao, a dark, dry, ancient splatter that fit with the crew member's wound. Hayden was becoming accustomed to seeing the violence, and he moved past it without the earlier nausea, starting the climb toward Section C. How was he going to know when he was on the right floor? He knew he had to be at least three or four decks below the Section, based on the relationship between Engineering and Metro, and Metro and the secret underground stash. He was sure he would know when he found the right hatch.

It would be the one with the bloody handprint below it.

He started climbing, taking the stairs one at a time, careful not to make too much noise. He came across two more bodies on the steps, one soldier and one crew member, as well as a few remains of xenotrife. He had to step over the soldier, skipping two steps to get past.

He was nearing the door on the third deck when he froze, an echoing click sounding above him. He looked up through the flooring, able to just barely make out the bottom of one of the doors on an upper deck slowly swinging open. He stared at the space, unable to see anything joining him on the stairs before the door signaled its closure again.

He took a couple of steps on the ascent before freezing again. A sound was echoing down from the steps above. Footsteps, one after another in a cadence that matched human feet.

His heart leaped out ahead of him, and he drew in a breath, ready to throw away any thought of caution, There was nobody else alive out here. It had to be Natalia!

"Nat," he shouted, his voice echoing in the shaft. "Nat, it's me. Nat. Wait."

He bounded up the steps, taking them two or three at a time. He could hear the other footfalls between bounces. They had picked up speed, trying to escape.

Could she not hear him? Did she think it was a trick? If she had been wandering around the ship since she had disappeared, she might be exhausted and confused.

"Natalia," he shouted again. "It's Hayden. Stop. Wait."

A door further up opened and closed. Hayden kept climbing, ascending another five decks before coming to a halt, leaning over and gasping for air. He had tears in his eyes. Why hadn't she stopped?

She didn't know what she was doing. She didn't know he wasn't a threat. He felt the pain of it in his gut. He could barely handle the idea that she was frightened and alone. But which deck had she escaped onto? She had been too far away from him. If he had reached the stairs five minutes earlier, they might have been reunited already. Damn it.

His composure was crumbling, his strength and sanity eroding with it. He should have told her about the tapping. He should have gone with her to check the damage to Section C. He should have found a way to reach her sooner.

He lowered his head, nearly sobbing into his hand. He

had to pull himself together. He had to regroup. He couldn't help either of them if he stood there and felt sorry for himself. He looked at the stairwell door. The writing on it had been scratched out, just like the rest of the labels. Looking up, he could see the end of the stairwell above, and he counted down. Deck Five. Had Natalia gone up to Deck One? Should he look for her there?

He had to pick a door. Should he start at the top and work his way down, or should he stick with his original plan? Find the Section C access hatch and make a fresh decision from there.

He had to find the hatch first. If he assumed that there was at least one deck above Metro, beyond the elementals and the membrane sky, then the massive hold that contained the city would begin on Deck Two and end somewhere around Deck Fifteen. He tried to recount how many steps he had taken, and his rough estimate seemed about right. Section C most likely translated to Deck Seven or Eight, which meant he needed to go back down.

Or stay up and try one of these doors. But the Pilgrim was a massive ship, easily four to six kilometers long and at least a kilometer wide. Multiplied by as many as thirty decks, it left over one hundred square kilometers to search for a potentially moving target.

In other words, impossible.

But he had learned the Pilgrim was a manned vessel, and not as autonomous as he had once believed. Since there was a crew, that meant there was likely a bridge, or at least a command center. There was also likely some sort of intercom system; a means to transmit information ship-wide. If he could find that, he could call out to her. But how would that help? She couldn't come to him. She wasn't armed or armored like he was. But what if there were stations where she could call in and tell him where she was. That had to be better than chasing blindly after her.

He wiped the tears from his eyes. First things first. He had to determine whether or not she had survived the first few minutes after the secured hatch opened. He could swear he had heard her footsteps. He felt certain he was chasing her, and at the same time, he didn't quite trust that he wasn't the one hallucinating. The explosion had knocked him for a pretty big loop. What if he were hearing what he wanted to hear, and seeing what he wanted to see?

There was only one way to be sure.

He sighed thickly, glancing up at the doors above him before turning and descending two more decks.

He opened the door slowly, moving back out into a corridor nearly identical to the last, save for the position of the corpses resting forever silenced against the wall.

He never noticed the pair of human eyes tracking him, watching his every move as he abandoned the chase.

34

Hayden moved along Deck Seven, rifle up and ready. His heart was telling him to run, to go as fast as he could to where the deck's secure hatch should be and prove to himself that Natalia was still alive.

His head knew better. The ship was still crawling with xenotrife, and who knew what else? In his excitement on the stairs, he had forgotten what Natalia had said to him before she disappeared. She had found a body. A human body. A corpse that didn't belong to anyone in Metro.

He could have been chasing anybody, calling out Natalia's name in a fit of desperation that might have gotten him killed.

But if there were other people besides colonists and crew aboard, where the hell had they come from?

He couldn't even begin to guess. Stowaways on the Generation ship that had somehow managed to avoid the xenotrife? A second ship that had managed to catch up with and dock to theirs? The Pilgrim was the first of its kind, but that didn't mean it was the only one.

Or maybe there was another explanation? What if the

hatches had opened before? What if a group of Metro citizens had gone out into the ship? What if they had survived? They had been in space for almost four hundred years. It could be just another piece of history that had been buried and forgotten.

What if there were no humans at all? What if what Natalia had seen was another xenotrife, and she had assumed it was human? The demons were humanoid in shape and could be mistaken for a person in a split-second glance.

But he had heard the footsteps, and someone had climbed the stairs.

His mind was running in circles, trying to solve the riddle. He forced himself to stay focused, to keep his eyes and ears at attention, listening for anything that might be coming his way. He was getting close, and-

A xenotrife turned the corner right in front of him, as surprised by his presence as he was by it. They both froze for a moment, startled, regaining themselves at the same time.

Hayden pulled the trigger on the rifle, his burst tearing into the creature's shoulder, the impact pushing it backward. It hissed and scrambled back around the corner, leaving him to give chase. He took five quick steps to the junction, spinning to his left.

It was gone.

That couldn't be possible.

His eyes scanned the corridor. One of the grates for the ventilation shaft was on the floor. Had it gone in there? He didn't see any blood near the opening.

He swept his rifle across the passage, looking at the shadows on the ceiling, but seeing nothing. Where the hell was it?

Something dark and warm dropped onto the side of his head, sliding down his face.

Damn it.

He threw the rifle and his head back and up, getting a quick glimpse of the creature suspended from the ceiling and ready to drop.

Pop. Pop. Pop. Its head vanished suddenly in a spray of flesh and bone and brains, heavy slugs slamming into it and reducing it to mist. The lifeless body lost its grip on the ceiling, dropping on him. He caught it on his shoulder, pushing it off and to the ground.

He hadn't fired, which meant someone else had.

He spun again, back the way he had come. Someone was standing there.

They sure as hell looked human. But then again, it was hard to tell.

They were wearing headgear of some kind, with large oval eyes attached to a rubbery face mask that angled out of the mouth into a tube, which wrapped around behind their back. Long, tight, rubbery sleeves emerged from a looser fitting, dirty robe cinched at the waist. They carried a pistol of some kind, a dull chrome thing with a huge barrel, the weapon so large it looked like it barely fit in their gloved hands. It was aimed right at him. Not at his armored chest. At his head.

"Drop your weapon," they said in his language, muffled by the mask. "Do it, or you can say goodbye to your face."

Hayden continued to stare. Natalia had been right. There were other humans on the Pilgrim.

"Who are you?" he asked.

"I said drop it, meat sack."

They pulled back on part of the gun, causing it to click. It sounded threatening enough.

"What are you doing here?" Hayden asked. "How did you get out here?"

"Drop the grepping gun, or I blow off your grepping face."

The words came out harsh, and Hayden wasn't an idiot.

Whoever this person was, they didn't want to talk. But they wanted something from him. They had killed the xenotrife to keep it from killing him.

"Pozz," Hayden said, beginning to lower the rifle.

He didn't trust them at all. He kept his eyes steady on them as he brought the rifle down close to the pistol on his hip, hoping the stranger hadn't seen it or didn't realize how easily he could retrieve it.

The person took a step toward him, holding the pistol out further, shaking it threateningly. Hayden opened his hand, letting the rifle clatter onto the ground, still keeping eye contact.

At the same time, his hand fell to the pistol, and he grabbed it, raising it and firing in one quick motion.

The round caught the stranger off-guard, hitting them in the chest. The gun fell immediately from their hand, their body collapsing to the ground.

"Damn it," Hayden said, out loud this time.

He didn't want to have to kill them. He didn't want to have to kill anybody. He walked over, keeping the pistol trained on them.

He stood over the body. The front of the robe was staining with their blood. He couldn't see eyes past the dark orbs of the mask. He couldn't see a face at all. He leaned over, grabbing at it to pull it off.

It didn't come easily, but it slid away from the face as he pulled. He cursed again when he saw the person he had shot. A girl. She was just a girl. She looked to be around Sarah's age.

The same question filled his thoughts. Where had she come from?

He followed the tube of the mask around to the girl's back. He shifted her slightly so he could see the small device there, feeding oxygen into the mask. Why was she wearing it? To prevent contamination from the xenotrife?

Had Malcolm been telling the truth after all?

He patted her down, looking for anything else that might give him a clue about her. He found a pocket in her robe. There were six shells that looked like they went with the pistol she was carrying and a stack of torn paper inside. Every piece of it had been stamped with the all too familiar eagle logo of the USSF.

But what did it mean?

He had no idea. It didn't matter right now. He had learned there were other humans alive on the Pilgrim.

He had also learned they weren't friendly.

He leaned back down to push the girl's eyelids closed. Then he grabbed her pistol and the shells. It seemed like a more powerful alternative to the handgun he was already carrying. He snapped it to his waist in front of Baby.

Then he left her behind, more attentive and alert than ever. It wasn't only the xenotrife he had to worry about, but these outsiders, too. If they had come across Natalia, was there any hope she was still alive?

35

Hayden's body trembled as he stared down at the bloodstain on the floor of Deck Seven. It was heavy and red, human blood. It had been smeared from the secure access hatch into Section C back and away from the entrance, a corpse dragged along the floor and away from the scene. A pair of boots preceded it. Large boots. Way too big to belong to Natalia.

There was no sign of her. Not unless the blood on the floor had been hers.

In his mind, he wanted to force himself to admit she was gone. That everything he had done was for nothing. He wanted to let her go, let himself grieve, and then do what he could to get the Pilgrim back on track and deliver the colony to their new home. If that meant killing everything out here that wasn't him?

So be it.

In his heart, he knew that wasn't an option. He had to believe Natalia was still alive, and that he would find her. He couldn't rest. Only her cold, dead body in his arms would convince him hope was lost. Once he found her, they could work on saving the Pilgrim together. He knew their odds would be much better with her skillset to lean on.

The streak of blood moved down the corridor adjacent to the hatch. Now that Hayden had his bearings, he was able to visualize the area of Engineering only a handful of centimeters away. So close, and at the same time so far. It might as well have been another universe. He knew the section moved in that direction, and if the corridor remained relatively straight, it would come close to the waste system that he had gone to inspect. The area where he had heard the tapping.

He started in that direction, still walking carefully through the corridors. He had put the rifle on his back, preferring the stranger's pistol instead. The size and shape of it was substantial in his hand and gave him a greater sense of security. One round from the cannon could reduce a xenotrife's head to mush. He had checked the chambers, replacing the three missing rounds with the shells he had taken from the girl's pockets. He had nine bullets total, and he figured with his aim he could take out nine of the demons with it.

He paused at one of the doors on the north side of the corridor. It was slightly open. He didn't hear any noise from it, but its position made him curious. He leaned in, looking through the crack. There were a few MRE wrappers on the ground, and a dozen crates had been opened and picked through. More supplies. Someone had taken them recently.

He backed out, scanning the hallway. The main blood stain had faded after a dozen meters or so, but there were still smudges along the center of the hallway where little bits of blood and bodily fluid had leaked from the corpse. He could see it continued further down, and there was another door on the south side of the corridor fifty meters away, adjacent to Section C. It was approximately in line with the waste disposal system, making it the most likely source of the tapping. It also seemed to be where they had brought the body.

He moved to the south side of the passage, staying tight against the wall. Whoever had dragged the body could still be in there, and there was nothing he had experienced to suggest they wouldn't kill him on sight.

He got closer to the hatch, noticing that this one was also hanging slightly open. He could hear noise from it, too. Soft whispers of low voices speaking to one another. He paused, listening. He couldn't make out the words, but he was able to hear the different tones and pitches. There were at least four people inside, and he guessed three men and woman. Not Natalia. The voice was too familiar. Too comfortable.

He could also smell something. It was a scent he vaguely recognized but couldn't place. It wafted out through the hatch to him, a stronger sense than the sound.

He eased closer, remaining pressed against the wall as he approached, keeping the revolver up near his face. He reached the edge of the hatch, turning his head slightly to see inside from the corner of his right eye.

The room was different from the others. It had a stairwell just inside the hatch, which led down into a bigger space where a pair of large tanks were resting near the wall, pipes running away from them and into the floor. Hayden wasn't an Engineer, but he was willing to bet they were related to the waste system somehow.

He could see the people now. Three men and a woman. They weren't wearing masks like the girl, but they were dressed similarly. Threadbare robes over fitted clothing, over bodies lean from either a lot of exercise or not a lot of food. All of their heads were shaved, and one of the men had what looked like a tattoo on the side of his face. Hayden was too far away to make out what it was.

There was a small device sitting in the middle of them, the top of it glowing red with heat.

On top of the device was a leg.

A human leg.

Hayden turned back, covering his mouth to keep from gagging. His heart leaped into his throat, his pulse pounding. It was one thing if she were dead. Another if they were eating her.

That didn't mean it was Natalia's leg. They had dragged the other body away for a reason. Was this how they had survived on the outside for so long?

He swallowed the rise in his throat, repositioning himself to take another look. He forced himself to set his eyes on the cooktop. The leg was too big to be Natalia's.

He felt the relief, despite the grotesqueness of it all. What the hell was their existence like that it had driven them to eat another human being? He wanted to kill them all, and he could from here. Four shots from the rifle and they would put them all to rest. Except, it was possible they knew what had happened to his wife.

He had to try to talk to them.

He returned the revolver to his hip and grabbed the rifle from his back, remembering to scan the corridor again as he did. The people inside were laughing now, and he thought he heard one of them say, "Smells so good. So much better than Hisser."

He bit his lip to keep from gagging. Hisser? Did he mean xenotrife? These people ate them, too?

"Toko will be missed," he heard the woman say.

He crouched down, using his shoulder to begin brushing open the hatch. It moved easily and quietly, giving him enough space to slink into the room. The kept his eyes locked on the people below, making sure they didn't notice him. He wondered why they felt so secure down there with the hatch open and the smell making its way out. Weren't they afraid the xenotrife would find them?

Unless they had already killed all of the creatures in the area. If they gathered in smaller, competitive groups, it might be possible to wipe them out one nest at a time.

He stood slowly, getting the rifle up and over the railing to the steps. He swept his reticle across all four of them, preparing his firing path. He repeated it a couple of times, still unnoticed. Then he tapped the muzzle of the rifle against the metal rail.

The speaking stopped. The man with the tattoo started to turn his head in Hayden's direction. "Gizzie, is that - who the grep are you?"

Hayden's body shook slightly, a sudden chill of fear running through it. The other side of the man's face was heavily scarred, as though it had been melted.

"I'll ask the questions," Hayden said, forcing the words out without quivering. "None of you move."

The man turned his head back to the others. "You see that shit?" he asked. "Who the grep does this grepper think he is?"

The rest of the group started to laugh. Hayden shifted his aim and squeezed the trigger. The round hit the floor right beside the man.

"I'm not joking with you," Hayden said.

"No?" Tatoo asked. "You look pretty comical to me."

The man beside Tattoo was shifting, reaching for something. Hayden adjusted his aim again and fired. The man's head snapped back, and he toppled over, a half-drawn gun in his hand.

"Think it's funny?" Hayden asked, getting angry. "Want to keep laughing?"

The remaining members of the group quieted, except for Tattoo.

"You have no grepping idea what you just done," he said. "You kill one of the Scrappers; you have to deal with us all."

Hayden didn't hesitate. He shifted the rifle and fired again. The second member of the group died.

"I will if I have to," Hayden said. "I'm already having a bad day."

"It's going to get worse for you, then."

What was he doing? He wasn't sure. Killing people was getting easier. Could it get too easy? Or maybe it had to be to survive out here. Compassion had been in short supply since Natalia had disappeared. Not from the Governor, not from his deputies, not from the girl he assumed was probably Gizzie, and not from these assholes.

"Answer my questions," Hayden said.

"Or what?" Tattoo replied. "You kill me? Grep you."

Hayden shifted his reticle to the man but didn't shoot. "There was a woman. She found a body. That one, I think." He motioned to the leg on the cooktop. "Have you seen her?"

Tattoo's face changed, softening with a sudden understanding. He smiled wide. "Oh. Shit. Now I get it. You're like her. You come from Inside. You come looking for her, mate? You her bitch?"

Hayden tried to keep himself calm. His heart was pulsing at the news that this guy had seen her and that she had been alive when he did.

"You're worth a pretty penny, Insider," Tattoo said. "Grepping treasure indeed. You got out. On purpose. Which means you know how to get back in."

Hayden stared at the man, trying to decompile what he was saying. His eyes focused on the tattoo, finally identifying it.

An eagle. The USSF logo.

He heard a whisper from below, and he shifted his attention to the woman. She was leaning down, holding something in her hand and talking into it. A transceiver of some kind.

"You don't know grep-all about grep, mate," Tattoo said. "That uni will fetch a grepping treasure in the market; I'll tell you that."

Hayden fired again, hitting the woman in the side of the head. She collapsed.

"I can't wait to cut your grepping head off and take it from you," Tattoo finished. "But not till you shows me how to get inside."

Hayden's reticle landed on the man's forehead. Tattoo was still smiling. Unafraid.

Hayden heard the echoes of feet approaching, too many to count, all coming toward the room at a run. The noise distracted him, and when he pulled the trigger, the bullet grazed Tattoo's face instead, ripping a gash across the eagle.

Tattoo didn't react. He didn't even blink. He just stood there, smiling and unconcerned.

"Better run, Insider," he said.

36

HAYDEN BACKED OUT OF THE HATCH, TURNING HIS HEAD BACK the way he had come. Ten men were rushing toward him, still a good two hundred meters away. It looked like they were armed, and the suspicion was confirmed when a slug hit the wall a few meters in front of him.

"Shit," Hayden said, cradling the rifle.

He was tempted to use the secondary trigger, to send one of the explosive balls out to greet the men. But Metro's waste system was just on the other side, and if it damaged the wall, he could wind up killing everyone inside.

He followed Tattoo's advice, instead.

He ran.

He broke to the west, rushing headlong down the corridor at a sprint, thankful for the added boost of strength the body armor provided. He had gone a hundred meters when he heard a heavy crack behind him, and a moment later something hit him in the back. The impact threw him forward, sending him sprawling to the ground, the rifle coming from his hands. He felt the sharp sting on his muscles, but he didn't think the round had pierced the plating. He pulled himself up as quickly as he could, risking a glance back.

Tattoo was standing in the doorway to the room, a revolver similar to the one he had taken from the girl in his hand.

Hayden bounced back to his feet, finding an intersection a few meters ahead. He sprinted toward it, laying out in the air to dive around the corner as Tattoo fired his cannon again. The round whizzed past Hayden's ear, close enough he could hear it, before slamming into the opposite wall, punching right through.

Damn, he was an incredible shot.

Hayden got up again, running north along the new corridor. He had a headstart on the Scrappers, or whatever the hell they called themselves, but if Tattoo made it to the junction before he was out of sight? He didn't know if the man would miss again.

He charged down the corridor, the threat of xenotrife forgotten. One enemy at a time. Malcolm had warned him about leaving Metro, but he doubted the Governor knew the full extent of it. A lot had happened on the Pilgrim over the years.

He shouldn't have shot first. It was a mistake. He had pissed them off instead of trying to make allies. With cannibals? Besides, he had already killed the girl. The matching weapons made him pretty sure she was the one Tattoo had called Gizzie. He had been screwed before he entered the room.

He raced another fifty meters, coming to another intersection. Which way? He looked to the right. A dead crew member was splayed out on the floor. He looked to the left, back to the eastern side of the ship. Port, if he was facing the bow. He didn't know if he was. It looked clear.

He turned that way. The more walls he could put between himself and the Scrappers, the better his chance of escaping.

He kept moving, desperate to keep ahead of them. He crossed another series of hatches, passing them without slowing. He heard one of them swing open, and when he looked back, there were a pair of xenotrife bounding toward him, their long limbs and light frames carrying them faster than he could run.

Damn it.

He grabbed the pistol on his hip, not trusting his aim with the revolver while running. He turned enough to fire back at them, more rounds missing than not. He emptied the magazine to drop them, taking them out before they could catch up.

He made another intersection, turning north. He kept going, another two hundred meters until he reached a central column, a circular room with a cylinder in the center. A lift. This was the main hub, which he assumed meant he was moving toward the bow of the starship.

A bullet hit the wall a half-meter ahead of him. He dove to the ground as more rounds smacked the area where he had been. He looked up, finding a fresh trio of Scrappers coming out of one of the other passages. One of them was carrying a transceiver of some kind, along with a gun. The other two had what looked like spears in their hands, wires running from the weapons to their backs. They were all wearing masks like the girl. Were they some kind of hunting party?

The man put the transceiver onto his hip, along with the spent pistol, reaching behind and withdrawing a similar spear. Hayden got to his feet as they approached, catching one of them with the pistol while reaching for Baby.

The apparent leader lashed out with the spear, using the butt of it to slap his gun hand. Hayden felt a shock from the blow, and his whole hand went numb, forcing him to drop the weapon. The other Scrapper moved in from the side, lashing out with the tip of the weapon, hitting the armor plating. A web of energy flared around it, but it didn't pierce the protection.

"Pig wants him alive," the leader said, stepping back cautiously as Hayden got Baby out in his good hand.

It was also his off hand, leaving him feeling incredibly exposed. He didn't have time to linger on these two, not when Tattoo was close behind.

"He's got Gizzie's popper," the other man said, confirming that was the girl he had killed.

Hayden faced off against them, waving Baby to keep their spears at bay. He needed to figure something out if he was going to survive. He glanced over to the lift. The control panel was close. Could he reach it?

He had to try. He faked a slash with Baby, and then dove sideways, barely avoiding the spears that slapped down toward his feet. He reached out, hitting the control panel with his hand. It lit up, the word ASCENDING appearing on the display. It worked!

He stood with his back to the door as the leader came at him with the spear. He knew the plating on the armor would protect him, so he brought his forearm up, using it to deflect the weapon. He slashed out with Baby, nearly catching the man in the hip as he backed away again.

The second man had retreated, picking up his dropped pistol.

"Hey, frekton," the Scrapper said, getting Hayden's attention.

The weapon was aimed at his head.

The door to the lift opened behind him.

"Don't," the man said.

Hayden stood motionless ahead of the open lift door. He couldn't let them catch him. He had to risk it.

He threw himself backward. The Scrapper fired, the bullet hitting the armored collar of the uniform, cracking the plating before deflecting away. As Hayden fell into the lift, he saw the Scrapper's head vanish in a spray of blood and bone.

"I said alive!" Tattoo roared, entering the area.

Hayden pushed himself to his knees, reaching out for the panel with his left hand.

A blue light appeared, stretching across to the identification chip beneath the sleeve of the uniform. The display changed.

CONFIRMED.

The door slid closed as Pig's face appeared in front of it, an expression of both displeasure and mirth mixing on his face as he raised the middle finger of his free hand.

"I seen your bitch, Insider. She's on her way. You want her? Come and get her."

37

HAYDEN LET HIMSELF FALL BACK ONTO THE FLOOR OF THE LIFT, breathing heavily as it descended. His right hand was tingling, the feeling starting to return to it. His body was burning, sore and tired.

He had escaped. Just barely. The lift had scanned the chip he took from the Governor, and it was taking him - where?

At the moment, he didn't care. He was grateful to be alive.

Natalia was alive too, if the Scrapper, Pig, was to be believed. His words echoed in Hayden's mind. She's on her way. What the hell did that mean?

They knew about Metro. About the city inside the Pilgrim's hold. They wanted to get in, but couldn't. They must have known the door opened because of the turbs. Maybe the body she had found, Toko, had tried to get in, and was attacked by a xenotrife before he made it? Maybe the other Scrappers hadn't been far behind, and had grabbed her before it closed again?

Pig knew Hayden had come out on his own. He was too well prepared for his exodus to be a mistake. Maybe that was something he could use.

Could he barter Malcolm's identification chip for Natalia's life?

Should he?

The possibility sent a chill through him because he knew he would trade every last one of them for her. He didn't have to think that hard about it.

Then again, would Pig agree to that kind of deal? He seemed like the sort of man who would accept the terms and then renege as soon as it was convenient, killing him and keeping Natalia for whatever it was they wanted her to do. If they knew she was an Engineer, he could imagine they would find her incredibly valuable.

Besides, even if Pig didn't stab him in the back, then what? They were all trapped on the Pilgrim together, and what kind of life would they have hiding from xenotrife and the Scrappers on the starship? The ultimate solution was still the same. He had to recover Natalia, and together they would find a way to get the ship back on course. To get them to their destination. Once they had a future, a real future, all of their options would expand.

What if that's where she was right now? What if the Scrappers had taken her to the bridge, or to the engine room? What if they were already using her to find a way to get them to their new home?

It wasn't crazy to think they had a shared goal. Nobody wanted to be drifting through space until the power went out, and Malcolm had suggested that was going to happen sooner rather than later. It was possible Natalia was not only still alive, but being treated fairly well.

He had to believe that. It was the most logical position, and it allowed him to continue to hold onto hope, even against what felt like crushing odds. He would find her. Knowing she was alive gave him fresh strength and motivation.

The lift came to a stop. Hayden looked up at the display on the control panel to see what deck they were on. Instead of a number, it read "RESEARCH."

He didn't linger; certain Pig would call the lift back up. When the door slid open, he pushed himself up and stumbled out, collapsing on the other side. The door closed behind him, and he could hear the lift rising again.

He wasn't worried about the Scrappers reaching this level. The system had scanned the chip. This area was locked down.

He was safe. For now, anyway. He knew he couldn't stay here forever, but if this area had been secured, there was a reason it was secured. Was there another weapons cache hiding down here?

He leaned back against the side of the lift, surveying the area. There wasn't much to it. The hub was similar to Deck Seven, a rounded space with the lift in the center. Except there weren't four corridors leading off in each direction. There was one directly ahead of the lift, sealed off by a hatch with a plate hanging on the wall beside it. The writing hadn't been scratched off it because nothing had been down here.

In how many years?

Since the colonists had been sealed into Metro, at least. He was the first to enter the area in centuries.

He stood up, reaching for the closure to the armor and pulling it down. The suit expanded as he unzipped it, giving his body room to move in it again. He pulled it off, resting it beside the lift. The armor had saved his life multiple times, but he enjoyed the feeling of freedom to be out of it, and besides, he had to use the bathroom, an impossible task in the uniform.

He wasn't sure where to relieve himself, so he moved to the other side of the lift and went. It smelled awful. So much worse than he remembered. Was it a result of the infection?

He had almost forgotten about that. Three months, Malcolm had said. He still didn't want to believe it was true, but everything suggested it was. The Scrappers wore masks to protect themselves from the disease. Where had they gotten them?

Pig hadn't been wearing a mask. Did that mean he was infected? Immune? Did that mean maybe they had a cure? He couldn't imagine them living with the creatures for so long unless they could inoculate themselves somehow. The lift had called this place Research. Maybe there were no weapons down here, but a cure to whatever disease the xenotrife carried. Maybe the crew of the Pilgrim had been working on it when they were forced to lock themselves in Metro.

If they had abandoned this deck, maybe it wasn't as safe as he thought?

He returned to the armor, pulling it back on. There was no reason to risk it, not now that his bowels and bladder were clear. He had lost both the rifle and the pistol, which didn't make him happy. At least he had the revolver and Baby. At least he wasn't completely unarmed. Still, it wasn't nearly enough to confront the Scrappers again. It wasn't nearly enough to wade back into an unknown number of xenotrife. He needed more. Could he find it here?

He headed to the hatch.

It slid open as he approached.

38

HAYDEN HELD THE REVOLVER IN HIS HAND, READY TO USE IT IF needed. He didn't think he would have to, but he didn't want to be caught unprepared. He walked through the corridor that connected Research with the lift, covering a hundred meters before reaching a second hatch that slid open ahead of him.

The room beyond it was dark at first, but the opening hatch seemed to signal it to come to life, a series of interior lights flickering on overhead and revealing a command center of some sort.

It reminded him of Engineering. Workstations with displays suspended in front of them. A board at the front to show information to all of the workers in the area. They all began to activate as he entered, the displays showing the USSF logo before switching over to individualized interfaces, all of the stations locked and requesting a passcode.

He stood at the entrance to the room and stared. It was nearly identical to Engineering, save for the fact that it was immaculately clean. Everything was white and silver, and while he would have expected a layer of dust to have settled over it after all of these years, it remained pristine and fresh, the particles filtered out of the area.

His eyes shifted to the lead station near the back of the room. It was on a slightly raised dais, giving the team lead a full view of everyone else from the position, and also the best view of the master display. It was the same area where Natalia had spent the most time, when she hadn't been moving station to station, asking questions and encouraging her subordinates. She was a fantastic leader. So much better than he was. He could picture her there, looking up and smiling at him. Welcoming him to her department.

Only this wasn't that. This was something else entirely. He didn't understand what. The Pilgrim was a colony ship. What were they researching? Was it anything he could use?

He made his way to the lead station. The display was on, beckoning for a password. Jonas had given him Metro's master code. Would it work down here?

He typed it in. The screen changed.

WELCOME ADMIN.

Admin? Was that the name of the head researcher? It didn't matter. He was in.

The interface reminded him of the PASS. A query tool, and direct access to systems he didn't understand displayed on the left. He stared at the screen, trying to decide what to ask it for.

"Query Pilgrim schematic," he said, unsure if it had a voice module like the PASS in the Law Station. A map of the ship would be incredibly useful to help him get his bearings.

It did, responding to his query a moment later.

NO RESULTS.

It didn't have the schematic or anything like it. It was a secured system inside a secured area. A third network, then? But sharing the same master code as Metro? He wasn't an

Engineer. He didn't know if that was normal or not. It was what it was.

"Query personnel records in Research," he said. He had used that command in the Law Station plenty of times to access his deputies' files. He could write to those records, adding reviews, commendations, that sort of thing.

A list of names and positions appeared on the display. The head of Research wasn't named Admin after all. Ironically, their name was Hope. Senior Special Officer Hope Mendez. Age: Thirty-seven. Status: Suspended.

Suspended? Normally, status was either living or deceased. He didn't know there was a third option.

He didn't drill deeper into her file yet, reading more of the names from the list, instead. Special Officer Kyle Noah. Special Officer Jennifer Kazlaski. Junior Special Officer Ramshit Shah. They all had ranks of some kind. But the Pilgrim was supposed to be civ -

He stopped himself. It was stupid to keep assuming any part of the the ship's history was the truth. Not after everything else he had learned. Maybe the Pilgrim was a colony ship. But maybe it was also something else. There was enough firepower under Metro to level the city. What about elsewhere in the ship? And this secured area? Research? He still wanted to know what kind.

He went back to Senior Special Officer Mendez, opening her file. The display split in half, one side showed a three-dimensional, lifelike image of her over the eagle logo and the USSF abbreviation. The other side had a more detailed description of her.

Divorced. A specialist in bio-engineering and infectious diseases. She had gotten her Doctorate at Harvard University. She had risen through the Special Officer ranks of the USSF quickly, going from junior to senior in a few years. She had published a number of papers on the topic of genetics, genetic engineering, and the role of gene mutation in both weaponizing and neutralizing disease.

As far as Hayden was concerned, she was a frightening individual. She toyed with the building blocks of life like they were grains of sand on a playground, and had the education to create things that killed.

Like the xenotrife?

He couldn't rule it out. Not with what little he knew about the creatures. Maybe they hadn't found their way onto the Pilgrim, but had been created within it? That was a frightening thought, too.

"Query mission logs, Senior Officer Hope Mendez," Hayden said, wondering if she had recorded her progress the same way the Captain had.

She had. A list of recordings displayed, each with a timestamp. He chose the first result, the last entry she had made, noting the date was a few days after Captain Bradshaw had been killed.

Mendez's face appeared on the display. She was an ordinary looking woman, with dark hair and intelligent eyes. Unlike Bradshaw, she looked composed on the recording. Unconcerned with the creatures overwhelming the ship.

"Research Log Four Hundred Seventeen," she said. "We've finished securing the Research module. It was more work than we expected, and the number of modifications needed to route proper filtration and seal off the ducts from intrusion cost many people their lives. The entire Fourth Squad was assigned to the area, and we've only survived because of their bravery."

She paused for a long time, her eyes glistening at the thought. Hayden couldn't help but wonder what had happened down here. Or how.

"Our research has gone as far as we can take it. Without access to the colonists, we can't continue to test any of the mutagens, and without access to the trife, we can't test our toxins. We had hoped to come up with something before the clock ran out. A cure. A poison. Anything to stop their spread. We had hoped to seal the ship, keep them out and provide an answer before we had to abandon the planet. We've failed at both. I can only hope our counterparts on the other Generation class vessels have more success, and I mourn for the billions of souls already lost in this senseless conflict."

She stopped again. Tears were running from her eyes. Hayden felt cold, his body shivering from her words. The PASS had always insisted that the Pilgrim had left the planet of its own volition. That the colonization program was voluntary.

Of course, the PASS lied.

What the hell had happened to Earth?

"I don't know if anyone will ever hear this log. I don't know if anyone will ever see my face again. I hope that if and when you do, the Pilgrim will be free of the xenotrife. I hope the ship will have set down on New Gaia, the secured hatches will have unsealed, and you'll be discovering this area a long time after you've begun to dismantle the city and move it outside. I hope that you'll have already found us, sleeping in our hibernation pods. I hope you'll have woken us up so that we can rejoin you as members of a new society.

"If not. If the trife survive our best efforts. If the Pilgrim drifts across the universe until the end of time... I hope never to wake up at all."

The recording ended. Hayden stared at the interface containing the query results for nearly a minute, trying to process what she had said, and slowly piecing together a vague outline of events.

The trife had come from outside the Pilgrim. From Earth. Mendez and her team had been working to find a way to stop them, using colonists as test subjects for their experiments. Apparently, there were other ships and other researchers doing the same. And when they failed? That's when the ships had left Earth. But the Pilgrim still had a bug problem, one they had decided not to carry to their new home. The ship was drifting, waiting for the creatures to die. Not only had they survived, but it also appeared they were still reproducing.

And now here he was.

Here they all were.

Had any of the ships found a cure? Had any found a way to destroy the demons? Had they made it to their new home? Hayden felt a pang of jealousy at the idea that some other ship full of colonists was out there on New Gaia, enjoying the splendor of a clean world where anything was possible instead of facing a future that was anything but sure.

He looked at Special Officer Mendez's image on the display. She had said she and her team had taken to hibernation pods. That they were sleeping. The suspended status made more sense to him now. She had hoped they would make it to their new home and be woken then. She didn't want to be taken out of hibernation otherwise.

Too damn bad.

39

It took Hayden some time to find the hibernation pods. Research was larger than he expected, accounting for close to half a square kilometer. He had come across a number of hatches along the way, and while he had no idea what a hibernation pod looked like, he knew what it wasn't.

The whole area was self-sufficient, just like Metro but on a much smaller scale. He found cubes for the research team, a dozen of them, but they were tiny bunks in the wall just big enough to house a small mattress. He found a shared shower and bathroom, embarrassed about voiding on the floor outside when he did. He found a laboratory stocked with all kinds of fancy equipment whose function he didn't understand. He found more external hatches that had been sealed with heavy solder to keep them from opening to adjacent corridors, and roughly patched shafts altered to keep the xenotrife away.

In a discovery that sent his body to shivering again, he had also come across a room of cells, a prison like the one in Metro, eight separate cages in all. Seven of them had corpses in them. Bodies that he imagined had once been human.

Something had happened to each of them, leaving them in a state of distressed mutation. On one, the skull was much too large. On another, it appeared as though the muscles had grown beyond control. He knew from Special Officer Mendez's log that each of the apparent prisoners had been colonists. Had they volunteered for the experiments or had the soldiers on board taken them against their will?

It was one of the many questions circulating in his mind. He expected to ask Mendez all of them once he got her up.

The hibernation pods were tucked into the northernmost corner of the Research module. The room they were in was cold, much colder than anywhere else he had been on the ship. A wash of freezing air had exploded out of it when Hayden opened the hatch, having to enter the master code on the door's panel to convince it to slide away. Once the mist had cleared, he was able to make out the twelve pods arranged in groups of six on either side of the main aisle. They were roughly bed shaped, flat on the bottom and rounded on top, with tubes entering at multiple points along the back. Displays sat over each of them, frosted over by the cold, moist air and leaving their contents invisible. He guessed each display would list the name of the occupant and their vitals, important because the pods had no transparencies to view the state of the bodies inside.

He approached the closest pod on his left. Natalia would have loved to see this technology and to try to understand how it all worked. He didn't much care for the inner workings of things, and especially not for these things. Not right now. All he wanted to know was how to turn it off.

He reached up to the display, putting a finger to the freezing surface. He had never touched anything so cold, and the sensation of it caused him to draw his hand back. There was nothing in Metro like this. He overcame the shock quickly, scraping his hand across the display, watching as the heat of his body overcame the frost and began to clear it from the glass. He wasn't sure what to think as it became clear of the frozen condensation.

The display was empty. Blank.

Dead.

Conserving power? He tapped on it a few times, thinking it might activate with his touch.

It didn't.

He stared at it, a sense of dread starting to filter in. He looked over the pod, studying it more closely. It had to have a manual release of some kind, didn't it? He bent down to see beneath it, looking at the frosted tubes running from it to the wall. He scraped some of the frost off. They appeared to be empty. He had a feeling they weren't supposed to be.

He was pretty sure the pod had failed. Just like so many things in Metro had failed.

He went to the next one, scraping the frost off its display. Again, it was blank. He examined its tubes. This pod was dead as well.

He went to the third, and then the fourth. They were the same. Each time he discovered a dead pod his heart sank a little more. He needed one of the researchers to be alive, damn it.

The fifth was dead. So was the sixth. He crossed to the other side. The seventh and eighth were both offline.

He rubbed the frost from the display of the ninth. He was so prepared for it to be inoperable that when he saw the red text across the black background, he almost didn't recognize what it meant. He bent to check the tubes, realizing that there was a clear fluid moving in and out of the pod.

He stood back up, his eyes landing on the display again, his heart pulsing.

KAZLASKI, J.

A small graph ran below the name, measuring something

inside the pod. It wasn't flat, which Hayden assumed was good. At least one of the researchers was alive!

He didn't look for a way to open the pod. Not yet. Instead, he went to the remaining three, wiping the frost from each.

There was only one survivor. Senior Officer Mendez had gotten her wish.

She was never going to wake up.

He returned to the operable pod. He reached up and tapped on the display. It changed beneath his finger.

HIBERNATION SEQUENCE ACTIVATED. ENGAGE MANUAL OVERRIDE?

A pair of buttons appeared. YES or NO. He tapped on YES.

ENTER ACCESS CODE.

He put in the master code.

MANUAL OVERRIDE SELECTED. CONFIRM?

Again, YES or NO. He tapped on YES.

The text turned green.

THAWING PROCESS ACTIVATED. STANDBY.

A timer appeared beneath it. Ten minutes. The pod started to hum.

Hayden took a step back from it, holding his breath. The other pods had all failed. What if this one died during the thawing process?

He shook as he watched the timer count down. The hum from the pod was getting louder, and he could see the layer of frost surrounding it turning to water as it warmed up. The air in the room was getting warmer too, signaling that the system was aware only one pod was functional.

When the timer reached five minutes, a sucking sound came from the inside, which he could see in the tubes below was the fluid draining from the system. That took another minute to happen.

He wasn't sure what it was doing after that, but the display was on 3:38 when it suddenly, inexplicably fell dark.

There was no warning. No flashing lights. No indication of failure or emergency. One moment, the whole thing was working. The next, it had all stopped, going dark and silent. Dead.

"No," Hayden said, stepping toward it and tapping on the display. "Come on, damn it. No." He smacked the side of the screen a few times. What the hell had happened to it?

Three more minutes. It only had three more minutes. Had the person inside been revived? He needed to open it up. There had to be a way.

He crouched in front of it, grabbing the tubes and pulling as hard as he could. When that didn't work, he grabbed Baby, slashing and cutting at the lines until he got them disconnected. The pod still didn't open. He banged the handle of the blade against the seam, hoping he could dislodge it. He couldn't.

He stopped hitting it, staring at it. How could he get it open? He was close. So damn close. He put his forehead in his hand, rubbing at it and trying to think.

Something knocked on the pod.

From inside.

He moved back to it.

"Hello?" he shouted.

The knocking came again.

"Hello? Can you hear me?"

Silence.

"Hello?" Hayden shouted. "I can't figure out how to open-"

The seams hissed. Hayden jumped back. The top of the pod started to move, lifting open from the back. No, not lifting on its own. Being lifted. Two small hands gripped the sides of it, trying to push it out of the way. He rushed to help, grabbing one side and pulling it up. It was heavier than he would have guessed.

He strained to keep it raised. He could see the woman inside. She was completely naked, and she moved in a way that suggested she had almost forgotten how.

She wasn't paying attention to him. She was struggling to get her muscles working, to get herself out of the pod. She faced away from him, leaning over the opposite side. She was still wet from the fluid, a shimmering gel that coated her bare, completely hairless flesh. She got herself to the edge and tumbled over, hitting the cold floor with a wet slap.

40

Hayden rushed to her, reaching out to help her to her feet.

She looked in his direction, putting her hand out and trying to push herself away from him.

He stopped moving when he saw she was afraid of him.

"It's okay," he said. "I'm not going to hurt you. It's okay. My name is Sheriff Hayden Duke. From Metro."

Her eyes were moving back and forth. She couldn't see him, not clearly. Even so, his words seemed to calm her some. She stopped trying to push herself away, changing her effort to covering her breasts and groin with her hands instead.

"I'm sorry," Hayden said. "I didn't know you were naked in there or I would have brought something to cover you. I can go and get something."

"No," she said, the word viscous in her throat.

She coughed, shifting her hands to lean on the ground while she spit out clear fluid onto it. She continued to hack for a good minute, her body heaving. When she had cleared the gel from her mouth, she looked up at him again, blinking rapidly. Her eyes seemed more focus now, her vision returning.

She didn't try to cover herself again. She had decided her modesty was less important than not being alone.

"Sheriff?" she said, her voice a little stronger.

"Hayden Duke," he repeated. "From Metro. Inside the Pilgrim."

A small smile started to creep onto her face. "The Pilgrim? Then, we've arrived? New Gaia?"

Hayden froze. He knew she was going to be crushed, and there was nothing he could do about it.

"No," he said softly. "I'm sorry. We haven't reached New Gaia. We haven't reached anywhere. I don't know if we ever will. That's why I woke you. I need your help."

She lowered her head again, shaking it. "Senior Officer Mendez?" she asked.

"I don't know how to tell you this in a way that doesn't hurt," Hayden replied. "The pods. They all broke. Yours was the only one that was still functional, and it didn't complete the thawing process."

She gave out a short cry, lowering herself to the floor. Her body shook with her sobs, and he stepped forward again with the intention of comforting her.

She stopped shaking almost immediately, pushing herself back up. She reached up and wiped her eyes.

"No," she said. "Don't touch me. Just give me a minute."

"I can leave?"

"No. Stay with me, Sheriff. I don't want to be alone. Just. Wait."

He turned around to give her some privacy, standing there while she breathed. Ragged at first, but slowly calming.

"It's a lot to take in," she said after a few minutes.

"Tell me about it," he said.

"My name is Special Officer Jennifer Kazlaski," she said. "United States Special Operations, Disease Control."

"I'd say it's a pleasure to meet you, Officer Kazlaski, but honestly, I wish you were still asleep."

She looked up at him, holding out her hand. "So do I, but you woke me for a reason. Help me up. It's cold in here."

He grabbed her hand and pulled her to her feet. He did his best to keep his eyes off her body. He didn't want her to think he was that kind of man.

"I give new meaning to the term hairless ape, don't I, Sheriff?" she said as she stood.

"I don't know what you mean."

"It's an old expression. The sensors on the hibernation pod have trouble with hair, so it had to all come off before I went in. It'll grow back in time. Assuming we have time. My bunk is this way. I can pick up clothes there." She paused, looking down at their still connected hands. "You haven't been exposed to the trife, have you?"

Hayden pulled his hand away. "Yes, ma'am," he replied. "I've been killing them."

She didn't look happy. "They're still on the ship?"

"Yes, ma'am. I don't know much about what's going on, but I know you were hoping they would die out. It's been almost four hundred years. They haven't."

"Four hundred years," Jennifer said, her voice heavy with the idea of it. "Damn. We were afraid they might be regenerative. Their DNA suggested it was a possibility."

"What do you mean?" Hayden asked.

"They thrive on radiation, Sheriff," she said. "It doesn't even seem to matter which kind. We knew it was their food source, but we were split on whether or not it would keep them alive indefinitely."

"It might not. I saw a nest. There were small ones growing in some kind of sticky gel."

"Reproducing? Then their resource pool has increased. Or a number of them are dying. You said you've been exposed to them?"

"Yes, ma'am."

"Have you been bitten?"

"No."

"Then you aren't contagious. That's good."

"But I am sick?"

"If you've engaged them, you've gotten close enough to them to get the disease. Whether or not it will ever manifest? That's up to your immune system. Ninety percent of those exposed to the disease died within three months."

"Shit."

"Yes. Follow me."

Jennifer led him out of the room, moving through the corridors like she had done it a thousand times. He supposed she had.

"So," she said as they walked. "What's our situation?"

"I'm not completely sure," Hayden said. "I barely understand what's happening. Two days ago, I was in Metro doing the job the way I'd been taught, waiting for the Pilgrim to reach our new homeworld. Then a massive turb hit, one of the secured hatches opened, my wife disappeared, and a xenotrife got into the city."

She paused again, looking at him. "A trife got into the city?"

"I killed it."

"Good. The hatch?"

"Not so good. The Governor killed hundreds of people because he said they were exposed. You said the disease isn't contagious unless they were bitten?"

"Airborne contagious, no. It's a slightly different mutation on the same viral strain. But if the residents were sick and exchanged bodily fluids, you might have been facing a major outbreak within a few months. I'm guessing you don't understand, but the protocols were put in place for a reason. You should be thankful your Governor had the balls to follow through. We always worried they would balk in an emergency situation like that. The hatch?"

Hayden was silent for a moment, digesting the fact that Malcolm had acted purely as had been prescribed. He didn't think he would have been able to do the same.

"The hatch, Sheriff?" Jennifer repeated.

"It closed after the turbs. I don't know how long it was open for. Twenty seconds? A minute?"

She seemed satisfied. She continued walking. "Turbs?"

"Turbulence of some kind. It comes and goes almost at random. It shakes the entire ship. My wife is an Engineer. She was out checking on potential damage from them when one of the secure hatches opened."

"There's no turbulence in space."

"Yeah, that always confused Nat, too, but it's there, Officer Kazlaski. I promise."

"I believe you. Please, call me Jen or Jenny. You've seen me naked, after all. I think that puts us at least on the level of friendly acquaintance."

"Pozz," Hayden said without thinking.

"Pozz? New words for old things. I like it."

They reached the row of bunks. She stopped at one of them, pressing the space below one it. A drawer slid out, revealing three rows of identical uniforms. She grabbed one and put it on the bunk, beginning to dress.

"The Pilgrim never went to New Gaia because the xenotrife didn't die," she said. "Hope helped Captain Bradshaw program that protocol. You said the Pilgrim's been out here four hundred years?"

"Close enough. Three ninety-six."

"Which means there are only about one hundred years left on the reactor."

"So I've heard."

"And you said your wife was taken?"

"Yes."

"The xenotrife don't take prisoners. The only thing they use humans for is killing."

"Pozz that. It wasn't the demons. It was people."

Jennifer finished putting on her clothes. A pair of fitted blue pants, a white blouse, and a long white coat over it. A pair of standard issue boots similar to what he was wearing. She looked better in clothes. There was something disconcerting about the absence of hair.

"People? Sheriff, the Pilgrim is a closed ecosystem."

"I know. They call themselves the Scrappers. I don't know how many there are, but they have weird clothes, and they wear masks. I think to keep them from breathing in the contagion? One of them, their leader I think, his name is Pig. He's got a tattoo on his face. The same eagle that's on all the screens."

"United States Space Force?" she said.

"If that's what it means."

"It is. If he has that tattoo, he's military. Or the descendant of military. We thought all of the soldiers were killed, but some of them stayed outside while we sealed the area, so we didn't have any proof. It's incredible if they survived. Even more incredible if they reproduced." She considered it. "Then again, they would have had access to the main medical facilities and the full stores of emergency rations. If they could find a place to batten the hatches against the trife, it could be they've been riding this out. The Pilgrim is a big ship."

"Maybe. If they have, I think they're getting desperate.

They want to get into Metro real bad. And I witnessed them eating one of their own before they attacked me."

"Cannibalism?"

He nodded.

"Don't judge them for it, Sheriff. You don't know what they may have been through, forced to survive out here."

"That's easy for you to say. I told you, they took my wife. They tried to kill me until they realized I came from Metro, and then they wanted to grab me."

"Did you try talking to them?"

"Twice. The first one nearly shot me. The second, Pig and his followers? I've been a Sheriff a long time, and my father was Sheriff before me. I know when people are up to no good. They had malice in their eyes. I don't care what they've been through, Jenny. That kind of look? It's barely human."

She was silent. Hayden figured she was working out the implications on her own terms.

"So, you know my situation," Hayden said, not waiting for her to finish. "I want to know what happened to get us here. I also want to know what I can do to get us out of it. Foremost, I need to get my wife back from the Scrappers. Maybe you can help me figure out where they've got her? If nothing else, maybe you can help me get some more guns and ammo?"

"They belong on this ship, just like you do, Sheriff," Jennifer said. "Do you really want to kill them?"

"They started it, Jenny. I just want Natalia. I'm damn certain they aren't going to give her back if I ask nicely."

She didn't look happy with the answer, but she nodded. "I'll help you as best I can."

"Good. Start at the beginning, and keep it short and simple. Time isn't on our side."

41

"We don't know where the Xenotrife came from," Jennifer said. She beckoned him to follow while she spoke, leading him away from the bunk where she had retrieved her clothes. "Besides space, I mean." She paused a moment. "It feels weird to talk about it. It feels weird to be here. We never had time to think about what was happening while it was happening. We reacted to the situation as it developed."

"By we, you mean?" Hayden asked.

"The world," she said. "Every government on Earth. I'm sorry, Sheriff. I'm getting ahead of myself. We spent years sending transmissions into space, hoping that something would respond. And they did. At least, we think that's how they figured out we were there. But they didn't pull up in a flying saucer to greet us. At first, we thought they were asteroids. They had the same general size and shape. Their trajectories were bringing them past the planet. They were near-Earth events but nothing that any of the space agencies were worried about. We all thought they would fly harmlessly by."

"Until they didn't," Hayden said.

"They changed course at the last minute. We never

detected anything even remotely resembling engines, but their vectors shifted as they approached, just enough to start spreading them across the planet's surface. Even then, we didn't think they were dangerous. They were small and would likely break up on the way down. I was fourteen when it happened. I still remember watching them hit the thermosphere. The light show was incredible. They burned up, just like the scientists expected. At least, most of them did.

"I woke up the next morning, and when I looked outside, it was like a dust storm had gone through overnight. There were particles. Spores. The remnants of the objects. They were heavier than the air, and they started to settle soon enough. I lived on a farm in Montana. I remember riding to school with my father, marveling at the layer of glistening dust across the wheat fields. It was beautiful. And dangerous. Of course, the government sent scientists to collect samples. Every government did. You can guess what they were shocked to discover."

"The particles were xenotrife?" Hayden said.

"Bingo. Every single one was an alien life form. A xenotrife. Trillions and trillions of them." She smiled sardonically. "You can't imagine what that's like. I know because I can't, and I was there. In one day, our planet was completely overrun with aliens, and we had no way to get rid of them all. We tried. We did our best. Open spaces were burned. Forests were razed. It was a global effort to remove the spores from the surface. An impossible effort. To make matters worse, we tried to nuke them out of existence in the largest open expanses. We didn't know how they responded to radiation then."

"How long did it take them to mature?"

"About two months. Less in the areas where radiation was high. Entire swarms of the things would turn up almost overnight, eager to attack any humans they encountered.

Hundreds of thousands were dead within sixty days of first contact. We didn't realize at first they were carrying the disease. By the six month mark, nearly four billion were dead."

Hayden couldn't wrap his head around a number that large. But he could imagine what kind of chaos an onslaught like that would cause.

"I never thought we would make it much longer than that," Jennifer said. "A year, at most. But the one thing humankind has always been good at is rallying around a common enemy. The governments of the world came together, and we started building weapons of war from entrenched positions around the globe. We learned to fight back, and for six years we managed to keep the xenotrife from destroying us completely. But we lost more people than we created every day, and our time to maturity was much too slow. By year eight, we knew the planet was lost."

"Where does the Pilgrim fit in with that?" Hayden asked.

"A number of governments had been working on Generation ships before the xenotrife arrived. The interest in settling the stars has always been there, and we had the technology. We had the volunteers. We had identified nearly two dozen hospitable destinations within range of our newest reactors. When the xenotrife showed up, we had all the motivation we needed to push the programs forward. I don't know about all of the countries, but the United States had four Generation ships in development. The Pilgrim was one of them. As our strongholds began to fall, the mission parameters were changed. The civilian volunteers were vetted based on education and skillset and then mingled with military families and VIPs. Research teams were sent to each of the ships, equipped with the best tools available, and sequestered in the lab to continue working on a way to stop the virus, and a way to kill the aliens. Our tertiary mission parameter was to create a mutagen that would let us enhance a human soldier. To make them more than human, and able to stand up to hundreds of xenotrife alone. We no longer had the facilities to build tanks and mechs and guns. We needed pure, brute strength."

"I saw cells on my way to the hibernation pods," Hayden said. "The people inside-"

"Were failed attempts to succeed in the tertiary mission. We were making progress on the mutagen. We were making progress on the cure. Not enough progress. We had three months to come up with something, or we had the go-ahead to leave Earth behind. To launch the Pilgrim and hope we had better luck on a new planet. In our case, New Gaia, in the Trappist system."

"Except the xenotrife got on board."

"Yes. I still don't know how. But they managed to breach our defenses and bypass our security. They got onto the ship, and we weren't able to dislodge them. The decision was made to secure Research and Metro and hope the trife would die. We didn't know what else to do."

"What about the PASS?" Hayden asked. "It was altered. So much was erased."

"Can you imagine living in a place where you know death is waiting right on the other side of the walls? Where you know you have a fixed number of years before certain death? We were trying to protect the people inside."

"But didn't they know the truth?"

"The first Generation did. And they took it to their graves. They knew what was at stake for their offspring. What parent would want their child to live that way?"

Hayden nodded. If Natalia had brought their son to full term, would he have wanted his child to know what lay in store for him?

Not a chance.

"And now the Pilgrim is drifting," Hayden said.

"A year distant from New Gaia," Jennifer replied. "That's the way we programmed the computer."

They entered the Command Center. Hayden hadn't realized that's where they were headed. He was too engrossed in her story. She headed over to one of the stations there, tapping the projected keys and entering her password.

WELCOME JENNIFER.

"If I had access to the lead console, I could show you more, but this will have to do."

She kept entering commands until the large display turned on. It showed a three-dimensional outline of the Pilgrim, the schematic he had failed to find earlier.

"We built a sensor that can detect the xenotrife based on their unique chemistry and dietary needs. Every red dot that appears is one of them."

Hayden watched as the ship began to fill in with red dots. Ten at first. Then a hundred. Then four hundred. In the beginning, he expected that there would be thousands of the things, reproducing unfettered for four hundred years. But when the dots stopped appearing, he felt an almost palpable relief.

"Interesting," Jennifer said, staring at the schematic. "There are fewer of them now than there were when we launched. It seems these Scrappers you're so eager to kill have been doing an incredible job of keeping them under control."

"But not eliminated," Hayden said.

"If they are the descendants of soldiers, you might want to consider your position, Sheriff. We left a cache of military gear below Metro. I know you've seen it because you're wearing some of the armor. Think about what these people could do with that equipment."

"I have. They could kill everyone inside the city."

"Or they could finish killing the trife. When those dots are gone, the computer will automatically put the Pilgrim back on course. We'll all be able to go home."

"Is that what you would do, Jen?" he asked, still looking at the red dots. "Let the cannibals into Metro so they can use the gear down there to finish off the xenotrife? Is that what you think I should do?"

"What are the alternatives, Sheriff?" she replied. "Die out here, so close to safety and yet so far?"

"At what point is your life worth more than your humanity? I told you, the Scrappers are killers. How do we know they haven't kept the trife alive as a food source? I heard them talking about eating the things."

The statement took her by surprise. "You did? Trife are poisonous to humans. The levels of radiation would kill them."

"Maybe they've built up an immunity?" he suggested. "A mutation of their own to survive out here. What if they don't know killing them all would get them home?"

"It's possible," she said. "If you don't want to try to reason with them, then what else do you suggest?"

"I did try to reason with them," Hayden said. "It didn't get me anywhere." He pointed at the screen. "Six hundred of those things, give or take. What if I go back to Metro and tell the Governor what we've got? I'm sure we can find some able-bodied citizens to do the rest of the dirty work with the munitions we have on board."

And he was sure Malcolm would forgive him for removing his hand if he brought them back a way to get to their destination.

Jennifer laughed. "I had almost forgotten you got out of Metro through a secured hatch. How did you do that, anyway, Sheriff?"

"It's a long story," Hayden said. "And we don't have time

for it. The important part is that I got out, and I can get back in. There are just two problems."

"Which are?"

"One, if you're right about the Scrappers being the descendants of military, and based on how good a shot Pig is I'm inclined to agree, nobody on Metro will be equipped to deal with them. I don't know if they have it in them to kill another human being, even one that's trying to kill them."

"You did."

"I'm the Sheriff. I do what needs to be done, whether I like it or not."

"And two?"

"Those assholes still have Natalia, and I'm not going back to Metro without her."

"Is she really worth that much to you, Sheriff? I'm sure there are other women in Metro, and that's one loyalty that has no place in a universe like ours."

Hayden's eyes flipped to her, his face flaring with heat. He could have screamed at her, but he held the emotion in check.

"Have you ever been in love, Jenny?" he asked.

"Probably not the way you're thinking," she replied, recognizing she had made him angry. "I'm sorry, Sheriff, but on the Earth I escaped from, love is a luxury few can afford. If you want to save the colony, that's a lesson you need to learn."

"I'd rather save Natalia than save the colony."

She stared at him, not able to understand his perspective. He was okay with that. He couldn't understand hers, either.

"But I think maybe we can save both. The sensor that identifies the trife, can it pick up humans, too? It would be incredibly helpful if I knew how many Scrappers there are, and where they're located."

"No," she said. "There's a standard sensor suite on board,

but the only access to it is through the bridge, and nobody can get into-" She paused. "That's not true, is it, Sheriff? You got out of Metro. You got in here. You can get to the bridge. It's secured with the same sequence."

"Now you're talking. You're saying there's a system there that can show me the position of humans on the ship?"

She nodded. "Yes. But you would need to have an admin password to access it. You can probably get it from Bradshaw's quarters. He liked to keep written copies of everything. He always said he didn't trust machines."

Hayden had no intention of telling her he already had a master code, since she didn't seem to know it. He wanted to trust her, but their differences made him wary.

"I can get with that sentiment," he said. "Where are we in relation to both?"

Jennifer brought the same view of the ship on the smaller display, using her fingers to manipulate it and turn it in space. She pressed a button, and all of the red dots vanished, giving him a decent outline of the Pilgrim.

"We're here, on Deck Eighteen," she said, pointing to a section of the ship. "The Research module was designed as a drop in for this segment of the ship, as were all of the decks from nineteen to thirty. They weren't all sealed, but they are by design a little harder to reach. Only one way in and out from bow to stern." She pointed at the bottom of the ship, right before the hull. "Deck Thirty's module is a hangar. It has four Landers and a few large capacity trucks in it for helping move the city out into the open on the new world." She moved her finger up slightly. "Deck Twenty-nine, that's the one you want. It's a USMC equipment module."

"USMC?" he asked.

"United States Marine Corp. A military branch. The Space Force was founded after the xenotrife arrived. All of the combat units that were assigned to the Generation ships were pulled into the USSF from the USMC, but their equipment was essentially the same. The stuff you found under Metro came from the module. The stuff that would fit through the connecting corridors. Some of it was taken apart and put back together. Anyway, it has a lift down to Deck Thirty to unload. If you want guns and ammo, then that's where you need to go."

"The Scrappers have probably taken everything from it already." He lifted the revolver from his hip. "What about this? Have you seen a weapon like this before?"

She looked at it. "No. But some of the jarheads brought their personal firearms on board. It could be one of theirs. You're right, the Scrappers probably have raided the module already. It may be they spent all the ammunition years ago."

"I've only got eight rounds for this thing," he said. "And a blade."

"Maybe you should reconsider my suggestion to try the Scrappers again? If you tell them you want the same thing they do-"

Hayden put up his hand. "I'm not convinced I want the same thing they do. That option isn't on the table."

Her lips tightened into a firm line, but she didn't argue. She pointed at the schematic again. "Okay, here's the bridge," she said, tapping her finger on a spot near the bow of the Pilgrim, on Deck Four.

"I thought it would be up on top," he said.

"Have you noticed the Pilgrim has no windows?" Jennifer said.

"I've been too busy running to notice."

"Windows don't make sense on starships, despite what you may have seen or read. High-resolution cameras are more than capable. The bridge is here. We can take the central lift here up to Deck Four and-"

"No, we can't take the central lift. That's where I left Pig. He's sure to keep a guard there, waiting for me to turn up."

She was silent for a moment. "Okay, then we can try this route. Central lift down to Deck Twenty-eight, across the mechanical access points here, and then up the bow lift to Deck Four. Or you can take the smaller stairwell here if you're worried about the Scrappers. Bradshaw's quarters are close to the bridge. On the same Deck, here." She pointed to a relatively large suite close to the bridge before showing him the route, tracing it with her finger.

"Can you turn the trife scanner back on?" he asked.

She nodded. The red dots slowly reappeared. A large concentration of them were along the route she had given him.

"Damned if you do and damned if you don't," he said.

"It makes sense. There's more radiation moving through there, and it's not the most hospitable environment for humans." She looked at him. "The good news is, there's a chance Deck Twenty-nine is still stocked. There's enough trife moving through there even the Scrappers may not have tried to run the gauntlet for those supplies. Pick your poison, Sheriff."

"We'll have to take our chances with the xenotrife," he said. "At least they don't have guns."

"You'll have to take your chances," Jennifer said. "I can't go through there. I'm not infected, and I don't plan to be."

"I can't leave you here alone," Hayden said.

"Why not? I've been down here alone for almost four hundred years. This area is secure."

"Okay," he agreed. "Is there anything else down here that might come in handy? Anything at all I can use as a weapon against the trife?"

She considered for a moment.

"I want to show you something."

42

She led him out of the Control Center, through the corridors to the laboratory. He had peeked inside before, but only for long enough to identify it wasn't the hibernation pods.

"I told you before that we had three different mission directives. One, stop the xenotrife virus. Two, create a pathogen to kill the xenotrife. Three, create a mutagen to make humans better able to stand up to the trife."

"I remember," Hayden said. "You said you failed at all three."

"We did," she agreed. "But we were close on the mutagen."

"You were close? I saw the bodies in the cells." He paused. "Tell me something, Jenny."

"What?"

"The colonists you used for the experiments. Were they volunteers?"

She stared back at him, biting her lip. Then she shook her head. "No. Not all of them. We needed a diverse genetic sample, and we only had so many pools to pull from."

"I don't know what that means."

"Different races. Different genetic origins. For example, people with Aboriginal progenitors were more resistant to infection by up to twenty percent."

"Aboriginal?"

"Native Australians. Ten were brought to the Pilgrim with the Research team and integrated into the colony. Unfortunately, none of them survived."

"You were experimenting on people against their will?"

"We were fighting for the continuation of the human race," she said. "Don't you even dare think you can judge me or anyone on the Research team for that."

It wasn't right. Hayden knew it, and he had a feeling she knew it, too. But what choices did they have? He didn't push.

"And you think the mutagen can help me?" he asked.

"Maybe," she said. "That depends."

"On what?"

"You saw what happened to the last round of samples."

"They all died."

"Yes, but not right away." She moved to one of the workstations in the lab, activating it and entering her passcode.

HELLO JENNIFER.

She typed onto the projected keyboard until the display shifted to a video of one of the subjects. He was slight of frame, standing naked in front of one of the hatches Hayden was pretty sure had been sealed.

The door started to open. A pair of xenotrife ducked beneath it as it rose, rushing right toward the man. He didn't move as they approached, remaining still.

The first one reached him. It slashed out at him with its claws.

He moved, slipping aside, his body a hair's breadth from the claws. His hand lashed out, crashing into the trife's skull. A loud crack and the creature fell dead.

The second tried to come at him from behind. He ducked

as it pounced at him, backing up, grabbing its head and twisting. Another crack and it too fell dead.

The man turned to face the camera.

"How was that?" he asked.

A third xenotrife rushed in from the doorway. The man couldn't possibly see it. There was no warning. It was diving toward him when he ducked, bringing his arms up and grabbing it on the way over him and slamming it hard into the floor, breaking its hollow bones and killing it.

Jennifer stopped the recording.

"What am I looking at?" Hayden said.

"One of the mutagen samples. G71C. It was a mutation that made the nervous system more sensitive to the radiation given off by the trife. Kind of like trife lidar. It gave the subject an advantage in agility against them, allowing him to sense their movements, sometimes before they made them. It was one of the most successful alterations, but it was judged too limited. Against three, it was effective. Against thirty?"

"What happened to him?"

"He died like the rest. The mutations typically wind up causing either an enhanced immune response or a higher incidence of cancer. Either outcome was fatal within a number of weeks."

"But if I'm already infected?"

"All of the mutagens provide a secondary benefit of immunity to the contagion. That's why we were working on it as a tertiary directive. The problem was we weren't able to eliminate the side effects that lead to an equally premature death."

"So the disease won't kill me, but the mutation will?"

"Exactly."

"And that's why it depends. Because I have a ten percent chance of surviving the infection."

"Yes."

"What are my odds of surviving the mutation?"

"None of the subjects survived."

"But if you give me this, I'll have a better chance of making it through the xenotrife."

"Yes."

Hayden sighed. Ten percent was lousy, but it was something. What were the chances both he and Natalia beat those odds? Slim was still more than none. Nothing was nothing. No chance for him at all. But he could still save her. He could still get her back. She wasn't contagious unless she was bitten, and he doubted she had been bitten. Once Jennifer told Malcolm the whole truth about the contagion he would let her back in, and if Hayden could take care of the xenotrife? She would have a chance to make it to New Gaia. A ten percent chance. Maybe more. She had some Asian blood in her. Did that give her better odds? What if Jen could continue her research and come up with a cure before time was up? It was a longshot, but it wasn't impossible.

Or maybe Jenny was right? Maybe he should give the Scrappers another chance? Maybe they weren't too far gone to accept that helping one another would give them all a fresh start? He thought back to his encounter with Gizzie. He didn't understand why the girl had been so ready to kill him after the Insiders and the Outsiders had been parted for so many years. And then when he had confronted Pig, they had laughed in his face as though they were enemies, not long separated friends. They wanted to force him to act, not work with him. How could they hold such animosity toward the colonists when they were all stuck on the Pilgrim together?

Unless they had been abandoned? Was it possible the soldiers had been left behind, left for dead and trapped with the xenotrife? That would have made him plenty angry, too. And what if not all of the Scrappers were as violent as Pig? If he took away their primary food source and killed their leader, could he negotiate peace with the rest?

What if he could make it to Deck Twenty-nine and the USMC equipment there? If he could pick up fresh supplies, reach the bridge and get an accurate view of the opposition, it would be a major step in the right direction.

He looked at the schematic again, following the red dots along the suggested route.

First, he had to get there.

"Sheriff?" Jennifer said, waiting for his response.

He was the one who had gotten Outside. He was the one who could make things right.

He could sacrifice himself to save her.

He could sacrifice himself to save them all.

He looked at Jennifer. He wasn't sure it was the right thing to do. Maybe the whole thing was a huge mistake. What were the chances he would be able to accomplish all of that on his own?

It might be the only way to save Natalia.

He had to try.

"It won't kill me?" he asked.

"Not immediately, no."

"How long does it take to start working?"

"About four hours. It'll knock you out for a while, but you're safe down here."

"That's a long time."

"You know the options. It's your call, Sheriff."

He thought about Natalia.

He had to try.

"Do it," he said.

She nodded, heading over to the corner of the room and opening the front of a large, stainless steel box. A freezer. Hayden could see hundreds of vials stored in it, marked with different colored labels depending on what kind of chemical concoction they were.

"Are you sure they're still good?" he asked.

"Yes. I'm just glad the freezer didn't break down."

She took a syringe from a nearby cabinet, using the needle to pull some of the clear liquid from the vial into it. He watched it pool there, still trying to decide if he was doing the right thing.

"What will it feel like?" he asked.

"The subject described it as 'seeing fire.' He could feel the movement of the trife around him as a burning on his skin. The reaction to it came naturally."

"Seeing fire. Right. Am I doing the right thing, Jenny?"

She glanced up at him. "You know what I think, Sheriff. You took that option off the table."

Hayden didn't respond. He didn't know why he had asked.

"You'll need to roll down the armor so I can get to your arm," she said.

He nodded, unzipping the body armor. He pulled it away from his chest and shoulders, careful the identification chip didn't get dislodged from its spot below his wrist.

"You promise this will work?" he said.

"You pulled me out of hibernation for a reason," she replied.

"For answers."

"I gave you my answers."

"I have to be honest; I didn't like them all that much."

She smirked. "I don't like them either. It is what it is."

"Well said."

"Keep your arm relaxed," she said, pushing a small amount of the mutagen from the tip of the needle.

He shook it out to relax the muscles. She stood beside him, running her hand on his arm to find the vein.

"Ready?"

He nodded. "Yeah."

She jabbed it into him. He could feel the liquid spilling out into his arm.

He hoped he was doing the right thing.

"You'll start to get sleepy within a few minutes," she said. "And your muscles will feel weak. It's normal."

"Pozz that," he said. He was already starting to feel warmer.

She stepped back, putting the syringe next to the small vial she had pulled the mutagen from. His eyes followed it, stopping when they landed on the vial. The label was white. The text printed on it said 'Ketalar.'

He looked from the vial to her and back to the vial. She was staring at him.

"That's not the mutagen," he said, realizing she had given him something else.

"No," she admitted. "G71C would have killed you within a few days, and I couldn't bring myself to do that to you. This is an anesthetic. It's going to put you to sleep."

He wanted to push himself to his feet and pull the armor back on, but he found he didn't have the energy or the will to do it.

"Why?" he said. "I trusted you."

"You trusted me to a point. I don't know why you let me inject anything into you, but you didn't admit you know the admin code, or that you have security clearance implanted in your identification chip. Only the Governor is supposed to have that, but I guess he made an exception for you?"

Hayden struggled not to tell her the truth about the chip. His ability to resist anything was fading. "I just want to save my wife and Metro."

"I want to save Metro, too, Sheriff. I want to save as many of the people on the Pilgrim as I can, including myself. The

Scrappers are trained soldiers. They're survivors. Once they have access to the supplies under Metro, they'll finish off the xenotrife, and we can all go home."

"They'll kill the civilians," Hayden said, his voice weakening, the light fading away from his eyes. "I'm telling you."

"They won't kill one another, and they won't kill me," she replied. "I'm willing to risk it. That's the difference between you and me."

"I woke you up," Hayden said.

"And you think I owe you something for that? You brought me into your fucking nightmare. Thanks a whole lot. You didn't do yourself any favors, but you did help out the people you swore to protect. Somebody is going to live because of you; it just might not be you or your wife. I'm sorry if you regret it now."

She turned away, leaving the laboratory. Hayden tried to stand, finding his legs had no strength and stumbling onto the floor.

His world went dark.

43

HAYDEN'S EYES OPENED TO A WORLD OF BLURRY WHITE BOXES resting on narrow metal legs, a hard gray floor, and a horrible headache.

"Natalia," he said, his first thought of his wife.

A sense of panic crept over him when he realized he wasn't in his bed back in his cube, and she wasn't there with him.

It calmed only slightly a moment later when he remembered where he was. Special Officer Jennifer Kozlaski. She had drugged him. Knocked him out on his ass.

He pushed himself to his knees. The body armor was heavy on him, gathered at his back where he had shifted it so she could inject his arm. What the hell had he been thinking? He was going to let her dope him up with a gene mutating serum. Was he getting that desperate?

He was.

He heard rattling, and something fell off the counter, landing beside him.

Huh?

He tried to stand, but the ship was moving beneath him, trying to knock him back off-balance.

Turbs, he realized. He had never experienced them from anywhere other than Metro. They seemed more subdued here, where there was less equipment to knock loose. Not that it made it any easier to stand.

He tried to shake the sleep from his eyes. How long was he out? There was a clock on the terminal a few meters ahead of him. He stumbled toward it, catching himself on his hands when he fell forward. Thirty minutes. He had only been out for thirty minutes.

He struggled to pull the armor back on, getting it straight on his back and letting himself fall against a counter to ride out the shaking. It was already fading. Had he slept through the worst of it?

He grabbed at the armor's zipper and pulled it all the way up, the motion signaling it to condense against his body. It hurt where it pressed against the injection site, but he ignored it.

Stupid. He was so stupid. He felt for the identification chip beneath his wrist. It was still there. He was lucky Jenny had decided not to cut off his wrist, thinking his chip was keyed with the security clearance. He was lucky she hadn't discovered Malcolm's chip, either.

But then, where the hell had she gone?

He felt a pang of guilt. He knew where she had gone. To find the Scrappers. To talk to Pig. Maybe to bring him back down here? Did her code give her access to this area?

For all he knew, they were on their way.

He reached up, grabbing the edge of the counter and yanking himself to his feet. His legs were still unsteady, but he managed to stay upright, hanging onto nearby equipment to guide himself to the door. There was no time.

He moved out into the corridor. There was only one way

out of the area. He had to go back to the lift, even if the Scrappers might be coming for him from the same place.

He leaned against the wall, pushing his legs to move as quickly as he could manage. It wasn't very fast at all. They were weak and tired and unprepared. He made it thirty meters before he fell again, his left leg refusing to hold him up.

"Come on, damn it," he said to himself, smacking his leg with his arm. He got up and kept going, racing for the lift.

The turbs continued to lessen, fading away to the softest of vibrations. He hobbled through the corridor, wondering what he was going to do when he made it to the lift. It was crazy to descend, to take the path Jennifer had suggested. There were too many xenotrife, and he was too damn weak. What else could he do? He wasn't going up, and there were no other directions.

He reached the Command Center, the door opening at his approach. Just as he stumbled inside, the hatch on the other side of the room started to open.

He dove behind one of the workstations to avoid being seen. He crouched there, looking through a small crack between the legs of the desk to the center of the room. Two pairs of dirty boots appeared there a moment later.

"I don't think I've seen anything this clean in my life," one of the wearers said.

"That's because you been wandering too long, mate," the other said.

Hayden cursed under his breath. Damn it. He hadn't made it in time.

"That was something, the way Pig did that bitch," the first one said. "Right in front of everybody like that. And not a lick of hair on her entire body."

"I've never seen an adult woman like that before. I wish I could've got me a turn."

"Don't worry mate. I'm sure she'll taste just as good cooked."

The first one laughed. "Oldest woman he ever did. That's what he said. Har har."

The second one joined him. "Prime aged beef," he said, laughing. "Like a fine wine."

Hayden felt sick. Jennifer had left him unconscious down here to find the Scrappers and try to reason with them. Instead, they had taken what she had to give before attacking her.

He wanted to say he was surprised, but he wasn't. He had read them right the first time. It didn't stop him from being guilty or angry, emotions he had every intention of taking out on the two men. He could only hope she hadn't told Pig his plan.

"Let's just find the Insider and get back to Pig. The sooner we can get out of here, the happier I'll be."

"Aww, are you afraid of a few bugs?"

"It's been more than a few. And yeah, I think it's only a matter of time before one of them gets its claws into me."

"I don't see him in here, do you?"

"Are you kidding? Let's go that way."

He watched the boots start moving, heading for the corridor he had just emerged from. There was no way they were going to walk past without noticing him.

He reached for the revolver, moving as slowly and deliberately as he dared so he wouldn't make a sound. The Scrappers were drawing nearer, reaching the other side of the station he was hiding behind.

Hayden grabbed Baby with his other hand, moving his arm behind his body so he could get some momentum going in any swing. The first Scrapper reached his position, head up and looking out toward the corridor beyond. He was carrying one of the electric spears in his hands, ready to use it.

His head turned as Hayden threw his arm forward, swinging Baby in a short arc toward the Scrapper's leg. It caught on the man's calf, digging in deep and taking him by surprise.

"Ah, my grepping leg," the man shouted, at the same time Hayden brought the revolver around. At this range, it was impossible to miss.

He pulled the trigger, the large shell punching into the Scrapper's gut and exploding out of his back, continuing into one of the workstations and destroying it in a shower of sparks. The body started to collapse as Hayden rotated his gun hand toward the second Scrapper.

He was caught as unaware as the first, and he scrambled to stab out at Hayden with his spear, his attack nowhere near close to making contact. Hayden raised the revolver and fired, the round destroying his opponent's chest.

If they were military, they weren't very skilled military.

He leaned over the first, quickly rifling through the pocket in his robe and checking him for weapons. The man was only carrying the spear, which attached to a pack he wore on his back. It was too big and bulky to be useful.

Hayden crouched beside the second body, finding it was armed similarly to the first. Had Pig taken their guns to ensure they wouldn't kill him? It wasn't out of the question.

He continued toward the lift, his body still waking up. It was getting easier to move, but he was nowhere near one hundred percent.

The hatch to the lift opened ahead of him. Two more Scrappers were rushing his way, responding to the gunshots they had heard. Neither seemed to be carrying a gun because when Hayden raised the revolver in their direction, they both looked surprised and afraid. The weapon echoed in the passage, twin cracks that saw both the remaining Scrappers drop in sprays of blood and bone.

He paused beside each, checking them. He pulled more of the torn pieces of paper from one of their pockets, and a pair of smaller caliber bullets from the other. The rounds were useless without a matching weapon, so he dropped them on the floor. He was getting to his feet when a crackle of static next to one of the bodies alerted him to a transceiver.

He moved to that Scrapper, pushing the man's robes out of the way and finding the device. It was roughly square, with a long, wide antenna extending from the top of it. He picked it up.

"Sergeant Dunn, what's your status?" Pig's voice was like gravel over the transceiver. "Sergeant Dunn, come in." There was a pause before the man repeated the message.

Hayden brought the box to his face. It had a trigger on the side, and he depressed it to speak.

"You didn't have to kill her," he said.

"Insider," Pig said, sounding almost happy to hear from him. "Is that you?"

"I'm afraid so," Hayden replied.

"I did have to kill her, my friend. Nobody, and I mean nobody, likes a snitch. And she gave you up to me like a whore gives up her nethers. Negotiate? Grep that. We take what we want. I take what I want. I assume my boys are dead?"

"Very," Hayden said.

"A little more pain I owe you, then. If your woman was still with me, I'd make her pay for your indiscretion. She might even enjoy it."

"Where is she?" Hayden asked, clenching his teeth.

"I told you, friend. She's on her way."

"What the hell does that mean?"

"I'm on Deck Three. Come on up, and I'll show you."

"If you hurt her, I'll-"

Hayden stopped talking when Pig interrupted in a fit of laughter.

"That's cute. Real cute. You aren't going to do a grepping thing to me. Do you know why? Because you're soft, and I'm hard. You're paper, and I'm steel. But don't worry Sheriff, we wouldn't dream of hurting an Engineer of any kind. We have needs, and bitches like your wife? They're the key to the future. You want to talk more, come on up. I'll be waiting."

The transceiver clicked as Pig disconnected. Hayden stood there trembling with anger. What else had Jennifer told the Scrapper about him before he killed her?

It didn't matter. One of them was going to die. That much was guaranteed.

He reached the lift, activating the control panel and calling it to him. He backed away, propping one of the Scrapper corpses up in front of him and aiming the revolver while he waited for it to arrive. He expected an ambush when the doors opened, but none came. The lift wasn't empty, though.

Special Officer Jennifer Kazlaski's naked and bloody body was lying face up inside. The stomach had been cut with a knife, scarred with the word 'bitch.' Only the 'b' had been crossed out with a line and 'sn' added above it.

More surprising was that the cutting wasn't the worst of it. Her left hand was missing, cut off above the wrist. There was no question Pig was sending him a message. He knew about the identification chip, and what it could do. He didn't need to take Hayden alive. Not anymore. He was going to take what he wanted.

Hayden huffed out a breath, fighting against the disgust. He stepped into the lift, leaving Jennifer's body in place as he keyed in '29.'

44

He had the revolver reloaded and in his left hand, Baby in his right, when the lift reached Deck Twenty-nine. According to the schematic he had seen, he would only be a hundred meters or so from the USMC module that had been loaded into the ship beneath Research.

A hundred meters populated by at least twenty xenotrife.

That fact hadn't caused him to hesitate to descend instead of heading uplevel and taking his chances with the Scrappers. He could hear the evil in Pig's voice. The arrogant malice. He didn't know how many people the tyrant had with him, but he knew Pig scared him more than the trife did.

His only regret was that Jennifer hadn't given him the mutation she had promised. Or more importantly, it wasn't as effective as she had promised. She said he would have been dead in a few days. Maybe it would have been worth it?

Her time had been cut short. Incredibly short. She had gambled and lost, refusing to listen to him or any of his warnings about the Scrappers. He didn't blame her. Not completely. She was right; he had woken her up to a nightmare. One she just wanted to escape from.

He glanced down at her body. It was a reminder of what Pig and the Scrappers were capable of. More than cannibalism. More than murder. Outsiders were objects to them. Things to use and discard. Whatever had happened to them over the years to make them that way, it wasn't an excuse. They had turned to evil by choice.

At least the xenotrife were being what they were supposed to be and doing what they were supposed to do.

The lift slowed as it reached the deck. Hayden's body was almost awake again, and he knew he would need every ounce of his strength. He couldn't fight that many trife on his own. He had to run, and hope he made it to the module's hatch.

Even that might not be enough.

He tried to prepare himself to accept death, but he found it impossible. He couldn't accept it. Not until Natalia was away from the Scrappers. Not until she was safe.

The lift stopped. Hayden crouched, testing his legs, preparing them to run. He raised Baby into position to swing the blade. He had used four of his nine rounds, leaving the revolver with an empty chamber.

The door slid open.

He pushed off, leaving Jennifer's body behind, catching sight of the module hatch directly ahead, a mass of darkness to its left. He managed two steps before the mass changed, shifting and moving, the trife unwrapping themselves from one another.

He didn't make it to them before he was attacked. There were trife on the other side of the lift, and they hissed at his back, forcing him to turn his attention that way. They rushed toward him, and he swung his left arm back and fired the revolver. A single round blasted through the first of them, his luck holding as the bullet exploded through it and into a second, knocking both down.

He counted each footstep, his eyes dancing around the hub. He could feel the increased warmth down here. He could smell the trife, sweet and sticky like the reproductive gel that had gotten onto him.

He covered ten meters. The bundle of trife revealed half a dozen, though they were moving slower than he expected as they reacted from a relaxed state. He fired the revolver again, into the mass, the slug tearing through parts of three of them, barely slowed by their hollow bones. They hissed and screeched.

One of them dove at him from his left. He caught it on the corner of the armor, its claws skidding off the shoulder plate. He rolled it past him, not letting it slow his momentum. He heard a hiss over his head, looking up as one dropped toward him. He raised Baby over his head, letting the creature impale itself on the weapon and then swinging it and throwing it forward, into one of the demons ahead of him.

He jumped over them both, still charging for the hatch. One of them reached up, catching his leg as he passed, claws digging into the softer armored material. It got stuck on something, and Hayden was brought face-first to the ground.

He kicked back, hitting the arm and freeing himself, struggling desperately to get back to his feet. A trife jumped toward him, and he barely managed to get the revolver up to squeeze off a round, detonating its head in a spray of dark blood. He stood up, eyes flailing, realizing they were surrounding him, eight in all.

They were motionless around him. Two at his back. Two on the ceiling in front of the hatch. Two on either side. They had maneuvered intelligently, holding back to get into position instead of attacking.

Eight xenotrife. One bullet.

He looked back at the hatch. It was still fifty meters away.

Damn it.

He wasn't ready to die.

"Come on then," he said, shouting at them. "Come on. Do it. Let's go."

He waved Baby around himself, threatening them. They hissed in response. But it wasn't the same hiss he had heard before. It was in a variable burst of length and pitch.

They were talking to one another.

Then the hissing stopped. They all fell silent. Hayden could hear himself breathing, the air ragged through his throat. He gripped Baby a little tighter, tensing his legs again.

One of the trife screeched, and then they were all on the move. So was Hayden. He burst forward again, focused on the two by the hatch. They leaped from their positions, long jumps sending them arcing toward him. He only had one round. He raised the revolver and fired, hitting the first of them square in the chest and knocking it away. The second landed only a meter ahead of him, swinging its claws at the same time.

He barely ducked beneath them, slashing at the demon with Baby. It shifted aside, avoiding the blow, turning and lashing out with a foot. It caught Hayden in the side, sending him reeling toward the pair in that direction.

He spun off-balance, letting himself fall, dropping the gun and using his now free hand to stop himself on the floor, pivoting on the hand and swinging the blade. It caught one of the trife in the neck, nearly severing its head as it was thrown aside. He shouted in triumph as he stabbed the second, driving Baby hard into its chest and then kicking it away.

He started rotating back toward the hatch, five of the trife remaining.

Out of the corner of his eye, he saw the lift door slide open again.

A handful of Scrappers were inside. They poured out of the lift, guns in hand. Pig wasn't with them, but that didn't make them any less dangerous.

The crack of gunfire followed. Hayden didn't look back. He sprinted for the hatch, hearing the bullets whizzing past him. One round caught his armor at the calf, hitting a plate there. Another grazed his shoulder, sending a feeling of moist warmth along his arm. Had it made it through the armor? Dozens of rounds punched into the trife, dropping them in a fading chorus of hissing.

The hatch slid open as he approached, just like in the Research module on the next deck up. He stopped on the other side, finding the door control. The trife in the hub were dead, the Scrappers turning their attention to him. They were all wearing the robes and masks, trying to keep themselves from getting the creature's disease.

Hayden tapped on the control, quickly entering the master admin code into the panel. Bullets began to hit the area around him, a few of them striking his armor. He put his other arm in front of his head to protect it, rewarded when a round struck the small ballistic plate on the back of his hand.

He finished keying in the code, hoping his luck would hold out and it would have the effect he wanted. He nearly cried out in triumph again as the hatch slid closed in front of him.

He breathed heavily, slumping against the wall. A few rounds pinged off the metal of the hatch, followed by a few seconds of silence. Then the Scrappers started thumping against the door, trying to convince it to open with brute force. Then the thumping stopped.

Hayden was still for a few seconds, but only a few

seconds. He hurried back to his feet, turning to face the inside of the module. He was sure the Scrappers hadn't given up.

There were two more entrances to the module not counting the ventilation shafts.

He wasn't even close to being safe.

45

HAYDEN MOVED THROUGH THE ENTRANCE CORRIDOR OF THE module, reaching the second hatch only a dozen meters in. It opened as he neared, and where the Research module had placed a command center, he discovered a mess instead.

Metal tables and chairs sat abandoned in the room, a few thrown into the corner but most of them still in place, with enough seats for an entire platoon of soldiers. A small kitchen sat on the right in front of a bartop with indents for different foods. A large refrigeration unit sat behind it, dark and silent.

There were two hatches connecting to the mess. A dead soldier lay in the middle of one of them, preventing the hatch from closing. That didn't stop it from sliding back and forth, and by the looks of it, the thing had been repeating the motion for a long time. Hayden found he was able to appreciate the irony of the hatch. So many other things on the ship had broken. The food refrigerator here. Eleven of the twelve hibernation pods on the deck above. Countless pieces of technology in Metro.

The door kept going after countless repetitions.

Hayden approached the soldier, leaning down and reaching for the rifle at his side. He noticed the blood when he did, a stain of it marking the edge of the body armor. It didn't hurt all that much. He turned his arm over, checking the wound. A bullet had grazed him, just enough to draw blood. It was one of too many that had hit him; his life preserved only by the design of the armor he was wearing.

He returned his attention to the rifle, picking it up. The power was switched on. The display was dead. He grabbed the magazine and pulled it out. Empty. It wasn't carrying a secondary magazine with the explosive spheres inside.

He moved past the soldier, into the area beyond. A long, narrow corridor with two levels of bunks on either side, a slim locker beside each. He opened a couple of them, finding nothing useful inside. Hangers for uniforms, some fading photographs. One locker had a torn and cracked image of a woman standing on a beach, the sun setting behind her. She was wearing a white dress, her hair bent and folded on top of her head, her feet invisible in the water. Another had a larger image of a naked woman, her breasts way out of proportion to the size of her body. Hayden didn't understand why it was there.

He bypassed the room, heading into the adjacent one. It too was long and narrow, a series of spigots reaching out from the walls and a drain in the floor. A shower, followed by a latrine. The smell was horrible, and he turned around and went back the other way. What he was looking for was likely in the other direction.

He passed the mess and through the second hatch, into a long corridor with doors on either side. What looked like an Officer's office. A small conference room, a larger meeting room. There was a hatch at the other end which led into a small connecting segment with a third hatch on the side. It slid open, revealing the target of his desire.

An open space greeted him. Lockers like the ones below Metro sat against one wall. On the opposite side three hundred meters away, a pair of lanes with targets at the end. Next to that was a rack.

It was loaded with weapons.

Hayden's eyes widened at the sight of it. There were rifles, the same kind he had carried before. But there were other weapons, too. Different kinds of pistols, larger long guns, and a few other things with triggers but no obvious ammunition. It was all arranged neatly, ready to be lifted and fired at the targets on the far end. A rack of magazines and cartridges of different shapes and sizes sat beside it.

He couldn't believe his luck. All of these years and the room had gone unnoticed. Undisturbed. The United States Marine Corp equipment was all present and intact. He didn't quite understand how that could be. Didn't the Scrappers know this was down here? Why hadn't their forebears taken the weapons and used them against the xenotrife? Or did they know the cache was here, but they had never needed to make use of it? They seemed to be doing just fine without it, why not leave it in place and save it for an emergency?

He was going to make a move for the weapons, but that was when he noticed the floor in the center of the room vanished into shadow and light. He remembered what Jennifer had said about the lift between this deck and the next, installed to transport the equipment more efficiently to the vehicles in what should be the hangar below.

He moved to the edge and looked down.

A pile of debris rested on the floor of the hangar, two dozen or so suits of some kind of metal armor flung across the ground, along with heavier equipment and ordnance. Massive guns too large to carry, small projectiles spilled from broken containers. Bits and pieces of other broken equipment he couldn't identify.

And a mass of xenotrife resting beside it.

He froze at the sight of them. The group was much bigger than the one he had discovered earlier, at least a hundred or more pressing tightly against one another. While it was heavily coated in the creature's thick reproductive slime, it was also currently motionless.

The lift must have collapsed during one of the turbs. Age and wear had probably caused the mechanism to fail, the weight of the abandoned armor and weaponry on top putting added pressure on the systems. It appeared the trife had moved in after that, surrounding an area near the collapse. Why had they gathered here, of all places?

They thrived on radiation. Something down there had to be giving off some form of it.

Hayden backed away from the edge. He turned his eyes back to the lockers, and then to the guns in the corner. He needed those weapons. He just had to be quiet and careful.

He walked over to them, watching every step he took to make sure he didn't trip over anything. His boots were clicking on the floor, and he hoped the trife's state would prevent them from noticing the sound. He couldn't go too slowly. The Scrappers were making their way back to him, and they were sure to be eager to stop him from taking their guns. He had to find the right balance of speed and silence, and at a minimum be ready to confront whichever enemy confronted him.

He made it over to the rack and looked over the weapons. He quickly grabbed a pair of pistols that matched the indents in his armor, loading them with fresh magazines, careful to tuck them under his arms and turn his back on the trife nest as he did to minimize the noise. He also picked up a fresh rifle, adding a regular magazine to it before discovering there were no explosive rounds to be had. It probably didn't make sense to let the soldiers fire such damaging ammunition at targets inside a spacecraft. It didn't make much sense to let soldiers waste ammunition on target practice at all. The module was probably a standard design, one that could be dropped into more than just starships. He could imagine a number of them being linked together to form bases for larger armies.

He snapped the rifle onto his back, having to adjust it a few times to get it to stick. The plating there had been hit multiple times, saving his life but damaging the magnets or whatever held the weapon in the process. After that, he looked over the guns he didn't recognize.

One had a long barrel and a small chamber at the back. It took Hayden a few seconds to locate the ammunition for it, picking up a cylindrical cartridge from the shelves beside the rack. The letters L-I-N were etched into it. He thought it was a curious weapon because it was light in his hand, and the cartridge barely had any weight at all. How could something like this do much damage? He wasn't sure how it worked, but he held onto it anyway, the lack of weight making it easy to carry.

He picked up a second firearm. A pistol. This one was also fairly light and didn't seem to carry any ammunition. It had a switch on the side, and when he flipped it a small display on the top showed a count of 0 with a hollow battery icon below it, indicating it was out of power. He searched the ammunition for a moment, finding a rounded rectangular piece that matched one in the gun's grip. He figured out how to eject the first and loaded the fresh one, turning it on and seeing in now registered one hundred from a full charge.

One hundred what?

He was tempted to keep at it, but he had been ticking off seconds in his head, and he had a feeling his time was running short. He had to decide if he should return to the lift behind him or continue to the hatch he knew would be at the bow end of the ship. It was possible, even likely, that Pig had stationed Scrappers at both ends. He had reloaded, but that didn't make him any more impervious to their bullets.

He started moving back the way he had come, remaining cautious where he stepped. He glanced down at the xenotrife nest below, ensuring the creatures were still distracted by the afterglow of their reproductive cycle, or whatever the hell it was.

He reached the hatch where he had entered, at the point where he had to make a final decision about his path forward.

He heard an echo behind him, back at the entrance to the module. The supposedly locked hatch sliding open. His thoughts dialed back to Jennifer's severed hand.

She had clearance to the USMC module?

The decision had been made for him. He started moving around the edge of the collapsed floor, his pace a little quicker. He could hear the boots echoing in the corridors behind him, the Scrappers getting closer.

He heard motion in front of him as well. More footfalls. More of the murderous gang.

He was surrounded.

He cradled the strange, lighter rifle he had claimed. It didn't fire projectiles; he knew that much. Whatever came out of the barrel, would it make a sound? If the xenotrife nest below him became active, they were all going to be in a shitload of trouble.

The first of the Scrappers emerged from the corridor ahead of him. A woman, judging by her size, though she was impossible to see beneath the mask and goggles. She wasn't alone, flanked by a pair of larger men with more bringing up the rear. They were armed with revolvers and rifles that looked pitiful compared to the cache he had found.

The second group of Scrappers poured out behind him at

nearly the same time, close to a dozen, leaving him to wonder how many of them there were. He still didn't see Pig among them. Where was their leader in all of this?

He raised the muzzle of the rifle to his lips before motioning to the hole in the floor by flicking his head. The female Scrapper followed his motion, glancing down. Hayden couldn't see her face, but he noticed how her body tensed at the sight of the nest.

The Scrappers behind him saw it, too. They moved toward him more quietly, doing their best not to make a sound. The first group followed suit, closing in on him in silence.

He was surrounded, the noose tightening inch by inch. He looked down at his weapon. Why had he picked it up if he wasn't going to use it?

He squeezed the trigger.

He heard a soft whoosh, a motor somewhere in the gun spinning up and firing out a jet of compressed air. That air was mixed with whatever was in the cartridge, and an instant later a stream of freezing gas exploded from the muzzle, reaching out and hitting the lead Scrapper ahead of him, still four meters away.

It took about two seconds, and then she started screaming, turning and trying to escape from the gas, which moved around her and into the group of Scrappers behind. They turned away in fear as well, trying to avoid the nearly invisible cloud that suddenly seemed to be coating their robes.

Hayden spun around, redirecting the weapon toward the Scrappers behind him. They were caught off-guard by his attack and hesitant to fire their guns and wake the xenotrife. The blast of super-frigid air reached them, forcing them to turn away.

He looked down into the hangar below at the mass of

trife. At first, he didn't think the screaming was enough to disturb them. Then they started to slowly untangle.

He heard the click of a revolver's hammer locking back in preparation. He didn't know what he had thought was going to happen, but it wasn't like he had a plan. He was completely dependent on instinct, luck, and a massive will to live.

As he threw himself over the edge of the collapsed floor toward the deck below, he hoped it would be enough.

46

Without the armor, the fall probably would have caused him to break at least one of his legs, and probably a few of his ribs.

With the armor, he still found himself engulfed in burning pain, his limbs slamming down on the uneven surface, his back cracking on the solid arm of one of the spilled metal suits at the bottom.

He rolled off the obstacle without hesitating, pulling himself away from the floor above as gunfire rained down on him. The Scrappers' aim wasn't great, and while a couple of the bullets scored hits on his body armor's plating, most of them kicked up settled dirt and dust around him.

And served to wake the xenotrife.

He couldn't believe the Scrappers were that stupid, but it seemed the screaming from the front lines and the subsequent motion from the trife had convinced them they were screwed anyway. Hayden had seen what Pig did to soldiers who didn't follow orders, and he could imagine the same fate would await them if they went home empty-handed.

Too bad.

He got out from under the line of fire, pushing himself to his feet and continuing to back away. He glanced back to get a feel for the hangar. It was bigger than he had expected, stretching back beneath Deck Twenty-nine for at least six hundred meters. There were vehicles lined up back there, four huge wheeled behemoths with massive flat backs, which supposedly had some means of pulling pieces of Metro out of the ship and onto the flat earth of their new homeworld if they ever reached it. The size of the trucks was the reason his fall had been almost twenty meters instead of the usual three or four. The hangar was cavernous.

And dangerous.

The top layer of xenotrife were climbing down from their nest group, still moving fairly slowly. A fresh round of cracks from above and they stuttered and stumbled, knocked back by the fire from the recovering Scrappers, who had forgotten about him for the moment, at least.

The demons didn't. He heard a hiss from his left, and one of them came out from behind a large, rectangular vehicle with four landing skids instead of wheels and what looked like huge rocket motors jutting out from the rear. It scampered toward him on all four, springing off its back feet and spreading its front claws as it neared.

Hayden lifted his weapon and pulled the trigger, sending a gout of gas out toward the xenotrife. It howled in sudden agony, its flesh shriveling beneath the assault. Even after Hayden turned the weapon away, it continued to hiss and shrink and die, its physiology unable to stand up to the attack.

What the hell?

He looked down at the weapon. Why was this the only one of these guns he had seen when it seemed so incredibly effective against the trife? Was it experimental?

If so, the experiment was a success.

He turned around, watching as more of the trife spread away from the nest, breaking up and scaling the walls, able to cling to the top of the ceiling on their way to confront the Scrappers. More of them had caught sight of him as well, and they unfurled from the pile, casting off the sticky goop and rushing toward him en masse.

He scanned the hangar for an exit to the rest of the deck, finding one at the rear of the space past all of the massive loaders. He started running, painfully aware of the trife at his back as he charged toward what he hoped would be freedom.

Then that hatch slid open, revealing another contingent of Scrappers behind it. They charged into the space, aiming rifles that looked more modern than what the first group carried. Hayden changed direction immediately, rushing to get behind cover as the bullets started to fly.

A dozen trife were dead in seconds, knocked down by the sudden onslaught. Then they too adjusted to the new threat, breaking apart and surging behind cover in an effort to reach the enemy unharmed. A pair of them rushed toward Hayden, and he triggered his weapon, watching with satisfaction as they hissed and died.

The Scrappers on the floor above started to scream. Hayden looked back toward the nest in time to see one fall from the height, his lifeless corpse crashing to the floor. More bullets and hisses followed, and the constant muzzle flashes lit up the hangar like a celebration.

Hayden peered out from the corner of the loader, around the side of a huge tire. The Scrappers had taken defensive positions closer to the hatch, blocking off his chance at escape. Meanwhile, the trife were closing in on him, catching him in between two hostile armies.

He charged back toward the debris, and back toward the nest. Trife hissed and charged, but he engulfed them in the freezing mist, sending them to their deaths.

Gunfire rattled around him, bullets kicking up the destruction nearby. Hissing and screaming filled his ears. He started climbing the pile of debris, turning his head and locating another hatch in the direction of the bow.

Another strong hiss alerted him to an incoming trife. Hayden saw it almost too late, barely managing to catch its teeth on his shoulder plate instead of his neck, turning it with his body and shoving the gun in its gut. He pulled the trigger, and it jumped back, crumpling to the ground.

Another one took its place. Then another. And then another. In seconds, nearly fifteen of the creatures were surrounding him, their sharp hisses angry. Hayden could see the battle wasn't going well for the Scrappers, either. Everyone from Deck Twenty-nine had either vanished or was dead on the hangar floor. The secondary force was still holed up near the first hatch, but the second was almost clear.

He just had to get past the trife.

They were cautious with him, just like before, giving him some room to maneuver but ultimately keeping him close. As he backed up, he realized he was getting close to the edge of the nest. He turned quickly, spinning just in time to catch the group of demons preparing to jump him. A wave of cold launched from his gun, too far away to hit them, close enough to warn. It did hit the nest, though, and the trife screeched as it did, clearly unhappy with any damage to the thick gel material.

He looked at it, and then looked at them. They had backed off further when he damaged the nest, showing almost human concern for the embryos locked inside.

He started moving laterally, searching for a path past the creatures and the Scrappers. He wanted to cut around the loaders and use them as cover, but right now he couldn't get close.

He was stuck between a rock and a hard place. A growing number of xenotrife were surrounding him, including the group that had climbed the walls to reach the Scrappers. He was vastly outnumbered, and it seemed to him as if all of the remaining creatures had found their way to his position. Bullets still screamed in from the Scrappers' defensive placement, but they were becoming fewer and further between, more pot shots than a real effort to hurt him.

He triggered his weapon a few times, sending bursts of cold toward the nest. The xenotrife complained each time, but they didn't draw too close. It was a standoff of the worst kind. At some point either they would jump him to protect the nest, or he would attack the nest to keep them from jumping him.

Could he make it to the distant hatch before that happened?

His question was answered almost as soon as he considered it. There was a sudden commotion near the hatch, a shout rising from the Scrappers as reinforcements arrived. Even from across the hangar, Hayden could see the lead soldier was cradling something in his arms, and he knelt at the entrance, shifting it to his shoulder. A long cylinder, with a red-tipped projectile shoved into the front.

The xenotrife cried out at the same time a gout of smoke escaped from the cylinder, and a loud thunk signaled the launch of the warhead. It burst from the device, whistling down the row of loaders, soaring past Hayden and detonating on the other side of the nest.

The explosion knocked Hayden forward and off his feet and scattered pieces of xenotrife and hardened gel all around him. His back was burning, his ears ringing.

The Scrappers were emboldened by the assault, and they broke from their defenses, charging down the aisle toward him with guns and spears in hand. He saw them coming, almost taking too long to fight his way back to his feet and triggering the weapon.

Nothing happened.

He cursed, throwing it aside without another thought, pulling his pistol and taking aim, firing one round after another. Four of the Scrappers fell, and then they were nearly on him.

He grabbed Baby, firing again and dropping two more before his magazine was emptied. With no time to reload, he returned the pistol to his armor, switching Baby in his hands and grabbing the other one. Then the xenotrife seemed to recover, joining him in the fight and pouncing on the humans.

The hatch was still far away, but it was also undefended, both of his enemies' attention drawn to one another. A trife appeared beside him, hissing and raising its claws. Hayden shifted his arm to shoot it, surprised when it shoved him aside and hit an incoming Scrapper before their spear could hit him.

Had it just saved him? He didn't pause to think about it. He ran for the hatch, sprinting as hard as his legs would allow. He shifted position to cross beneath the heavy loaders, hearing rounds striking the metal around him but ultimately missing him on the way past. He took a few shots at the Scrappers on the way by, dropping two of them with wounds to their legs, leaving them to be finished off by the trife. People and demons were dying all around him, but he didn't look back.

Not until he reached the hatch. He stopped on the other side, tapping on the control panel. It wouldn't keep either group away for long, but it would slow them down. He eyed the carnage as he keyed in the admin code. The Scrappers and trife were both running out of combatants, whittling one another down to nothing.

Had Pig really sent so many of his people down to attack the creatures? Hayden doubted it. The lead Scrapper wanted to get into Metro and was willing to sacrifice dozens to capture him. They had a keen sense of self-preservation, forgetting him in the scrum.

He finished entering the code. The hatch slid closed and locked. He didn't wait to catch his breath, remembering the Pilgrim's schematic.

He was going to make it to the bridge.

Based on how many Scrappers had died down here, and how many Pig likely had remaining, would it even matter?

47

Hayden rode the forward lift to Deck Four, slumping against the back of it as it ascended. His back was still burning, and when he reached behind to feel the area, he could tell something had pierced his armor and lodged itself into his flesh. He brought his hand back with traces of blood on it. It wasn't bad enough that he was about to bleed to death, but it wasn't exactly comfortable either.

He would worry about it later. He hadn't come this far to drop now.

He put Baby back on his hip, reloaded his empty pistol, and checked the rest of his weaponry. Then he looked himself over for any other damage.

The armor had been a cream color with dark armor plating when he first put it on. Now it was stained dark with blood and sweat, had numerous tears in the softer ballistic fabric, and plenty of scuffs, marks, dents, and cracks along the thicker, solid plates. It had saved his life more times than he could count, absorbing damage that would have killed him quickly and allowing him to stay on course to the bridge.

It didn't keep his muscles from being sore or bruised. He was sure the next time he took the armor off his entire body would be discolored in an ugly rainbow of blacks and blues, yellows and browns.

It would all be worth it once Natalia was safe.

He figured Pig would have guards at as many Decks as he could afford, waiting outside the lifts for his arrival. When the transport stopped at Deck Four, and the doors slid open, he wasn't surprised to find a squad of Scrappers on the other side.

They cocked their weapons and stared into what they thought was an empty space, until Hayden swung around the corner, both pistols in his hands, firing quickly and with deadly accuracy. He didn't go right for their heads or chests, taking them down with rounds to the knees and legs first, and then finishing them off as they howled and stumbled. He could vaguely remember the guilt he had felt about the man he killed in Metro, a man whose body reacted violently to being hit with his stunner. There was no guilt in his killing now. No remorse. Especially after what they had done to Jennifer.

The xenotrife were less monster than these people.

They didn't deserve to be the ones to reach New Gaia. They didn't deserve to have a fresh new world to live and thrive on. They didn't deserve to see the Pilgrim reach her port of call. While the trife might be bugs to exterminate, they were the real demons, and they had to be expunged.

Once Hayden knew their number, once he knew where they were positioned, he could find Natalia. Then, when she was safe, he could go back to Malcolm with everything he had learned. He would apologize for cutting off the man's hand, but only in part. If he hadn't done it, they would all have perished waiting for the trife to die, and it was clear they never would on their own. He would get him to rally Law, to arm and equip the deputies and send them out into the Pilgrim. To search and destroy the remaining Scrappers, and then the remaining trife. They had the arms to do it, as long as they were smart about it.

Then the Pilgrim's computers would send the ship to their new homeworld, and within months they would be free of the failing technology, the rationed food and water, and the crumbling infrastructure. They would be free of the turbs.

It was almost too much for him to hope for, but as he stepped over the bodies of the Scrappers, it was a hope he refused to let go of.

He moved through the corridors of Deck Four, winding his way along the path Jennifer had pointed out to him, moving as quickly as he could. He knew the trife were few in the upper parts of the ship, but he had no idea where the Scrappers might be stationed. He was almost eager to come across them, though. Each one he killed now was one less they would have to kill later.

It didn't take him all that long to reach the entrance to the bridge, making it without interruption. It was easy to recognize despite the plate that had been scratched and worn away. It had a different hatch than any of the other rooms and corridors, a large, wide entrance that opened a pair of heavy doors to the left and right. Not that they opened when he approached. The doors were sealed, locked and waiting for Captain Bradshaw's code.

Or the master admin code.

He typed it in quickly, his heart racing as he finished. His breath caught in his throat until the light on the panel turned green, and he heard the doors unlock.

Only one of them moved, clicking loudly in its track as it was pulled into the wall. It traveled less than a meter before a sharp snap sounded inside the wall and it froze. The other was stuck, the motor that drove it dead, keeping it locked in place.

Hayden cursed under his breath. At least the opening was big enough for him to fit through. He turned sideways, starting to push his way in.

He cursed again when one of the plates on the body armor wedged against the door. He tried to shove it through a few times.

"Damn it," he whispered, realizing he didn't fit after all.

Not with the armor. He quickly shed the weapons from it, tossing them into the darkened room. Then he evacuated himself from the body armor, the agony in his back growing the more he moved his arms. His luck had been too good up until now. He should have guessed something was bound to go wrong.

He was careful not to lose Malcolm's identification chip as he pulled out of the arms of the armor, clutching it in his hand. He looked down at his arms, wincing at the sight of all the bruising. Then he finished removing the suit, stepping out, putting the boots back on, and then finally entering the bridge.

The backup lights went on as he entered, but he didn't see the space right away. He bent at the entrance, grabbing Baby and the pistols before standing upright.

The bridge wasn't all that different from any of the other control centers in the Pilgrim. A large display sat at the front of the room, with a few rows of workstations backing it and a lead station raised above them at the rear. The biggest difference was in the size of the primary display, which wrapped almost all the way around the room, and in the stations closest to the front, which appeared to have joysticks to help direct the thrust of the ship's main engines. The command station was also slightly different, home to a much larger number of displays and controls, and a much bigger surface to work from.

Hayden glanced back over his shoulder at the half-open door. He walked to the command station, dumping his remaining arms there, and then returned to the entrance to grab the body armor, pulling it inside and out of sight. He hadn't come across any more Scrappers on his way here, and he didn't think there were any nearby. Still, he had to be alert. The broken doors meant he couldn't hide if they happened to go past. He considered putting the body armor back on, but he didn't plan to linger here long.

Just long enough to figure out how to activate the sensors and count the number of humans outside of Metro, and then he would be gone.

He stood in front of the Captain's seat. The terminals had all come to life when he entered, and as before the display was asking him for a passcode. He typed it in.

WELCOME ADMIN.

The screen changed, three adjacent displays coming online with his login. They were filled with different options for different parts of operations, along with small boxes of readings that he was sure Captain Bradshaw would have understood but didn't make much sense to him.

He scanned the options on the left display, a row of menu items. He tapped on the one that said "sensors." It brought him to another menu, listing more sensors. He noticed "external cameras" among them. He wanted to see the universe outside, but he wanted to find Natalia more. He bypassed that option, selecting "internal life support."

There were nearly two dozen sensors listed there, from C02 and oxygen levels to air filtration status, and other terms he didn't recognize. He understood "oxygen usage patterns" well enough. It wasn't exactly a specific life form detection tool, but it would tell him where people were breathing, and how much.

He tapped on that option. A display of the Pilgrim appeared on the screen in front of him, showing him green blobs where the sensors detected breathing. He found Metro immediately, the blob large and dark green and positioned near the center of the ship. The rest of the locations were hard to make out on the small display, but he found an icon of a larger rectangle and tapped on it.

The main display at the front of the bridge turned on, the light of it hurting his eyes at first. He blinked a few times to clear his vision, staring at the large, three-dimensional view of the ship. He scanned it quickly, fighting to keep his eyes off Metro, as they were constantly drawn to the massive burst of color in the center. He could see smaller blobs spread around only a small part of the ship, most of them on the upper decks. He identified the lifts, where the Scrappers had been assigned, judging each of those blobs to be worth four or five people. From that, he was able to extrapolate the other blobs he saw.

Two hundred. That was the quick estimation he came to after looking at the display for a few seconds. The largest group was on Deck Three, maybe a dozen targets in all, positioned on the starboard side close to the center, a few decks above the city. Why were they grouping there? Was that where he would find Natalia?

His eyes drifted back to the aft portion of the ship, to the engines. He had always thought they might bring her there, but that entire area was clear. In fact, the entire back portion of the ship was void of human life.

He swept back across the display to the bow of the ship, locating the faintest of green marks near the front, on Deck Four, on the bridge. He had found himself. His eyes tracked around the area, thankful there were no Scrappers registering nearby.

He watched the blobs on the display for a few more seconds. He was going to head to the grouping on Deck Three to look for Natalia. It was the most likely place.

He left the Captain's station, grabbing the body armor and returning it to the doorway. Then he went back to the station to pick up his weapons. He glanced at the display as he did.

A second, faint green signature had appeared as if out of nowhere.

It was right outside the door.

"Sheriff, I'm hoooommmeeeee," Pig said.

48

HAYDEN REACHED FOR HIS GUNS, GRABBING TWO OF THE pistols at the same time he jerked his head back toward the bridge's entrance. Where the hell had the tattooed man come from, and how come he hadn't shown up on the sensors until he was right on top of him?

He saw Pig standing there, arm extended, revolver pointed at his head. He barely fell out of the way as the Scrapper fired, the round smashing into the Captain's station and destroying the electronics.

"I figured if you got past my boys you would come up here. That's what the little snitch said anyways when she got around to begging for her life."

Hayden remained behind cover. He could hear the larger man pushing hard against the stuck doors, and the squeal of the tracks as his brute force overpowered them.

"There's nowhere for you to run, Sheriff," Pig said. "There's only one way out of this room, and you have to get through me to make it."

Hayden looked back at the control surface of the station.

He had left Malcolm's chip up there, and he could still see it, sitting out in the open. He could never reach it without the Scrapper blowing him away.

"I'll tell you what," Pig said, his voice slightly closer as he entered the bridge. "You take that blade of yours. You cut off your left hand, and you throw it to me. Then I'll leave you alone. I promise."

"Your promise is worthless," Hayden said.

Was it a good thing that the Scrapper still thought it was his wrist that would open the hatch to Metro?

He crept to the other side of the station. There was another row of them ahead. If he could sneak around to it, maybe he could take the big man by surprise.

"It didn't have to be personal," Pig said. "We could've done business. But you had to go and kill what was mine."

"Gizzie tried to kill me first."

He laughed. "She always was a little impetuous; I'll give you that. Did you know she was my daughter?"

Hayden grimaced. Had he killed the man's child? No wonder Pig was pissed. Still, she would have killed him if he hadn't.

"For whatever it's worth, I'm sorry it came to that," Hayden said.

He swung around the side of the Captain's station, trying to make it forward a row without being seen.

He must have failed, because a pair of rounds slammed into the side of the station, nearly killing him as he dove away, landing on the opposite side. He had seen Pig shoot. He knew the man could have hit him if he had wanted to.

Why hadn't he?

He heard the Scrapper's boots closing fast. He pushed himself up, turning as he stood.

Pig was at the station, less than a meter away. He already

had Baby in his meaty hand, and he forced Hayden to pull back his arms as the blade whistled toward them before he could shoot.

"Sorry?" the man roared. "You're grepping sorry?"

Hayden stumbled away, hitting his back on the workstation behind him, the maneuver pressing on whatever had impaled him. He grunted in pain, rolling around the object in an effort to escape.

"She was my best girl," Pig said. "She always listened. She always did what I said."

He came around the side of the station, face red, Baby clutched in his hand. Hayden had never been so close to him. He couldn't believe how large the man was, in size and muscle.

"I was gonna marry her one day, make her an honest girl," Pig said. "That ain't gonna happen now."

Hayden continued to back away. He lifted his hand to shoot again, but the furious Scrapper's reach was incredible, and he slapped the gun away.

He was going to die. He was sure of it. Painfully. There was no escaping this monster.

He backed into the wall, trapped as Pig closed on him, dropping the revolver and reaching out, putting his massive hand around Hayden's neck and holding him. He lowered his head to Hayden's face, eyes bloodshot, face sweaty and flushed.

"You ain't dying quick, Sheriff," he growled. "That's too good for you. I'm gonna cut you, and I'm gonna let you watch me and my boys eat you, one piece at a time."

Hayden's heart pounded, his breath cut off. He could feel the tears welling in his eyes. From the pain in his body. From the pain of his failure.

"Natalia," he said.

Pig looked at him and laughed. "You've got a fixed mind, Sheriff. Your bitch is gone. Long gone. You never had a chance of finding her."

Gone? What did that mean? Was she dead after all? Had she been dead this entire time?

The big man braced his neck with his elbow, using his forearm to push him harder into the wall and his palm to push back his left arm. He held Baby in his other hand, preparing it to strike.

"This is gonna hurt," Pig warned.

Then he brought the blade forward, severing Hayden's hand in one smooth stroke. Hayden cried out in agony, screaming and crying at the same time.

"That's just the start," Pig promised. "You shoulda stayed Inside."

Hayden looked at Pig. If Natalia was dead, he was ready to die.

"Oh, I see that look in your eye, Sheriff," Pig said in response. "Sorry if I confused you. She ain't dead. I told you, Engineers are worth a grepping fortune out here. She's on her way." He paused for a moment, laughing. "I forgot, you don't know."

"Don't know what?" Hayden managed to ask.

Pig didn't get a chance to answer. His body convulsed, his grip evaporating as he was thrown violently to the side.

A xenotrife crouched where he had been. This one was bigger than the others, thicker and stronger.

Hayden slumped against the wall, looking at the creature through tear-filled eyes. It had snuck up on them both. At least it would kill him quickly, and spare him from the agonizing death Pig had promised.

Except it didn't kill him. It didn't attack him at all. It hissed at him. Not a threatening sound, but a vocalization like he had heard earlier between the xenotrife near the lift. Communication of some kind.

Between allies.

It pounced on Pig, claws out, swinging them at the large man. The Scrapper was bleeding, but he wasn't dead. He reached out a long hand, grabbing at the trife and throwing it over his shoulders. It rolled on the floor, getting back to its feet.

Hayden scanned the room desperately, finding one of his guns a few meters away. He threw himself at it, at the same time the trife charged Pig again.

A heavy roar followed, and the trife screeched as a round from the Scrapper's revolver hit it square in the chest, exploding through it with enough force to carry the creature backward.

Hayden landed on the floor, reaching out with his remaining hand and grabbing the pistol. It was the strange weapon that took the battery to charge. How the hell was he supposed to turn it on with one hand?

"What, did you screw that bug or something?" Pig said, getting back to his feet and turning with the revolver in hand.

Hayden brought the gun to his mouth, using his teeth to switch it on. He lay on his stomach, holding it close to his chest. He could sense the Scrapper behind him, approaching slowly.

"You alive, Sheriff?" Pig asked, kicking him in the side.

It hurt like hell, but Hayden didn't make a sound.

"I ain't an idiot," Pig said. "Your back is still bleeding, which means your heart is still pumping." He grabbed Hayden's shoulder, pulling him over. "I'll give you that, Sheriff. You're a tough man to-"

Hayden pulled the trigger, not knowing what to expect. A

bolt of energy launched from the weapon, into the bottom of Pig's head. It passed through without slowing, burning a perfectly round hole the diameter of the barrel through his chin, tongue, palate, skull, and brain.

49

The Scrapper's suddenly lifeless corpse collapsed onto him, the weight driving the metal in his back deeper into the tissue. He cried out in pain, at the same time he pushed back, struggling but managing to roll the dead man off him.

He stayed on the floor for a few seconds, trying to catch his breath. He clutched the laser pistol to his chest, working to calm his mind. He wasn't dead yet. Neither was Natalia.

It wasn't over.

He rolled over onto his knees, and then to his feet. He looked down at the dead Scrapper, as though the big man was going to come back to life. Then he looked down at the stump at the end of his left arm, feeling nauseous as he did. The wound was still bleeding. He would die if he didn't stop it.

He looked back at the gun in his hand. He had heard of cauterization. Would this work? What were his other options?

He stayed on his knees, lowering himself to put his stump slightly above the floor. He positioned the pistol over it. Then he depressed the trigger.

He didn't see anything, but his left wrist began to burn, quickly turning black. He kept the trigger down, sweeping the beam across the area, clenching his teeth against the pain. The burning hurt like nothing he had felt before, but it also sealed the wound and stopped the bleeding.

He leaned over and heaved once he was done, vomiting onto the floor.

He remained in place while a few more minutes passed. Then Hayden remembered the display and looked back up at it, quickly tracing all of the green blobs. His was the only one near the bridge. He found the grouping near Deck Three. Pig had said Natalia was gone, but there was nowhere else she could be.

The Scrapper had been mocking him, teasing him to hurt him more. She was there. She had to be.

He looked down at the laser pistol. The counter had dropped to ninety-six because of his use. That was more shots than any other weapon he could carry in one hand.

He checked the display one last time, finding a route that would keep him away from any of the other green blobs. He could only hope there were no more trife nearby, or that if there were they were from the nest on Deck Thirty and might think he was a friend. He was still shocked by the xenotrife's actions, but he didn't have time to dwell on it now.

He stopped at the Captain's station, finding Malcolm's chip. He didn't know what else to do with it, so he stuck it in his mouth, tucking it in the back of the right side, behind his teeth. Then he made his way off the bridge, following the route he had traced with his eyes. He walked past the bridge, along the starboard side to an access stairwell there. He used his shoulder to push it open cautiously, leading with the pistol as he entered but finding it clear. He ascended one deck to Three, exiting out into the corridors there. Then he started to run, hurrying along the long connecting passage that would lead him toward the central part of the ship.

He slowed as he neared. It wouldn't help to rush headlong into the Scrappers there. He approached more slowly, the corridor curving slightly as it reached a small bulge in the ship's waist. He heard soft voices up ahead, along with other noises he didn't recognize. Snorts and exhales and the jangling of chains. What was that?

He reached the edge of the curve, pressing against the wall and leaning out slightly to see further around it. A pair of Scrappers were standing in front of an open hatch. The others had to be in the room behind them.

Was Natalia with them?

He was going to find out.

He shifted on the wall, putting his back to it and aiming sideways with his remaining hand, holding the laser pistol out and targeting down the barrel. Then he took three steps out to the center of the corridor, the curvature allowing him to get an angle on the two Scrappers. They were still talking to one another in low voices, and they didn't notice Hayden's sudden presence. Each of them toppled over a moment later, hit by an instantaneous, invisible blast of focused light that had no trouble cutting through their flesh and bone.

Hayden ran toward them, slowing in sudden confusion before he made it all the way. Not because the men weren't dead. They were. But a smell had risen from the hatch behind them, another that he didn't recognize. The strange noises were more clear now, too. Noises he didn't understand.

He reached the two bodies, coming around the corner with his laser pistol out and ready to fire.

He froze, his eyes giving sight to his earlier panic while his mind tried to make sense of the scene.

The hatch spilled out into a rectangular space. Inside the

space were a dozen creatures Hayden had never seen in person before, but that he knew the name and nature of through his usage of the PASS. They nickered and whined as he moved in front of them, stepping back cautiously in the face of the bloody and beaten stranger.

Hayden's eyes traveled past them, to the second hatch beyond. It was open, and he could see a long corridor stretching out toward a distant metal box at the far end.

Pig's words came back to him like a punch to the gut from one of the powerful man's meaty fists, his heart both pounding and stopping at the same time, the full truth of his situation quickly making itself clear.

"I forgot," Pig had said. "You don't know."

Just like that, Hayden did know, and it took all of his willpower to keep from falling to his knees and sobbing.

One of the horses sidled up to him, its head brushing along Hayden's suddenly frozen face. His eyes were still locked on the control center that sat two hundred meters opposite the midship airlock on Deck Three of the Pilgrim's starboard hull.

For three hundred ninety-six years, the people of Metro had been locked inside the belly of a starship they thought was on its way to a new home in the stars, living with the belief that one day they would reach their destination, and that their future generations would flourish and thrive on an unspoiled world.

Only they would never reach that unspoiled world. Not in three hundred years. Not in four hundred years. Not even if they were granted an eternity.

How could they make it to their new home when they had never left the old one?

50

HAYDEN HEARD THE SHOUTS DESPITE HIS SHOCK, COMING FROM the corridor beyond the airlock. Someone had noticed the two dead Scrappers. He broke free of the ice cold grip of reality that had frozen him, retreating to the second hatch and looking back into the Pilgrim. There were six Scrappers running toward him, reaching for the revolvers at their belts as they did.

His first instinct was to stand and fight, to move out into the passage and open fire, hoping for the best as he was killed in a blaze of glory.

But while the truth of the Pilgrim's situation was still sinking in, Pig had made the truth of his wife's whereabouts abundantly clear.

Too valuable to kill, she was on her way and long gone, spirited from the Pilgrim by the scavengers who had found their way to the place where it rested, who had boarded the starship in search of treasure and had come away with the greatest one of all:

Natalia.

He eyed the horse standing beside him. He had seen the

beasts before in the movies the colonists had brought with them. He knew John Wayne, Clint Eastwood, Gary Cooper. He knew the animals were for riding, and the saddles on their backs bore that out.

Could he do it? They made it look so easy, and this one seemed to like him.

He tucked his gun into his pants, glanced at the stirrup, and then lifted his foot and put it in, grabbing the saddle horn and pulling himself up. It was awkward and harder than it looked, especially with one hand. He slipped the first couple of times, having to try again. The horse didn't argue at all, docile and accepting of him on its back. Once steady in the saddle, he pulled his laser pistol again. He didn't dare drop it to take the reins, though. Instead, he shouted at the horse and kicked its sides with his boots.

It snorted, whined, and started walking, a little too slowly across the long, extended arm that connected the starship to its dock.

"Come on," Hayden said, digging his heels in a little harder.

The first of the Scrappers had reached the airlock, and he shouted to the others when he saw Hayden on the mount.

"There he is. He killed-"

The shout was cut short, a bolt from Hayden's pistol burning through the man's chest and killing him at once. The second Scrapper to turn the corner suffered the same fate, causing the rest of the group to slow and approach more carefully.

"I said, come on," Hayden shouted, kicking the horse harder.

It snorted again and took off, bolting forward and nearly knocking him from the saddle. He leaned forward, desperately wrapping his left elbow around the horn, staying low against the creature. The Scrappers heard the gallop and rushed forward, entering the airlock and taking quick shots from their revolvers. They all missed the moving target, but the shooting did serve to convince the horse to run faster.

Hayden looked back. The Scrappers were mounting the other horses to give chase. His mount was almost to the other side, and he could see how the small control station was connected by a small corridor leading to a rusted metal lift. He looked at the bridge beneath him, able to see through the grated bottom, one hundred fifty meters down. The Pilgrim was resting against a massive scaffolding apparatus on gigantic treads. There were different machines spread around it, loaders and cranes and dumpers, fuel trucks and water trucks sitting abandoned for all of these years, out of the elements and in great shape. There were people down there, too. More Scrappers who were working on the machines, trying to make them function. They looked up at the sound of gunfire and surely saw him crossing the gap.

Was Natalia down there? Had they taken her to help them fix the vehicles? He didn't think so. The Scrappers at the bottom seemed to know what they were doing. Why waste an Engineer on that?

He reached the other end of the platform. The horse didn't slow, and he wasn't about to argue with it. The creature made a straight line for the open lift, climbing inside and only then coming to a stop. It seemed it had made this trip a few times before.

Hayden stared at the inside of the cage the horse had put them in. There was no control pad in it. Only a single red button in the front corner. He kicked out with his foot, hitting it.

The cage started to close.

The world started to shake.

The horse whinnied, stomping its feet as the turb hit, the whole earth quivering. Hayden looked back toward the Pilgrim.

The ship was in a massive underground hangar. He could see part of the earth had collapsed above it, sending half of a mountain spilling onto the top and making it one with the ground it was buried below. He could see the shockwaves in that earth, spreading down to the ship and causing it to shake too.

Earthquakes? The turbs were earthquakes?

The cage rattled, bits of dust dislodged around it. There was shouting from below, the Scrappers warning one another about the coming temblors.

Hayden returned his attention to the Scrappers chasing him. They were nearly to the other side of the bridge. If the lift didn't start to raise, he would be a sitting duck.

It did start to raise, at the same time the forward gate locked into position. The ground shook again, the lift vibrating with it. The Scrappers started shooting, their bullets hitting the cage and ricocheting off.

Hayden and the horse rose away from them. The Scrappers shouted to one another, but they didn't move. There was no other easy way to reach him.

He wished he could have relaxed. It wasn't possible. His cauterized wrist hurt. His impaled back hurt. His muscles hurt. He was in a place he never expected he would be, and he wasn't capable of rationalizing any of it or even trying to come to terms with it. Natalia was gone, and he had no idea to where or how far he would have to track her, or how he would track her in a world he barely understood.

A world overrun by the xenotrife.

But there were still people here. Humankind hadn't died out completely. Were they all vicious killers like the Scrappers? Was that the only way to survive?

He clenched his teeth against the pain, tightening his grip on the laser pistol.

Whatever it took, he was going to find her.

The lift rose three hundred meters before finally reaching the top. Hayden could see the area ahead through the front cage as they rose to meet it. He was still inside, in a massive building of some kind. A cracked stone floor was spotted with tents and equipment, intermingled with different sized wheeled vehicles, some of which matched the ones he had seen below. They were arranged near another pair of lifts, both of them gigantic compared to the one he was in. They were the ones that had been used to bring equipment down to the Pilgrim.

There was also garbage piled in the corner of the space, a lot of garbage, suggesting the Scrappers had been here for some time. He smelled cooked flesh and recognized the bones of both trife and humans among the debris, bits of meat still clinging to them. Four Scrappers were standing at a table nearby, staring at something on top of it.

"It's about time for Pig to check in, isn't it?" one of them said.

"Shut your mouth," another one said. "Do you want it to hear us?"

The first man didn't respond.

There were dozens of Scrappers up here, but Hayden noticed they were all still and mostly silent, having stopped whatever they were doing while the earth rumbled around them. They looked over when the lift stopped with a clang, the cage rattling open to allow him out. He made eye contact with one of the men at the table.

He expected the man might shout or raise an alarm. He didn't. He stared at Hayden, a measure of disbelief gaining his face. He tapped the man next to him on the shoulder. He looked up and saw Hayden, too.

And then the lift doors were open. Hayden kicked the sides of the horse, and it continued its run, slowing slightly when the earth shook again, hard enough that it almost slipped.

He started through the space. The other Scrappers saw him, and they pulled their weapons but didn't fire. They looked concerned. Afraid.

"Hayden!"

The voice shocked him. He turned his head to the right, just in time to see a hand close over Natalia's mouth. They were standing next to one of the vehicles, and the door was open.

He kicked the horse on one side, hoping it would go the way he wanted. His heart was racing faster. She wasn't long gone. She was still here. She was still alive!

The horse kept going straight, heading for an open door at the end of the large building, where a light was filtering in along with dust from the shaking.

"I need to go that way," Hayden said, trying to decide how to grab the reins without dropping his gun. He kicked the horse harder on the right side, over and over again.

It finally decided to turn, slowing almost to a stop as it did. He was facing the vehicle. Facing the man holding Natalia. He was tall and lanky, dressed in a long white coat and a wide-brimmed white hat that cast a deep shadow across his face.

Hayden raised the laser pistol, aiming it at the man. He had Natalia in front of him. She was trying to escape his grasp, squirming in his strong grip. Hayden couldn't get a clear shot. He couldn't risk hitting her.

The man pulled her back and into the vehicle without a word, both of them vanishing inside. There was nothing Hayden could do to stop the abduction.

The vehicle powered on with a soft hum, and then it shot forward, heading toward the opening.

The Scrappers were closing in on him; guns exchanged

for spears. They still didn't say a word, remaining silent as they approached. Even the craft Natalia was being taken in was almost silent.

He aimed the pistol at the closest Scrapper. He didn't go for the kill, instead shooting the man in the leg.

The man started to scream in pain. The noise echoed in the large room and seemed to panic the other Scrappers. One of them stabbed him in the chest with the spear to shut him up.

Hayden fired the laser pistol into the Scrappers, not even trying to aim. The invisible bolts lashed into them, finding flesh and burning it, causing them to cry out.

The ground shook harder.

A loud crack of thunder echoed in the building as the first of the Scrappers gave up on silence in an effort to stop him. The bullet must have come to close to the horse, because it screamed and turned, bolting toward the door. If Hayden hadn't been holding its flanks to hard with his legs, it would have thrown him off. As it was, he was jerked back hard, and he dropped his pistol, grabbing the horn with his hand and holding on as they galloped toward the exit, following the vehicle that had stolen Natalia away.

"No guns, damn it," someone shouted behind him.

He looked back in time to see the top corner of the building peel away, the Scrappers all turning toward it in fear.

What the hell was going on?

Then the horse cleared the building. He was outside, truly outside, for the first time in his life. He immediately felt the heat of the sun and the dry air that surrounded him. They were surrounded by ridges and hills, rocky cliffs and crags. Everything was painted in brown and gold. A worn path spread out ahead of him, the dirt still unsettled where the vehicle had rolled over it. It went so far it vanished over the horizon.

He heard a deep groaning sound at his back. He craned his neck, careful to stay balanced on the horse as he risked a look behind them.

He nearly fell out of the saddle.

He had emerged from a building set against the base of a mountain. It was a rusted brown color that blended well with its surroundings, the exposed part was only a few hundred meters long, but he knew it extended further beneath the rock.

Standing beside it, directly over the collapsed portion of the hangar where the Pilgrim rested, was a creature that defied explanation or logic.

It was easily a hundred meters tall and humanoid in shape. It was naked and sexless, its flesh like a human's, only covered in what appeared to be millions of small barbs, mottled and weathered in grays and browns and reds, pressed tight against its muscles and bone, which were long and lean. Its head was oversized and twisted, the eyes positioned asymmetrically, the ears tiny and flat, its nose the same. Its mouth was open, revealing multiple rows of teeth that reminded him of a xenotrife, and as he watched it lifted its hand to it, a giant, barbed hand that had impaled three of the Scrappers on it. It shook the hand, sending them into its mouth while its other hand worked to pull off another part of the roof.

A second one was arriving through the haze in the distance, almost as large and just as terrifying. The ground trembled with every step it took.

The creature hadn't noticed the vehicle carrying Natalia, and it didn't notice him. Or if it did, it didn't think they were worth the effort when it had the Scrappers right in front of it. Hayden continued watching as it tore into the building, pulling frightened humans out and throwing them into its mouth. They tried shooting at it, but their weapons were worthless, the bullets barely able to dig into its flesh.

As he turned his head back to the road in front of them, he found he could barely breathe. The PASS had never mentioned anything like this. Neither had Jennifer. Did she know?

The nightmare of the alien invasion hadn't faded over time.

Somehow, it had gotten worse.

51

THE HORSE CONTINUED GALLOPING FOR NEARLY THIRTY minutes before finally starting to slow. The monsters had faded out of sight by then, as had the building and the Pilgrim's burial place. The vehicle carrying Natalia had fallen away into the horizon, the horse nowhere near able to match its speed.

Hayden slumped in the saddle. His face was wet with tears. His body screamed with every step. He was vaguely aware of the landscape changing around him, the dryness of the mountains slowly filling in with light vegetation.

His mind was everywhere and nowhere, focused and dispersed. Every time he tried to stay with one thought, it bounced to another, cycling through rounds of fear and desperation, pain and hope and sadness.

This was a world he didn't know. A world he didn't understand. Now that he was in it, he envied the citizens of Metro. He envied the life he had known. They were safe in their world, locked and hidden from the dangers that lurked outside. More than that, they were ignorant to the truth, blissfully unaware that the Pilgrim had never moved from the place where it had been built. They could hold onto the hope that one day they would arrive at their new world, to start a new life of peace and prosperity among the stars.

At least until the power went out. Since the ship's thrusters had never been fired, that could be quite a long time.

He shifted his tongue in his mouth, finding the identification chip still lodged inside. He lifted his hand, spitting the small device out. It was covered in blood. He held it up, staring at it for a long moment before casually flicking it away.

Some things were better off forgotten.

As for him, it was too late to forget. Too real to ignore. He had no idea if he was going to survive the coming night, but if he did?

He was going to find her.

Nothing was going to stop him.

ABOUT THE AUTHOR

M.R. Forbes is the creator of a growing catalog of science fiction and fantasy titles. He lives in the pacific northwest with his family, including a cat who thinks she's a dog, and a dog who thinks she's a cat. He eats too many donuts, and he's always happy to hear from readers.

To learn more about M.R. Forbes or just say hello:

Visit my website:
mrforbes.com

Send me an e-mail:
michael@mrforbes.com

Check out my Facebook page:
facebook.com/mrforbes.author

Chat with me on Facebook Messenger:
https://m.me/mrforbes.author